Piper,
Once & Again

Caroline E. Zani

Wyatt-MacKenzie Publishing
DEADWOOD, OREGON

Piper, Once & Again

Caroline E. Zani

ISBN: 978-1-942545-11-8

Library of Congress Control Number: 2016932378

Wyatt-MacKenzie Publishing
DEADWOOD, OREGON

Wyatt-MacKenzie Publishing, Inc.
www.WyattMacKenzie.com
Contact us: info@wyattmackenzie.com

"A beautifully written book that portrays the power and impor-
tance of a past life. Through the journey of Piper we experience
a magical memory of another time that deeply affects her
present life." — LYNN V. ANDREWS, *New York Times* Bestselling Author of
The Medicine Woman Series

"... lingers on my heart long after the book has been read, the
tea has been sipped, and the fire light has dimmed. It not only
entertains with its story of multi-generations told through the
lens of a rare heroine, but it is also a feast for the senses. I cannot see or smell lavender now without Piper riding through
my mind on her majestic steed. Piper feels real to me, as do
all great heroes and heroines of literature. Haunting, inspira-
tional, emotional, suspenseful, and sensual are words I use to
describe the unique perfume of this must-read novel."
— KELLY SULLIVAN WALDEN, Bestselling Author of *The Love, Sex &
Relationship Dream Dictionary,* and a Certified Clinical Hypnotherapist

"*Piper, Once & Again* is as emotionally complex and compelling
as the scents that seize its heroine, calling her back to another
life whose echoes she is feeling in this one. While Zani toggles
between two different lifetimes, a story of a young women's
rich inner life becomes connected to her outer. Zani's story-
telling is strong, adept and spare, like the sturdy horse barns
in which Piper finds solace. I couldn't put it down."
— LAURA PARKER ROERDEN, Author of *Salt From the Earth* blog

"I am enamored as much by words as by Lavender, and in this
book, I am overjoyed to have both. I was both surprised and
delighted by the superb writing of Ms. Zani—surprised that
she captured in words exactly the feelings I've had while picking Lavender for two months every year for 13 years. She truly
is a wordsmith, and I am grateful to find someone who could
put it so eloquently and elegantly."
— KRISTIN ORR, Lavender Farmer, Owner, Fort Hill Farms

"This is a wonderful story about the self, the soul, and the love that follows us from one lifetime into the next. Love never ends or dies but continues to follow us always. Such relatable characters, I couldn't put it down! This book is so wonderful—as I read it, I was reminded of my own childhood memories. It played like a movie across my mind's screen. Love. Love. Love it! I can't wait to see it on the big screen!"
— JACKIE WAITKUS, Spirit Medium, blendingtwoworlds.com

"These pages are a stunningly beautiful and fragrant voyage. I journeyed alongside Piper through the weaving of vivid lifetimes. The ethereal scenery calls me back to visit often and I find myself missing her. I felt her joys and her grief as if my own, understanding her plight at a level of my own soul, unknown to me prior to opening this wonderful story of time-less love. In many ways I am Piper and Piper is every woman."
— ANDREA VASSILIDIS, Host of Playing in the Matrix

"From the moment I began reading, I knew this story was one that belonged to every woman. Through devastation and life circumstances beyond her control, Piper learns she has a strength and dignity she hadn't yet known she possessed. Stretching our faith and preconceived notions about life and death, Piper leads us down a path we might not expect and like close friends we watch helplessly as she struggles and truly feel her angst as she goes from shattered to triumphant, faith-less to graceful, tarnished to the queen of her own court. This must grace the big screen one day!" — GINA CLAPPROOD, Personal Growth Coach and Advisor, www.ginaclapprood.com

"A wonderful love story on many levels—the love of a man and woman, husband and wife, the love of parents for their children, and the love of children for their parents, and the bond and love between horse and owner. It is a timeless story that I will read again for sure. I loved the ending... now that was a surprise. I was moved to tears for a lot of it. It truly touched my soul." — BONNIE S. KAVANAGH, R.N., Herbalist

Piper,
Once & Again

For Amanda, my pearl in the sand.
And for Piper for showing me the way.

Acknowledgements

THIS STORY IS ONE OF HOPE AND FAITH and is intended to seep into the parts of your heart that you might not know are there or perhaps have forgotten about.

Special thanks to Gina Clapprood of Intuitive Advisement who said to me, "Just sit at your computer and see what happens. You have a story in you. Others will connect to it. They need it."

Thanks also to Jackie Waitkus of Blending Two Worlds who has guided me on my journey since this book was written and has taught me much about Spirit and the understanding that indeed I chose to come here—with purpose, and for connecting me with such beautiful souls: David Reilly, Diana Fairfax, Kim Landini, Maribeth Cain, Michelle Cloutier, and Betty Applegate. You are all in my heart forever.

Thanks to Andrea Vassiliadis for her constant encouragement and guidance in all areas of life, including introducing me to the incredible author "Dr. Dream," Kelly Sullivan Walden, who introduced me to my agent Devra Jacobs, who connected me with my amazing publisher. Thank you to my publishing team, particularly Nancy Cleary. Her insight and experience are true gifts, her patience much appreciated and her enthusiasm is second to none. She is truly a visionary and I am grateful and humbled to have the chance to work with her. Thank you, Ladies, for being who you are and allowing me to be me.

Thanks to Andy Marcoux of Coachman's Delight who came into my life when I needed him most—before I knew I needed him.

Thanks to my dearest friend, Detective Ciara Maguire-Ryan, for helping me when I didn't think I needed it so that I could help her later when she didn't think she needed any more friends because it's funny how it all works.

Thank you to Brian Lozeau for finding me again in this lifetime. I have no doubt our connection precedes 1982. And though I still can't find the words on this keyboard to express what you mean to me, I'll keep trying. You are my heart of hearts. I love you.

Most important, thanks to my beautiful Amanda for changing my life in the ways that only a child can. You came here with purpose and I watch in awe as you find it.

And finally to my future great-great grandchildren, know that you are never alone. When you read this story, feel me there with you and learn to connect. It is your birthright and I look forward to being part of your Life.

"The wound is the place the Light enters you."

– Rumi

1

SITTING IN HER BOYFRIEND'S NEW 1970 Monte Carlo on Maple Street, Destiny Lynn Bohens wiped tears from her eyes and said a little prayer for herself, the unborn child she had just met, and for the uptight and righteous Elizabeth who, in her rigid ways, blocked the beautiful messages that wanted to be heard.

"I must have been born in the wrong century, *again*," Destiny said to the cross hanging on her rearview mirror. "I don't know why people think you can't believe in God and Jesus *and* be psychic; for crying out loud, they're all the same thing. She looked at her reflection in the mirror. "No, goddamn it, I'm not a freak! I just understand things most other people don't understand—yet." *Whatever, they paid me. Aaaaannd they don't burn girls at the stake anymore. Thaaaank God!* Her breath was slowing down as she counted the bills in her hand. She was starting to feel better but it always stung a little.

∽

"What? You hired a *fortune teller* to tell me the sex of my baby? I, I can't do that." Elizabeth didn't know if she should run, scream, punch, or say a rosary.

The woman in all black who went by the name of Destiny reached out with long, bony fingers. They reminded Elizabeth of the type that could poke your eye out, knit a shawl, and dial the deli down the street all in the same instant. They were cold and quick and decidedly witch-like. *Where does someone like this come from?* She was suddenly thankful for the upbringing she'd had. The staunch and religious Catholics could explain away all the ills of the world with a simple prayer.

"Now just lie still and hand me your wedding ring and I will tell you if your baby is a boy or a girl, dear."

Elizabeth took a breath and said, "What is that smell? Incense? Herbs?" She didn't know why she was going along with this malarkey, this nonsense, never mind how she failed to realize Helen had planned an entire party without her knowing. Helen couldn't do anything without someone's approval, particularly Elizabeth's. And this was just one more bit of evidence proving that Helen was really not the caliber of friend she ought to have in her life. Her mother was right about those "Protestant-types" and she figured this was just the proof in the pudding.

Elizabeth Ann Turchino took another deep breath and as she let it silently out of her lungs she could feel her baby. "Foolishness!" she said under her breath as she listened to the hushed whispers of the others. They crowded around as if to watch a show of sorts. "I'm glad my mother isn't here to see this."

The ring hung on the end of the string and was still. A little *too still* apparently, because Ms. Bones pulled up on the string ever so slightly to get it moving and at once the women took a collective breath that seemed to suck all movement and sound out of the tiny parlor in Helen's home.

They watched in amazement as the ring began to turn and pull the string out in a widening arc around Elizabeth's protruding belly. "Oh my God!" "I don't believe my eyes!" "Holy smoke, Elizabeth!" These were the things Elizabeth didn't hear. At that moment she was no longer Mrs. Anthony Turchino, new bride and mother-to-be. No, she wasn't any one person but the amalgamation of many—women's names and faces, their hair and eyes, their breath, joy and sadness, sorrow, and exhilaration filled the Elizabeth that lay on the sofa. Young faces, older ones, sun-wrinkled and creamy smooth, each one with a familiarity only a memory could bring.

One face in particular kept coming toward her mind's eye. It was one that she somehow knew would be the adult face of the child she carried in her belly. What a beautiful face—like Anthony's, but feminine and so strong and framed by silky black hair. *How could this be, how could she see her face forty years from now?* She couldn't speak. The face looked at her—for what seemed an eternity and a tenuous moment all at once—then slowly tilted to the side ever so slightly, blinked, and mouthed, "I forgive you, Mom."

"PIPER!"

Elizabeth struggled to sit up on the rust-colored sofa and looked around at the incredulity on the faces of the young women who invited her to tea but surprised her with a shower instead. At that moment she really wished she had some tea and was sitting with her husband at their small kitchen table at home. Feeling a bit embarrassed and not wanting anyone to confirm what she had just encountered, she kept her eyes on the hands of Destiny. Slowly she searched, one by one, the faces of her friends as if for an explanation as to what had just taken place.

After a few moments she began to hear the voices slowly coming back to her and realized then that they must have been talking all along, she just hadn't heard them. "A girl, Elizabeth!" "You're having a baby girl. I just knew it!" "I can't wait to shop for everything pink with you!" "Tony will be so happy—two ladies in the house to wait on him!"

Helen's face came into her view and the paleness it displayed confirmed for Elizabeth that she hadn't just imagined the last five or so minutes. Her best friend handed the witch some money and ushered her out to the porch even before she had a chance to explain what had happened.

"But I need to speak with her!" Destiny insisted as she looked deep into the eyes of Helen. "This doesn't happen often, you don't understand! That baby is different—she's a gift! You must let me tell her—PLEASE! The child she carries needs guidance, she needs to know!"

"Listen, you were great, your act and everything—really convincing." Helen shifted her weight back and forth. "Liz doesn't believe in any of that stuff so we just did it for fun!"

Destiny's heart sank.

"Would you like to take a piece of cake for your ride home?" Helen knew she would refuse the offer and was glad when the woman turned toward the street and waved her off.

The guests hugged her one last time before departing; it was Helen who asked, "Liz, Why did you yell 'Piper' when you sat up and opened your eyes?" Elizabeth shrugged as she nervously folded and unfolded the napkin in front of her at the dessert table.

"I don't remember saying that," she lied.

"Oh, well, I guess it must have been my imagination then."

Elizabeth, now wanting to bolt from the house, nodded back at Helen knowing that their friendship was too thready, too porous, too dangerous. With a reddened face and shaking voice she demanded, "I did not say it, Helen!"

When she finally fled the tiny cape house on Grove Street, Elizabeth knew she would never return, and that her friendship with Helen would have to end. *Anyone who believed in such witchcraft and sorcery would have to burn in hell without me. I just hope it's not too late to save myself.*

Destiny held her breath when she saw Elizabeth walking quickly across the lawn to her car nearby. For a moment, her hand lay on the door handle of the Monte and she thought, *I can try again—get her to hear me. I can help her see how amazing that little baby is.* She stopped herself when she saw Elizabeth make the sign of the cross with one hand and open her car with the other.

Elizabeth flung open the door of her car so forcefully that it swung back and closed before she could say "Amen." She looked through tears at the door handle and tried again. *What just happened? What was that back there? I can't tell Anthony, he would be so angry.* She seated herself behind the wheel and felt grateful to be on her way home to Anthony and their steadfast faith. When the motor came to life she rubbed her face with both hands, then pulled away from the curb and began a rosary that in a lot of ways would never really be finished.

2

OKAY. SO GOD SENDS BABIES to the Daddy and then he gives them to the Mommy? And then the doctor takes the baby out of the mother's stomach? So ... why can't Dad just give you another one?

Piper would have liked to ask her mother these things but the couple of times she tried, her mother made her feel as though she had done something wrong. But Piper remembered. She remembered being born and she remembered dying, too—before she was born.

"The other time—the one with my Mère who died in the night." That conversation resulted in a slap across her freshly washed four-year-old cheek and her mother's own cheeks drained of color. Piper, like most only children, yearned for a sister or brother to keep her company when she was growing up, but it never came to be. Her parents were sensitive to her desire and allowed her the horse, the dog, the cats, rabbits, anything she wanted except for what she really wanted. Elizabeth always marveled at her daughter's imagination in this area and told Piper—through tears once—about an imaginary friend that had kept Piper company when she was young. "But he went away, like your thumb-sucking and nail-biting."

Frightened by her mother's tears, she pretended to only vaguely remember the visits by a little boy when she was still in her crib but she remembered him as being real, not at all imagined. And she remembered every detail of his serious face, always showing concern for her. His hair, a blonde so light it was almost without color, his voice so familiar and comforting.

But his most distinguishing features by far were his eyes, a blue so bright that she could never find it in anything else in her world—not in the sky, the neighbor's pool, her box of sixty-four Crayolas. His voice brought serenity and calmed all her fears. She could listen to him for hours. But like the stories she and her grandfather used to make up at bedtime, he went the way of her childhood. The years slipped by, and Piper began to believe what she was told, that this beloved friend of hers had been nothing more than childhood fantasy.

His name was Vander; she knew that, like she knew her own name. He was slightly older than she, and he loved her. She was as sure of this as she was that her parents loved her. It was a constant in her young life, like breath, like water, like life itself. Vander came to sit with her when she couldn't sleep because of a bad dream or a fight she'd had with a classmate that day or because of a fever that was burning her up inside. He would put his cool hand on her forehead and tell her stories of a far-off village across the sea. "A very long time ago we both lived in that village together. Through the woods and down the lanes," he said. "We rode our horses out to the sea to watch my father bring in the day's catch. Along the sand we counted seashells from the backs of Pieferet and Henk, their long, curly manes covering our summer skin." He told her how they laughed and told jokes as the horses trod through the loose sand and up onto the dunes. "Sometimes we stayed long enough to watch the gulls come in to feed on whatever scraps were left behind when the fishermen went home to their families."

He told her stories of adventures they had had in the woods around their small village. The trees they had climbed without falling, the eggs they had stolen from nests to cook for their midday meal, the wild rabbits they had tried to catch and keep as pets, the berry bushes they had scoured, not caring how many scratches they had to endure, as long as they could have the sweet and tart taste of the red and blue berries on their tongues, and how they had been scolded at home for having stains on their clothing. These details were so real and so vivid it was as if Piper actually had memories of them. He told her of snowfall so great that everyone in the village had had to stay in their homes for days at a time and hope they had enough wood cut for the fire.

And then he told her about how one day he wouldn't come to visit anymore. "But don't worry, because even if you can't see me I will still be there with you—always with you," he whispered. Hot tears trickled down her fevered cheeks. "Why don't you want to come visit me anymore? What did I do wrong? Are you mad at me?" He wiped each tear as it slid down toward her pink chin. Vander smiled a smile that she would keep deep in her soul until the day she took her last breath, a smile so wide and so sweet she knew even at such a young age, that he was hers in some way she didn't quite understand.

He continued to visit her throughout the next couple of years, with longer periods of time between each visit until she turned seven on a snowy January night. After her birthday party was over and all the pink and yellow gift wrap was thrown away and all her friends had gone home, Piper was getting ready for bed, brushing her teeth, and thinking about her Shawn Cassidy cassette she had received and how she couldn't wait to listen to it the next morning. She got into bed, her cat Valentine curled up on her pink coverlet purring softly and not moving an inch to let Piper get comfortable. Remembering that she needed to say her prayers, she sprang back out of bed, kneeled on the hard floor and bowed her head. Without warning, Valentine jumped up and, hissing, leapt to the rocking chair at the foot of her bed. Piper was glad. It meant that when she opened her eyes, Vander would be there. And sure enough, as her eyes popped open, he was kneeling beside her.

He smiled at her and instantly the warm feeling he always brought filled her entire body, bottom to top. She knew this feeling well because it accompanied all his visits. What she didn't know then was that for the rest of her life she would be searching for that feeling of absolute love and light. And while she would come close on a couple of occasions, what she felt from others was never quite right, never enough. She opened her mouth to speak, wanting to tell him about all the gifts she had received for her birthday and the fun she'd had at her party. He just smiled back and nodded, looking at her hands still clasped in front of her on the edge of the bed. She looked at him for a moment longer, smiled back, and then continued her prayers. When she finished, she confided in him how much she had missed him. The floodgates opened then and the battery of questions washed away the silence of her bedroom. "Why have you been away for so long? Haven't you wondered what I've been up to? Do you know that I got a horse over the summer? His name was Cocoa but I renamed him Victory, because I like the sound the 'V' makes. Where do you go when you aren't here?"

He told her that he knew Victory and he liked him very much and asked her to promise that she would make sure she always cooled him off properly after riding and never to rush the process. "Horses need to be walked-out for a while after you ride—before eating, and drinking cold water." He made her promise to remember this. When she nodded, he touched her under her chin. Looking into his eyes she knew she needed to remember this. Then he smiled and she knew it was okay, that she was okay when he was near. She asked him how he knew so much about horses, and she wanted to know where he lived and why don't her parents believe her when she tells them about him and the stories he tells of the village and the fishermen and the berries. She wants to know why *he* doesn't have a mother and father, and a home for that matter. And why did his pants never reach past his knees and didn't his feet get cold without any shoes?

Piper stopped suddenly when she realized that she was making him sad with all her questions. Usually she just listened to Vander, but now she wanted to know so much about so many things. She could tell that he was feeling sad and asked him why. "Do you remember when I told you that I was not going to be able to visit forever?"

She looked down at the floorboards now, her excitement and wonder instantly evaporating. "I remember," she whispered. "What did I do?"

"Nothing Piper, nothing," he tried to reassure her, but she was crying now. The scent of lavender and burnt raisins reached behind her nose as he put his arms around her, joy and despair entwined in their hearts. The tears came fast and so furiously and she cried on his shoulder for some time. He held her close and whispered, "I will always love you. I have for so many lifetimes." She thought she heard footsteps in the hall. She didn't really understand what he meant but she knew that he loved her and didn't want her to be sad. Vander made her promise not to forget what he was about to say.

"Piper this is the last visit. I want to be able to visit forever, but I can't. One day you will know why. If I stay," he sighed, "people will think that something is wrong with you and it will get in the way of your life and your lessons. We all come here to learn—you'll see. You have to be patient, please. Do it for me, Piper."

Be patient? She didn't understand a word of what he said. She tried hard to concentrate, to focus on his words, but it was so difficult knowing that she had to study his face and try to absorb his voice into her memory, her being, if this was truly the last time she would see and hear him. His hair the color of sun-bleached straw, seemed so dull now; his eyes, usually so blue and bright, as if there was a light shining behind them, tonight were darker. When he did look at her, they were hazy, almost flickering.

He said, "You are mine and I am yours, God promised us that. I know you don't remember, but it's okay. You have to live *this* life now the best you can so that someday... someday...." His voice trailed off.

There was a knock at the bedroom door. "Piper, are you in bed yet birthday girl?" Piper jumped off the bed, surprised. "Hi, Daddy. I'm getting ready for bed now! She knew he wouldn't open her door if she were changing into her pajamas. He always tucked her in at night but she didn't want him to come in this sad night. She wanted only Vander.

She heard her father shift his weight back and forth in the hall, wooden floors gently sighing as he did. "I'll be back in little bit, Sweet Pea." Piper was relieved but sad to know her time with Vander was coming to an end. She hopped back onto her bed under the window that looked out over the small barn her dad and Uncle Guy built for Victory.

When the door opened fifteen minutes later and as the light from the hallway washed over her bed, Vander slipped from sight. For the first time in her life panic rose in her little chest, but at the same time she realized she could still feel his steady hand on her shoulder. Her dad bent down over her bed, wished her a happy birthday, told her how much he loved her, and kissed her on the forehead. And, as he did, Vander's hand slipped from her tiny shoulder. She wouldn't feel it again for what would seem a lifetime. "I love you, too," she whispered, but not to her dad, not this time.

3

"WHAT DO YOU MEAN YOU *smell* memories? What do memories smell like, Piper?" He always asked her questions in an accusatory tone. "In all of my years of teaching, I've never met a student who had so much potential and took so much pride in wasting it. And why is there hay in your hair, *again?*"

Piper was tired of trying to explain herself to adults who seemed to enjoy making her uncomfortable. "Maybe I was daydreaming. I don't really know what to call it. When you started talking about the Eiffel Tower I ... I started to smell ... I'm not sure what it was but ... it's a mixture of, umm, roses and something else—like cinnamon, I think." She shook her head until the offending piece of hay fell free of her long hair and spiraled to the floor.

How am I supposed to live like this? Why am I stuck here—in this dead town? Why does everyone go out of their way to make me miserable? These things had bothered Piper for so long. She wanted to say it all out loud but knew she couldn't without getting into more trouble. *Why did everyone else just stay here, work here, raise their kids here?* It made her stomach turn and she wanted out—now. She knew he didn't believe what she said. "I'm sorry, Mr. O'Connor, I'll pay more attention," she said, eyes on the floor, and then asked if she could leave. He nodded sternly.

This tiny little town in Massachusetts was like a cell to Piper, something that would smother the life breath out of her, something from which she needed to escape. She dreamed of bigger things. No, not marrying a prince or curing a disease or even become a rock star, just wanting something different, something just for her. She knew she deserved bigger and better things ... if she could only find them, or, she hoped, if they could find her. At seventeen, Piper could not stand another day of the town's drudgery, of teachers, of snooty girls who gauged status by the boys they dated, and of boys who did whatever it took to make the girls pay attention. Most of the kids in school were quite impressed with themselves, and regarded Piper as a nothing: someone perfect for a "do-over," though she had never considered anything of the sort. Even her own family members were strangers to her. She didn't seem to connect with anyone really, just her animals. Anyone who knew her knew the most important things in her life were a horse named Victory and a little brown dog with one eye she had found out in the woods while she was riding one day. He followed her home and that's where he stayed. Seemed to enjoy it quite a bit. Valiant taught her that one eye and a big heart were far better than two eyes and a nose in the air.

Her teachers didn't know what to do with her. Always late for class, seemingly apathetic, sometimes depressed, always had her nose in a book or was writing in a journal some very dark poetry that, in fact, frightened them: not for their sakes, but for hers. She had a couple of friends they saw her around town with, but they didn't attend the same school. She wasn't the kind of student that a teacher would have a chance to get to know; after all, she didn't cause trouble, but on the other hand, she wasn't an exceptional student, either. She had what the teachers called "potential." Piper knew it existed, didn't doubt it for a moment. She just couldn't see wasting it on textbooks and term papers. She had better things to do with her time. And because of this, she was thoroughly disgusted with her Senior English teacher when she asked Piper to stay after class on this already-gone-bad Tuesday afternoon.

Mrs. Karinnik slid a piece of notebook paper, the fringe still attached, out from under her blotter as if it were so secretive or perhaps so base that she didn't want it contaminating the other students' work. Piper recognized it as the assignment she had handed in the day before. The assignment was to write a poem with love as its central theme. And she did just that. Mrs. Karinnik looked at Piper and winced as she noticed the dark eye makeup that usually made Piper look sad, today making her look tired, almost old. There was a quality that she possessed some called "old soul" and others just called weird. She knew it wasn't because she had a tough life—quite the contrary. It's just that Piper didn't fit in any more than a Tupperware lid fits after it is introduced to the dishwasher.

Mrs. K, as everyone called her, said after a few moments hesitation, "Uh, Piper, honey, I wanted to talk with you about your work here. I'd like to help you."

Piper shifted her weight, folded her long arms on which hair stood at attention, straightened up her 5'10" frame and stared back down at this woman who knew nothing about her. She said nothing, only drawing in a deep breath, ready for battle. *For God's sake, why do adults, especially teachers, want to "help" me?*

Mrs. K, undaunted by Piper's defensive posture or impatience, said, "This is really quite good, Piper. You could really develop this talent, become a writer."

Piper tried to take the words in and see if she could somehow bend their meaning into a threat or a dig. She couldn't, of course, and, before she knew it, Mrs. K. had reached out and touched her arm gently. She looked deep into Piper's eyes, which were now squinting back at her, as she tried to think of something to say. "You know, this poetry is very sad, there's a feeling to it that is, well, really beautiful. Also I wanted to ask you if there was anything you'd like to talk about. Is everything okay at home?"

The kiss of death—when will teachers learn? No teenager, least of all, me, wants to "talk" to them. What could possibly come of a conversation with a woman who is three times my age, sometimes wears two different colored knee-high stockings with her skirts, never seems to keep up with the gray roots in her hair, and drinks Diet Coke like she really expects it to perform miracles on the spare tire around her soft middle? And for God's sake, she's a teacher—she didn't know anything about life or being young and misunderstood. Again, not wanting trouble, she simply said, "No, I don't have anything I want to talk about, thanks. I have to go; I have to feed my horse." This wasn't the first time she had used this as an excuse to leave the school at exactly 1:54 every day for the last three-and-a-half years. She couldn't imagine staying in that building, around all those people for a minute longer than was required by her parents, thereby delaying a ride on that particular day.

Many of her teachers admired her love of animals and her dedication to them as well as her talent for riding. They saw her galloping in the fields, seemingly one with her beautiful blood-bay horse, trotting along the railroad bed that could be seen only once the leaves fell from the trees, or contentedly leading her horse on the roadside as they drove past, out of town to go wherever it was that teachers live. They never stopped or waved. Some felt it would be inappropriate, an intrusion on something that was truly beautiful—a girl and her horse. Some of them actually envied her—tall, thin, and beautiful in a way that most girls are not. She had a unique way about her that defied definition. "She looked like she belonged," and that's where the thought always ended. Where did she look like she belonged? Certainly not here, in this small town that was going through growing pains, being invaded by a new breed of suburbanite—30-somethings drawn to a quaint town for the qualities it offers only to overbuild it, pave it, fill the wetlands, and fence off all the best places to ride. These intruders looked at people like Piper as if she ought to be removed from their idyllic town. She was a nuisance, someone whose horse's hooves destroyed lawns and left unpleasant "gifts" behind on their street; a street that was, only months before, a trail in the woods.

As for her looks, she wore her hair straight and parted on the side. Her coal black hair was shinier than any of the other girls', simply because she didn't do to it the things they did to theirs: perms, curling irons, hair spray, teasing, gel, protein packs, color. Piper simply used the same thing in her hair that she used on her horse's mane and tail—Cowboy Magic shampoo with a can of her father's Miller beer. Any horse product that was created for optimal hair and hoof growth would surely work on her was her logic and she was right. A little Hooflex here and a little Show Sheen there before leaving the house kept the comforting scent with her all day in the way some people find comfort from their grandmother's Jean Nate which she found quite unappealing. The beer always made Victory's coat seem to glow and his mane was easier to braid for shows with the added bonus of masking the floral scent of the shampoo. Flowers smelled like death and sadness to her but how could she explain that to anyone?

Super shiny and sleek was not a common sight with all the perming and bleaching going on. She would have gladly offered her simple recipe had anyone actually asked her. But no one ever did.

She thought people avoided her because she was different in a bad way; but really, people just didn't know how to approach her. On the back of a horse by day and absorbed in reading and designing her dream barn at night, she didn't give others much opportunity to interact, and she liked her solitude most of the time. Most adults, especially her teachers, knew that she would come into her own some day and be successful and loved and productive, but there was a process to this thing called life and it cannot be rushed. So some of them said silent prayers for her, some just shook their heads and thought, *Ah, to be so young and have your entire future ahead of you to figure it all out.* Most felt, however, that she could use a little help in the area of social skills, again not something you can force on a free spirit like Piper. She was unique, and, if given the opportunity, Mrs. K. would have freely shown her appreciation for the young talent and shared with her stories of when she was that age and the fact that she, too, rode quite a bit when she was younger and lived in North Carolina on her grandparents' farm. But Piper never gave her a chance.

When she walked out of the school that day, feeling the stale air of the empty corridors trying to hold her back, suck the life breath out of her, she knew she would never go back. She also had that strange experience again. In Mr. O'Connor's room it was so faint that she couldn't identify the scent. It usually happened every once in a blue moon when she least expected it, but here it was again. It was too powerful to ignore and yet so vague that it was difficult to describe in words. She had what she thought of as a scent memory. She thought everyone experienced these, but she never found anyone who recognized what she described. They weren't actually scents that were present in her immediate surroundings at the time; rather they seemed to come from behind her nose, or maybe from her mind, and were accompanied, always, by images that flooded her for only tiny fractions of time. She likened it to waking from a dream and not being able to hold onto it long enough to recall it, only to have little shards of it slice through her thoughts during the day. That, at least, seemed to happen to other people; but the "scent-ache" was something that no one else seemed to understand, so she stopped trying to describe it. When she was little she told her dad, "I can smell what it was like before in my other house." Her dad listened and encouraged her to continue, "What did it smell like, Sweet Pea?" "Like love, Dad." She smiled at the memory and her dad's response. "Oh, I see. That must have been nice!"

The smile faded from her face then as she recalled how it all changed. It happened the day her mother questioned her about the memories and the smells that triggered them. Piper was in third grade. She could remember it vividly, as if it had happened that morning. She walked into the kitchen after school and immediately heard her mother on the phone, which meant she could avoid the question and answer session about what she learned in school that day. Elizabeth smiled at her, held her hand over the phone receiver and whispered, "Hi, Sweetheart." Piper stopped but wanted to make her way quickly to the living room to watch 30 minutes of Tom and Jerry before heading out to the barn. Elizabeth raised her eyebrows and tilted her head, waiting for a response from Piper. "Mommy, you got tomato sauce on the ceiling."

When she reached the couch in the living room a few moments later, she felt her mother's hand grip her small shoulder and turn her around. "What did you say?!" Her mother's voice was shaking and Piper wondered if it was because her hand was also shaking. Elizabeth was surprised to see that her hand was out of control and immediately pulled it back and gripped it with her other shaking hand. Again she asked, this time a little calmer, a little quieter. "What did you just say when you came through the kitchen?" Piper looked up into her mother's pinched face and squinting eyes. Eyes that were searching for something in Piper's. "I just said you got tomato sauce on the ceiling. It's okay, Mommy. It'll come off." She looked down at her feet then, knowing her mother was still upset. "Piper, you didn't look up at the ceiling. You didn't. How do you know there's tomato sauce there?" Just then Piper closed her eyes for only a moment, as the scent of ocean air reached behind her nose. "I just knew it was there." Her mother shook her head. "No," was all Elizabeth could manage.

Piper said in a quiet voice, "Vander told me you took the lid off when Mrs. Grant came over and it bubbled everywhere." The scent of salty air came again and she smiled slightly as it comforted her. "Stop that," Elizabeth commanded in a harsh whisper. "Stop smiling," she begged. "Why are you smiling?" Piper answered, "The smells help me. They help me remember before." "Before *what*, Piper?" Elizabeth's voice decided shaking was warranted and this time she didn't try to hide it. "Before the time I was in your tummy."

The slap was severe and it stung like a horse tail stings your eye if you aren't careful. She didn't turn back to look at her mother. She focused on Mork and Mindy's faces smiling brightly from the TV Guide on the coffee table. She didn't know what was coming next but she bit her lip in anticipation. Elizabeth knelt down and grabbed Piper's thin arms. "Look at me. Look at me this instant." Piper's brown eyes looked up through the tears. She couldn't see the fear in her mother's eyes but sensed it.

"This stops now, Piper. Do you understand me? This nonsense stops *right now*. You weren't anything before you were in my tummy. Do you understand? Your life started just eight years ago. And those things you think you smell—those *ridiculous* make-believe *smells*—they give me a headache. Do you understand that?! Do you?!"

"Yes, Mommy. I won't smell them anymore. The smell aches. I won't."

The horn startled Piper and she looked up to see the school secretary waving to her. She raised her hand in response but didn't wave. The woman wasn't even looking her way. As she approached her red Jetta at the far end of the school parking lot, she was flooded with the scent of lavender and, in her mind, saw tiny fragments of time: a baby's cradle, a white blanket, sunlight slanting through an open window, a broom in the corner of a room. *What room, what window, whose baby? Whatever*, she thought. *I'm done for the day. I'm going home to ride.* The scent of lavender lingered behind her nose and filled her with a rare feeling of true happiness. Though fleeting, the happiness came when she needed it the most and for that she was grateful. She had a knowing that one day the happiness would settle down and stay a while. She turned up the radio and tore out of the school's parking lot for the last time.

4

DARRICK WAS LATE AGAIN—something Piper absolutely hated about him. It wasn't that she was perfect, but waiting was something that got under her skin like nothing else. She was much too busy for that, and, after all, she didn't make people wait for her.

And if they ever did, it would be for a good reason. Part of her felt that most people would not wait very long for her, much less look for her if she were missing; and part of her just thought it was simply very rude.

College had done wonders for Piper; high school had truly just been a waste for her and dropping out did nothing more than disappoint her parents. It devastated her mother in a way that Piper would never understand. Her plans were something she kept to herself and she never doubted she would be successful once she had a chance to take flight. She had to wait six months before being able to take the GED test and move on. And move on she did. She had met Darrick in an elective class called Myths, Monsters, and Mysteries at The University of New Hampshire taught by a woman who had a fervor and a passion for the subject. That, of course, is what makes learning fun and easy, something completely lost on most teachers who Piper had ever had the misfortune of having prior to college. Darrick was a good boyfriend, but from early on, Piper knew they wouldn't be together forever, hardly. They had dated for three-plus years and she was getting really very bored with their relationship, their routine. What was once exciting was now mundane; what was once a debate was now an argument; what was once a thought-provoking comment, now fighting words. She was admittedly a hothead, but a loving one just the same. Darrick was a good guy, nothing more than a run-of-the-mill good guy—liked his beer, football on Sundays, and lots of sex. Nothing unusual: guys like Darrick were a dime a dozen and Piper knew it.

It wasn't that she didn't have feelings for him because she truly did; it was just that the feelings she had in the beginning were being replaced with new feelings, and these were of the sort that are not conducive to a loving, lasting relationship.

Darrick finally pulled up in his black Celica and opened the window to whistle at her as she stood with her hands on her hips, a gesture he knew well to mean that she was pissed at him. She looked over her sunglasses at him, not wanting to say anything nasty in case he had a legitimate reason for being late, like saving a drowning man or stopping by church to light a candle for his grandmother who had passed away suddenly last year.

As she folded her lanky frame into the tiny car, she quickly glanced his way—his clothes were dry as a bone, and, as far as she knew, he would never spend $2.00 on a candle for someone alive never mind for someone who was no longer on earth. Her eyes opened wide when she saw the reason for his tardiness. He had gotten the car stereo installed. The one he had been obsessing over for a few months. When they had spoken on the phone over an hour and a half ago, he said his car was in the shop, and he would be at her apartment in 40 minutes. Not wanting him to have to wait for her, she left her work on her kitchen table and walked to the corner to wait for him ten minutes early and spent the next hour worrying that he was sitting in a dirty garage having some expensive engine work done. A wave of boiling blood coursed through her as she realized that not only had he not had to wait for a mechanic to extract hundreds of dollars from his wallet, but when he called her earlier, he said that instead of dinner and a movie as usual, they were just going to hang out because he was short on cash.

Now she could feel her temper begin to rise up and press behind her sternum as she tried to suppress her anger. Her heart was beating so hard that she could hear it in her ears and her hands began to sweat, her mouth dry as sand. She was so sick and tired of Darrick's self-centered, boyish behavior and she intended to put a stop to it. *Does he ever plan on growing up?*

He turned to her, with his unequivocally adorable smile and said, "Hey babe, what's shaking? Check it out—look what I got." He pointed to the ridiculously expensive stereo and started to rattle off all the various specifications and attributes he admired so much. She remembered a time when he talked about her that way. Her mind had a way of shutting down in times like this, a defense mechanism she learned in college when a particular professor stomped on his soapbox and ranted about one thing or ten thousand others. Piper was the type of student who, as long as she attended each class, did not need to study much in order to get exceptional grades. Her memory was a gift in that it was like a sponge, literally soaking up information and trapping it. Sometimes though, her memory was a weapon, as Darrick was about to find out.

"Babe, aren't you listening? I said, 6-CD changer—how cool is that? It's in the trunk, wanna see?" He reached for the door handle, but Piper grabbed his forearm and could feel heat through his sleeve. *Why is he sweating?*

She took her sunglasses off and turned in the small bucket seat to look at Darrick, really look at him. Something in her knew that this was going to be the last ride in the "love mobile" with Darrick. She had nothing left for him; he was never going to grow up and be the man she wanted.

"Darrick, do you remember what you said to me when you dropped me off at the end of our second date?" She felt a little bit badly when she realized he had that clueless look on his face that most men do when they don't know what their woman (mother, girlfriend, daughter, wife) is talking about. At the same time, that look started her blood simmering again. "I remember," she said, seemingly letting him off the hook. He looked relieved. "You said, 'Piper, you are so beautiful, how did I get so lucky? I have a feeling that we are going to be together for a very long time. I promise I won't disappoint you like Rob did." She raised her eyebrows to challenge him. *No response?*

At this point Darrick knew he was in trouble. If she was now going to say that he was acting even remotely like Rob, his former roommate, Piper's ex-boyfriend, then he knew he had really screwed up. As if on cue, Piper looked out the windshield of the car, seemingly at something in the tree next to the coffee shop they frequented. She didn't look back at Darrick as she said, "You know, I really believed you when you said that. I thought I had found my soul mate in you. I loved you at that moment and I couldn't ever imagine a time when I wouldn't feel that way. But lately you ... you've been acting like ... like Rob always did and treating me like an afterthought for a while now. I'm tired of it and I don't want this anymore. I want," she sighed and continued, "I want more than this."

Darrick looked at her, reached out and touched her face. She wished he wouldn't do that—she knew he was a good guy; he loved her in his own way. He gently tugged at her chin so that she would look at him. His good looks were even better when he was serious, and serious he was. And, as she took a breath, she noticed his cologne—the one he only wore on special occasions. She had given it to him on his birthday and made him promise to only wear it once in a while. "I love this cologne—but only on you," she had told him.

He dropped his gaze for a moment and then looked back up at her, her beautiful dark eyes, watery with tears now. He took a breath and whispered, "Don't do this, not now Piper. I love you. I need you."

She wriggled her chin out of his gentle grip and stared back out to the tree again. "I love you too, Darrick, but ... but I want more. I want to be with a grownup, not a child." He winced; she felt it more than saw it. "I'm sorry, Darrick, but I have to go. I'll call you later."

She grabbed the handle, felt his warm lips on her cheek for an instant as she pulled herself up and out of his car for the last time. She turned, bent down to look into the car, saw the tear on his cheek and said, "Darrick—" but there was nothing left to say. Suddenly a scent-ache, the first one in a long time, filled her with a feeling of contentment, not lavender and babies this time, but something else, something she couldn't grasp at first. She wasn't aware that she was grimacing until she saw the surprised look on Darrick's face. *Burnt raisins?* She stuck her tongue out and shook her head as if to clear the scent away. It wouldn't leave. Did she even know what burnt raisins smelled like? *Burnt raisins, indeed*, she thought as her mind was flooded with waves of images: bloody linens, a tall man holding a baby and smiling, an older man sitting close, with tears in his eyes. She was filled with a feeling of love amidst this time of sadness.

"Babe?" Darrick wanted to hold her close. He loved her quirks and the scent-aches she spoke of though he didn't really understand what she meant when she explained, "They are just there—doesn't everyone have them?"

"Darrick, it'll be okay, I'll call you ...." And with that she shut the door and walked home. She would never know that Darrick went home and cried for days and that in the trunk of his car was not only the 6-CD changer but a bottle of champagne and a diamond engagement ring.

5

SEVEN YEARS PASSED and Piper was in and out of several meaningless relationships with men who didn't want anything more from her than what she was willing to give them. She hated to admit it, but she really didn't want anything more from them, either. She was bored with the roller coaster ride her life had become: moments of high, clear views and exhilaration followed by a quick and often stomach-churning descent. She wanted stability and love and a family, but how was she ever going to find that when she couldn't stand the men she was with? She wondered if there was something wrong with her. All the women she knew were either married, in a serious relationship, or were hell-bent on getting into one. She felt envy but couldn't figure out if it was for what these women had or if it was for what she thought she should have but didn't.

Piper would have been hard pressed at 31 to put it all into words.

But she tried. She still scribbled bits of poetry when the mood struck her just so, which was not often in the last few years; but now that she was alone, save for her new pup Viceroy, she spent much of her free time brooding, listening to music, and writing. This wasn't a bad thing in and of itself, but certainly it did not lend itself to getting out and meeting anyone new. But did she want to meet another disappointment, another dead end, a man with promises to break?

She had often heard women say things like, "All the good men are either taken, gay, or dead." She would laugh. *Well, at least the taken ones will be available in about another ten years. And maybe even the dead one—in another lifetime.* This thought made her feel calm, though she wasn't sure she believed in having more than one go-round at life. In her adult life, Piper learned the hard way not to say too much in front of other women; she didn't trust many of them. That was something that really bothered her: She could tell a man anything at all, from secrets to desires and fantasies, rumors and fears. But women—women were so different, and she didn't really know why it had to be that way. They, especially a few she had worked with over the years, would so willingly listen to her, share things with her, and encourage her to spill it all, telling her that she would feel better if she did. And the next day, these same "friends" would hold it against her and proceed to promptly spread all of her most personal feelings all over the office, the lab, or stable, or wherever it was she happened to be working at that time.

Her favorite place to write was in the bedroom of her small apartment in Marblehead where the rent was so high that she could have easily moved a few miles west and saved at least $400 per month and lived in a larger space. But she loved the sea, the smell of the salt air, and the ocean breezes. It comforted her in a way that felt like home, though until now she hadn't lived within fifty miles of the coast.

On her bed she had a quilt that Darrick had bought for her on their first trip to Maine together so many years ago. It was navy blue and white with little sailboats on the border. That trip had been so exciting, their first weekend together, just the two of them in a sleepy little fishing village. In the first year after her breakup with Darrick, she had packed the quilt away, not being able to part with it completely, but not thinking that she would ever be able to take it out again. But slowly, as with most painful things, time tended not to wash it away but to soften its edges in such a way that it could be touched now and again without the threat of tearing you to shreds. Piper learned that even though remembering Darrick was sometimes hurtful, it also made her smile and she often said a little prayer in the hopes that it would find him well and happy. He was a good man, but she was certain he was never going to ask her to marry him, and that is how she justified never calling him after that day in front of the coffee shop. She knew that if she picked up the phone, heard his voice, the gentle way he had of asking how her how much did she love him, she would get weak and want to see him, and they would fall back into the old pattern of dating, keeping separate apartments, talking about the future that never seemed to come quickly enough for her. So she hoped and prayed for his happiness and for hers, too.

She wondered if he ever thought of her. She would remind herself of all the ways he showed his love for her. He always remembered her birthday and made a big deal out of Christmas and Valentine's Day—especially Valentine's Day. He knew she had a thing about the letter "V." He didn't know why; no one did. Not even Piper. But he indulged this little quirk of hers whenever he could. Anyone who knew Piper just knew that everything important in her life had a "V" in it if she had anything to say in the matter. There was her horse Victory, her new pup Viceroy, and even her cars were always Volkswagens and Volvos. She scribbled "Vs" on paper when she talked on the phone and in the sand at the beach. When asked, she would just shrug and say that it had no special meaning, just an easy letter to write over and over and over again. Sometimes in the shower, when she was in that state between waking and sleeping, she would squeeze the shampoo out onto her palm in a "V." Her favorite names for children that she now realized she would likely never have were Violet and Vincent.

She used to dream that she might have twins someday, you know, in that perfect world all twenty-three-year-olds live in. The one where you met your soul mate, fell in love, got engaged, soaked up the attention and the drama of looking for the perfect wedding gown, party favors and god-awful brides-maid dresses, got married with all of your friends and family present, went on a whirlwind honeymoon to the most romantic spots all over Europe and when you returned, you found the most stunning house to move into, just in time to find out you were expecting your first baby, or in Piper's world, twins.

A boy and a girl, she thought; what could be more perfect?

Sitting on the edge of her bed on this raw and misty October afternoon by the sea, Piper contemplated going grocery shopping at the Stop and Shop a couple of towns over, to avoid seeing anyone she knew. But leaving the house would mean having to take a shower, find clean underwear, a matching pair of socks (clean or otherwise), dig out her sneakers from under the bed where the puppy usually dragged them, take the puppy out to pee first, come back up the stairs to the second floor of the house, put the puppy back, find her car keys, and walk to the corner, hoping she didn't have a ticket on her windshield for parking too close to the fire hydrant. It all just seemed like too much work for a Sunday.

So she lay back on the bed, her long legs hanging down, her feet still flat on the hardwood floor of her small apartment. She liked the way her muscles felt stretched like that and had a fleeting thought of joining the gym again. But right now, she was enjoying being alone with her thoughts. She realized that she had spent a lot of time alone throughout her life and again wondered if this was normal. She shrugged her shoulders as if someone had had asked her this question aloud. Out of the blue, a tear drop pushed its way out from the corner of her eye and slowly made the trek down her cheek and onto the sail of one of the little boats on her quilt. She didn't often let herself cry, because when she did, she had a hard time stopping, and this time was no different.

The tears came hot and fast, each one chasing the last, faster and faster until she put her arm up over her face as if to hide her emotions from, what? The ceiling? She knew she needn't be ashamed; crying was normal. It's just that she didn't want it to be normal for her. She had hardened herself and now took pride in it as it had taken a lot of work. She knew from an early age that she could take care of herself and that she didn't really need anyone; it wasn't that she didn't want someone. Sometimes she wished she could let others see a little of her weakness—not too much, just a little softness, a little dilution. She wondered if it was too late to change, to really change, become something else, someone else. Sometimes when she was out in the world, on her way to the dog park, or perhaps in a store, Piper looked around and realized that she knew not one soul by name. This frightened her a little bit, but then told herself that she moved here only three years ago and that she was a little shy—it was not much of a consolation.

She would first notice all the couples. It seemed that everyone but she had someone. Some couples walked hand in hand, others had a way of walking so that one sort of shielded the other from passersby, the man sometimes guiding the woman around a slower couple, or perhaps a wayward child in the middle of an aisle. They seemed to have an easiness all their own, a language their bodies knew well from years of practice, an easy rhythm that they didn't even realize existed but that others could see. Something as simple as a slight hand movement by one person being received as a gesture that made the other person reach out and take his hand. No words: just ease. She longed for that knowing, for that connection.

Next she would look at the children and something inside her quickened a little. She wanted to be a mother. She had always wanted that, but it just seemed like one of those twenty-something ideals that was less and less likely to happen with each passing year. Piper was an only child and had always yearned for a sister or a brother to keep her company but got instead the horse, dog, rabbits, cats. Her mother, Elizabeth, told Piper—between sobs once, "Someday you will understand what a mother does for her child. Anything and everything, anything and everything—you'll see. And sometimes that means ... well, it means knowing when enough is enough. You are all Daddy and I need—just you, honey. You know, there are mothers and fathers in the world who send their children away when they misbehave. I know you don't want that now, do you?"

The 31-year-old Piper dried the last of her tears and rolled over onto her side, pulling her knees up onto the bed, her quilt damp in one spot from so many tears. She lay there like this for a few minutes before sitting up, feeling relieved, cleaner, more relaxed. She got up from the bed, pushed her long black hair back, and noticed in the mirror over her bed that her hair needed washing. She thought about hopping into the shower, but again, decided it would take too much effort. *And for what? For whom?* She didn't feel like going out today. Sharon had left her a message earlier asking if she'd like to get some lunch and prepare for their upcoming reviews at work. She thought about calling her back but then realized she could still hear rain hitting her window and savored the idea of making some tea and trimming Viceroy's nails. She thought maybe that was pathetic, and again shrugged her shoulders, turned on her CD player and grabbed her journal and a Valvoline pen she had slipped into her purse at the garage where she had her oil changed. The song that was playing fit her mood perfectly. A song called "Memories" by a Dutch band called Within Temptation. It was sad and sweet, and she loved it. She never got tired of listening to it.

She lay back down on her bed, avoiding the teary spots and, this time on her stomach, with her journal in front of her, knees bent, ankles crossed in the air above her. She often read a little of what she wrote previously prior to writing something new. But this time, she just opened to a blank page and began writing what she felt deep in her heart, not knowing really where the words came from, just obediently jotting down what was there—in her mind, her heart, her soul. Sometimes they just appeared seemingly from nowhere and not until she was done writing them did she realize what she had written.

> The wind calls your name
> And whispers a story
> Of a time gone by
> Of true love and glory
> Another place
> Another time
> When I find you
> Will you still be mine
> The years have passed
> I've cast off the sorrow
> Time marches on

I know I must follow
This journey is long
Mile after mile
Come take my hand
Rest here a while
The trail hasn't ended
Though many can't see
There's a path overgrown here
For you and for me
Let's ride it together
Though we're worlds apart
Take the reins in your hands
I'll take you in my heart
Watch the meadow turn green
Feel the warmth of the sun
God's always promised
A new day would come
Life is not measured
In numbers and days
But by love and by laughter
And kindhearted ways
You always believed this
Now I know that it's true
I no longer count days
Just memories of you
Did you tuck a note
'Neath the bluebird's wings
Is that why he visits
Is that why he sings?
He calls my name
And whispers a story
Of a time to come
Of patience and glory

Putting down her pen, a final tear falling onto the page, Piper felt better. Writing always made her feel better. Had she remembered Vander and his words, believed that he really existed not as an imaginary friend, but as a true soul, as real as anyone she knew on earth, she might have noticed that the solitary tear had fallen onto the word "patience," that it might be a reminder from him. Instead, she wiped the tear from the page, smearing the blue ink, giving the word wings, making it look as if it had fallen quickly from a far-away place, landing safely in her journal, just for her to see. She closed the journal and decided she did want lunch after all and headed for the shower.

Sharon was waiting for her at Jack-Tar Tavern on Washington Street down by the harbor and had ordered them a bottle of white Zinfandel. The atmosphere inside always made Piper feel like an invited guest, which is what she needed when the weather was like this.

"Hi Chickadee," chirped Sharon when she saw Piper approach the table by the window.

"Hey Lady, what's up?" She sat down with a sigh and a forced smile on her face. "Nice weather, huh?" she sneered.

Sharon rolled her eyes. "I know. And it gets dark so early. That reminds me, I have to pick up my happy pills on the way home."

"Do those things really work? I mean, how do you know?" Piper had often wondered if she was a candidate for anti-depressants but at the same time didn't really want to know.

Her closest friend poured them each a half glass of wine and said, "Well for starters I don't feel the urge to rip Mike's head off just for opening his mouth, if that's any indication."

Piper quickly swallowed the sip of wine she had just taken to avoid having it exit through her nose as it had on more than one occasion when Sharon was in a sarcastic mood.

"What else, though? I mean is there really a big difference between you with the meds and you without them?"

Her dirty-blonde confidant leaned back against the high back booth and thought for a moment.

"Oh most definitely, there's a difference: the difference between a size six jeans and a size ten, hello? And I was so bitchy! I hated everything and everyone got under my skin.

Don't you remember how I tortured Mike? The poor guy, it's a wonder he's stuck around as long as he has."

Piper nodded with one eyebrow raised. "Well, I guess that's what you do when you love someone."

Sharon perked up at the mention of love.

"Speaking of love ... how are things with Kevin? What's going on with the two of you?"

Piper rolled her eyes and shrugged her shoulders. "Not much. He's a nice guy, don't get me wrong. It's just ...."

"It's just what?" Sharon poured them some more wine.

"I don't know, I guess there's no real spark there."

With glass tilting in Piper's direction Sharon said, "You have to work at these things, guys are a lot of work. Hey, I'll tell ya what. I'll sell you half my prescription for thirty bucks if you think it might help."

Piper laughed and said, "No thanks, I like the way my jeans fit right now. But I appreciate your help. You're such a doll."

Their soup and sandwiches arrived and as soon as the waitress left their table Sharon joked, "Well they say it's better to be fat and happy than thin and miserable."

Piper tilted her head and replied, "Thanks, but I think I'll take my chances."

Sharon paused, contemplating. Then she raised her glass and smiled. "Well then, here's to skinny bitches!"

Work, for Piper, had always provided the stimulation that she needed to keep herself on track. She lived for her weekends, her time alone with her thoughts, time to sleep, or just to lie in bed dreaming of a day that she could roll out of bed, grab some jeans and a pair of boots, and ride out into the woods for a few hours, not seeing a single person the entire morning; the only sounds being the unmistakable sound of leather as it is stretched with each stride, hooves rustling in fallen leaves, and the steady breath of the horse beneath her. But spending alone even one day more than the weekend provided, left her feeling disconnected more than usual, a bit melancholy and out of sync with the world. As she grew into her adult self, she came to the realization that feeling this way helped her to be more introspective and creative in her writing. Who wants to read happy poems? And what about her favorite songs? Weren't they sad in nature? Isn't that why people connected with songs of lost loves and missed connections? But writing was not how she made her living. No, indeed, she knew she would starve if she *had* to write, especially if she had to write what someone told her to.

As an insurance agent in the equine industry, Piper needed to be detail oriented, shrewd, and sometimes more than a little suspicious of the very clients she was working for. Feelings of creativity and melancholy had no place there. She chose this career as a way to stay connected to something she had a passion for, something she was truly knowledgeable about. If there was one thing in life Piper knew well, it was horses and what made them tick.

The career she chose, unfortunately, also introduced her to the one thing that made most people tick. Money, she knew, was a force to be reckoned with; but to put money and an animal's life in the same column on the same spreadsheet always made her a little queasy. She didn't like it one bit, primarily because it usually meant that a horse had to suffer in some way or another in the name of someone's bank account. This is what made her widely respected in her field and feared by the most unscrupulous horse people. She didn't consider herself to be on the same plane as most horse people she knew. She loved these animals in a way that spoke to her admiration of God's divine perfection. She was more at ease on the back of a horse than in the presence of any human she had ever met. And, although she had owned two horses since Victory, she never found another gentle giant like him, one that she had such a strong bond with, a connection that seemed to continue even after his death at age twenty-seven.

While she made a decent living, she didn't feel that she could afford her rent *and* board to keep a horse at a stable, especially anywhere in the suburbs surrounding Boston where farmland had quickly transitioned from essential yet abundant, to commodity, to luxury in a matter of only a few decades. And besides, her dream was always to be able to keep any horse she owned at home, in her sight and care at all times. There was a time when she had dreamed that she and Darrick would have found a nice spot to settle, perhaps in the western part of the state or maybe Vermont, with some land and endless places to ride that were still untouched by McMansions and cul-de-sacs. And since her and Darrick's relationship ended, she never really pictured herself settling down with anyone she dated; at least, not in the long run anyway.

Piper seldom seemed to want what her peers did. She guessed that not a lot of people her age wanted to live in a way that she dreamed about. Quiet. Space. She wanted a lot of space. And a meadow! She would gladly trade the convenience of a coffee shop on every corner, great restaurants, and easy highway access for a long gravel driveway and four-stall barn with heated tack room and acre upon acre of open pasture. Any real estate she might consider purchasing in the future must have a meadow, or at least the potential for one. She didn't mind if her nearest neighbors were within walking distance, just not a walk that would make it especially easy for them to stop over, looking to borrow a cup of sugar.

Piper was friendly enough to people she knew and overly friendly to people she did not, really a requisite in the field she worked. But, by spending time with her, most people learned that she needed her alone time as much as she needed companionship and connection. She often grew quiet when she spent too much time with someone, be it a friend, family, or a date. Some suspected boredom, others snobbery, but those few who knew her well knew that she just had a side to her that was thoughtful, introspective, and she was easily overwhelmed by too much chatter about mundane things. She really did enjoy a night on the town now and again, and after a glass or three of wine had no problems playing the role of a successful young woman on the prowl, but it just wasn't her on the inside. She found herself most weekends at home alone. She knew that if she was out on a Friday night, she could still have Saturday night to herself. Getting dolled up and being on her best behavior two nights in a row seemed like a lot of work! This fact, though Piper had never been privy to it, and wouldn't have believed it if she had been, was much appreciated by the other young women out on the town trying to impress a handsome, single (or otherwise) man with deep pockets.

If attracting good-looking men had been a sport, and for some it seemed it was, one would not be wrong in saying that Piper had a natural ability in this area, one that can't be learned. She had an easygoing nature that men liked and women were surprised by in most situations. She could talk to anyone about any subject that she knew even just a little bit about. Asking questions was a very important part of her job. Equally important was listening to the answers given, reading body language, and deducing the unspoken messages that might imply fraud. It was no surprise that asking questions and putting people at ease came naturally to her in a conversation, giving the impression that she was truly interested in the subject at hand. And she usually was interested by the time the dialogue got rolling.

She did often notice, but didn't much care, that women sometimes became visibly uncomfortable with her ease around their boyfriends or husbands. She could get a little loose-lipped and flirtatious with the help of a little wine, and loved a dirty joke as much as the next person. Having been raised by a man who worked construction, she knew more than a fair share and didn't see a thing wrong with it. But she was harmless. The last thing Piper wanted was to take someone else's boyfriend home with her. She genuinely enjoyed learning what she could from whomever she met, whether it was a horse owner whose new mount happened to cost more than most people's vehicles or the cashier at Macy's shoe department whose accent struck Piper as comforting, even familiar, prompting her to make conversation outside the cashier's obligatory, "Will you be using your Macy's card today?"

The men who Piper dated more than once or twice learned quickly, however, and seemed somehow disappointed by the fact that she was much more comfortable spending time in the countryside—picking apples or pumpkins, fishing, canoeing, riding, stopping anywhere she saw a sign for a barn sale—than being in three-inch heels and at a five-star restaurant. Not that she didn't clean up very nicely; the only thing standing between her being beautiful and her being stunning was a string of pearls her grandmother left her and a really nice deep plum-colored lipstick called Ripe Raisin that whitened her teeth more than any dentist could ever hope to. Her hair always caught men's attention and was the envy of most women, though few vocalized these thoughts. Her thick black mane flowed gently past her shoulders and came to a "V" between her shoulder blades. She didn't do much with it because she didn't need to, and she always kept it long, feeling that this was one thing women had a right to, and should take advantage of. It was clearly a feminine trait that she enjoyed, and she noticed that it usually turned heads, whether she was in jeans and half-chaps or a skirt and blazer on the way to a meeting.

It was during one of these meetings that Piper met Paul. They were introduced by Sharon and there seemed to be a bit of a spark as they shook hands, Paul averting his gaze for a fraction of a second to see if there was a ring on her finger.

Paul was an agent with the same large insurance company that Piper had worked at for seven years, but he was only beginning to dabble in the equine division and had requested this office on a whim, mostly because it was far away from his former wife in New York and also because he was tired of being a closet Red Sox fan ever since, as a kid, he had watched Oil Can Boyd pitch a near perfect game against the Yankees. And, teetering on the cusp of forty, he felt he could use a change of scenery; what better way than to move hundreds of miles away from everything he knew because of the beautiful face of a woman he had seen on the company's website? He couldn't think of anything more romantic, or crazy for that matter. He wondered for a few seconds during their handshake if this could at all be considered rash or even a bit stalker-like, but shrugged it off, knowing himself too well. He was not impulsive in the least; but this move seemed to come at a time when he needed to make a break from the old and start anew.

Piper's eyes sparkled more than a little, which was unusual for a Thursday morning, with the weekend seeming close and yet too far away at the same time. Upon waking that morning she had known that the day would go well, but had had no idea how she knew it. Standing in the shower and letting the warm water saturate her hair, she stood still, eyes closed. The familiar scent of freshly turned soil and tomato plant leaves filled her seemingly from head to toe. Her shoulder blades twitched and she smiled.

"Okay Thursday. Let's see what you got."

Soon after arriving at work she glanced at her watch. *9:45? Really? Maybe I was wrong about you, Thursday.*

Piper never aspired to be in management in any way, shape, or form, but she knew that if by some bizarre turn of events she found herself there, she would not bore people to tears. *One meeting down, two to go.* She glanced at her day planner. 10:15 – Paul. *The new guy from New York. Hmm, maybe Thursday still has a chance.*

He walked into the conference room and immediately made eye contact with Piper. He fixed his tie nervously. "Good morning,"

"Hi. Good morning."

She realized she was smiling and tried to keep it to a friendly toothless grin. *Seems nice.*

Paul seemed a bit eager and she preferred to keep business matters just that: business matters.

"So, Piper, where would you recommend a newbie find the best martini in town?" They left the conference room after Sharon and the others. He stopped to let her through the doorway before him.

Here we go. Her mind flashed back to a guy she briefly dated. Stan. He worked in her office a few years back. She agreed to more than one date more out of boredom than any real interest. He seemed like a normal enough guy, a little older than she usually dated, balding, and more than a bit chubby, too. But she was consciously trying to change her dating criteria and date men who were different from those she was normally attracted to. She had read something online the previous month that suggested some women just needed to enhance their mate-choosing skills by using their heads more than their feelings or heart. She didn't usually take online fluff too seriously, but since Sharon had emailed the article to her, she thought maybe she ought to take the hint. Being a bit displeased with her own track record in the world of dating, Piper decided that she would assert this principle to her next potential relationship. She remembered her grandmother telling her more than once that, "Men learned to love the women they are attracted to and women learn to be attracted to the men they loved," much to the chagrin of both Piper's father and grandfather.

"Uh, well, I guess a newbie would want to try a few places and decide for himself." Piper realized her words came out wrong and she regretted it. "I could help?"

"Why am I flat ironing my hair for a casual, work related, no expectations dinner?" She looked over her shoulder at Viceroy. He was never more than a few feet from her when she was home. He tilted his head as if to ask her the same question. Memories crept in as she sprayed heat protectant on her silky raven hair. She couldn't help remembering more than a few awkward first dinner dates and other various courtship outings at which she couldn't, for the life of her, keep from making mental notes about the size of her date's diminutive hands, and how sweaty his hands and forehead would get when he dropped her off for the evening. She tried so hard to like the guy, but it was getting increasingly difficult for her. Mostly she was bored with a lot of them but with some ... she just could not bear the thought of them naked. It's not that Piper considered herself to be off limits. She did, however, feel there was a need for some modicum of attraction for it to work. *Come on now*, she would think to herself, *give a girl something to work with*. And she felt it important to go out of her way to present herself in a manner in which most people would find attractive, more for their sakes than hers. Her grandmother had for years told her that even though what's on the inside of a person is what matters most, people will judge you by what you choose to present. Of course, it didn't hurt that she'd inherited her grandmother's genes for height and for a narrow frame, making her height all that much more elegant and sexy. Piper felt her grandmother wouldn't have approved of any of the men who had been Piper's potential suitors. Presentation was completely lost on a few of them—particularly the guy from the office. What she really found tasteless was men showing interest in her just because of her looks; in fact, that was a big turn-off for women of substance, women like Piper. She had a lot of love and desire to offer the right man; it was simply a matter of finding him and she just didn't have the patience for it.

So she tried her best to make each man she dated "the right one," which she quickly learned is not a worthwhile exercise for a woman her age. She got the feeling that she could pretty much see someone's potential or lack thereof in the time it takes to order wine and an appetizer on the first date. Did he order her wine for her or ask her first what she'd like? Did he shave before their date, turn off his cell phone, clip his fingernails? Was he cordial to the waitress? And most important, did he stare at the waitress's chest as he ordered their spinach and artichoke dip?

Dating Stan had worn thin for her. The breaking point was when her sweaty, chubby, balding date asked when he was going to be able to see her wearing only her riding boots and carrying a whip. In fine Piper style, she took this disgusting little fact of life in stride, seeing it not as an insult, but as an opportunity. She took a deep breath and promptly responded by telling him that it was called a crop, not a whip, and that if she ever put her boots on without first putting on breeches, it would mean that she was too old and far too senile to want to be seen by even the handsomest of men, much less the likes of his perverted, disgusting self. And with that, Piper decided she would not date someone with whom she worked ever again. She smirked at herself in the mirror. She closed eyes for a moment and inhaled. *What is that? What is that smell?*

6

1848

T HE SUN WAS ALWAYS BRIGHTER on the days that he came to see her, the way it slanted through the window and fell gently, warmly on her face. She noticed things that she would have overlooked on any other ordinary day. The flowers in the dooryard were brighter, the floor was easier to sweep, the water from the well colder, cleaner somehow. The breeze found her in the open window making her feel unforgotten, a new feeling in her young life. She and Vander were going to the fair by the sea to celebrate the spring planting and the warm weather ahead. It did not matter how many times he knocked at her door, how many times he greeted her with a kiss on the cheek and a handful of freshly picked lavender: each time was like the first. What a difference in her heart, this kind of nervous fluttering. Until now, the only feelings to have visited her heart were heavy burden and mourning.

Piper and Vander had grown inseparable, their friendship growing over the years into something greater, though her father not allowing her to call it courting as yet. She thought that might change in the coming months with the feelings that Vander had been sharing with her. Prior to this springtime, if other girls had harbored any doubts that Vander and Piper would eventually have something other than friendship, those doubts melted away with the last of the lingering snow. Women and girls alike often waved their approval as the pair rode through the lanes on Vander's magnificent horses and headed toward the sea. And on market day, when Vander carried big armsful of freshly shorn wool, scratching and itching all the way only to trade it for a few sweets, a bit of ribbon, and a handful of lavender, it was clear to anyone for whom the wares were intended.

This quiet, handsome boy was quickly becoming a tall, broad-shouldered, and enviable young man. Many parents had their eye on him as a possible suitor for their daughters. His father Philip was honorable and hardworking, known for going out of his way for anyone in need. The men in the village often jokingly questioned this dark haired, stout man about his sons' paternity! Vander and his two older brothers were fair-haired and towered over their father. And his mother, Amélie was a woman other women wanted for a friend: quiet in her ways and honest in her deeds. Diminutive though her frame was, her spirit was as large and open as the spring skies at planting time. She raised three boys and a herd of sheep, kept two cows for milking, sold eggs at the market, mended her husband's fishing nets, and was known to be the gentlest of the village midwives. She quietly delighted in the honor of being the first person to touch many of the village's children as they made their passage from the womb into the world.

But those who thought they might bargain Amélie out of a fair price on her wool or perhaps play coy with her handsome sons, were quickly introduced to the side of her that questions not what is right and fair.

Philip pushed Vander to fish alongside him as he had done with his father, but Vander was not a man of the sea. He had a way with the land, the plow, and the animals. He dreamed of building his own home and farm outside the village on the land that was given to his father as a wedding gift. His brothers both had married and moved with their brides to a larger village where there was work for shoemakers, bakers, and milliners.

Piper and Vander had been childhood friends since she fell from a boulder at the edge of the meadow on the outskirts of the village when she was in her twelfth summer, Vander his fourteenth. He heard her cries in the woods and raced to find her before anyone else who might have dark intentions. He spoke kindly to her all the way through the meadow, into the village, and then gently helped her into her house. Drawing fresh water from the well and bandaging her bloody knee, he softly whispered a tune that put her at ease. It was a song she knew all too well. She had met him earlier that week but, being tongue-tied and unsure, hadn't spoken. She was taught to be afraid, afraid of those she did not know, especially boys. Her shiny, raven hair caught his eye the first time he had seen her at the market and the handful of other times he had seen her since. Her family had come to this village when her mother passed on and her father felt it better to return to the country he knew as a boy. He found work here as a tradesman building tables, chairs, brooms, and wine barrels that were shipped across the sea to be sold in markets Piper's father would never see. Young Piper had been skipping stones on the river when she was supposed to be washing her brother's trousers and bedclothes.

When Vander stopped to let his horses drink from the river, he asked her if he could show her a trick or two to help the stones skip farther, longer. She took one look at him and remembered what her father had told her about boys, being especially protective of her and her brother Marek since their mother's death; he did not like boys, or anyone for that matter, coming around to visit Piper, no matter how innocent. She shook her head no and looked away over the river bank into the sky as if she expected her mother's advice to be written in the clouds for her. She realized that Vander must be different from the boys her father warned about. He was quiet and treated his horse with such kindness. He kept his eyes downcast, showing Piper respect. She instantly felt sorry that she had shunned him, but her father had been adamant about boys and the things they can do to girls, especially when he was out of the village, perhaps on the sea, fishing. She wanted to tell him that indeed she would like to know how to skip the stones farther, that she had taught herself and for the life of her could not get them to skip more than twice, no matter what she tried. But when she looked back to the spot where he had been riding, he was gone. Her eyes quickly scanned the woods, up and down the riverbank but he was gone, his horses having had their fill of the cool, clean water.

Piper was a lonely girl and spent a lot of time by herself, washing, cooking, planting, mending, and trying to keep her brother out of trouble, which took more time than all the other chores put together. Disappointment was a companion that often whispered to her to come and play. Her mother suffered long with the sickness that finally took her when Piper was in her eighth autumn, and she knew nothing of a life outside of fetching cloths dipped in the coldest well water for her mother's feverish skin, feeding a younger brother what little bread there was after all of their father's wages went to medication that didn't work, and listening to father's cry in the night to a god who didn't answer.

Piper knew pain and she knew sorrow, but somehow she also knew it was going to be all right. Life was not all bad. Since they had come to this village, there was no sickness, no crying, and going to bed hungry didn't happen often. When it did, it was because of nervous butterflies, not for lack of food.

Piper had noticed Vander long before the day at the river. He was the boy who rode the fine black horses out to the meadow to let them graze on the days they weren't being used to pull a cart full of fish back from the seaside. He was the boy with the straw-colored hair and the shy eyes. The girls in the village were always giggling and whispering as he rode past, he seemingly unaware of them. Lyska, a piggish girl with hair the color of a rooster's comb, told Piper not to stare at him as he rode past, that it was shameful for a girl to notice a boy. But when Piper asked if Lyska had not noticed him first, she pushed Piper to the ground, bloodying her nose and dirtying her freshly washed dress, and knocking her out of one shoe. They had been her mother's shoes, a gift from her husband when they married. They were a bit too large for Piper's small feet, but they were the only ones she had or wanted. Lyska informed her that she was older than her by three summers; she had reached courting age and that Piper had better stop gawking.

She added, as if to cement the idea, that if Piper dared to quarrel about this, her mother would take care of it properly and without haste. What Lyska did not know, but was about to find out, was that Piper was not one to keep her thoughts to herself. Though she spent a lot of time alone, when given the chance, she let anyone in earshot know just what she thought, good, bad, or otherwise.

Piper picked herself up off the dirt lane, on the end of which sat her home with chores as yet undone. But before she had straightened up completely, she threw herself at the red-headed witch, who to Piper's way of thinking, was too ugly ever to catch the eye of someone as gentle and sweet as that boy, whoever he might be. She knocked Lyska down and straddled her, pinning her arms with her knees. Long ago she had learned that this was the only effective way to wash behind her brother's ears and it seemed to work in restraining this little red devil, too. She was quite pleased with the results. In the most authoritative voice she could muster, she told Lyska that patience is a virtue and she wasn't feeling very virtuous lately. She slapped Lyska's cheeks as hard as she could until the stunned girl was snorting and squealing like the piglet she was. Piper, realizing how this would sound to anyone coming down the lane, quickly jumped up and trotted back home to check on Marek; there was dirt covering the back of her dress, she clutched her shoe to her bosom, and blood dripped down her nose and into the corner of her mouth.

She caught a glimpse of Vander through the trees as he dismounted and turned his horses loose in the meadow. She loved how he quietly communicated with his horses. He knew that voices didn't have the same effect as gestures and that kindness begets obedience. Animals as grand as his had never been seen in this village until Vander's father brought them home from war in the east. He brought the majestic black horses home to his wife as a gift for staying true to him all the time he had been gone. The story in the village had it that Vander's father, though a fisherman here, was transformed into a great warrior on a battlefield far away across the sea. He had saved an entire town from being burned by an invading army, and in return for his bravery, the people of the town presented him with their two finest yearlings, as black as coal and as strong as oxen. He brought them across the sea on a ship two years after leaving home and finally returned to his family, the horses now three years old, ready to work. The everyday beasts of burden throughout the fields and stables of these fishing and farming villages were heavy horses, used to pull the plows and the fish carts, transport the harvest to the huge barns in the center of the village, and carry the dead to the burial yard; yet they were gentle enough for three or four children to ride at one time. They were simply working animals, beloved by their families no doubt, but necessity still. Vander's horses were far more beautiful and lighter, elegant yet broad shouldered, lifting their knees as they trotted, hooves reaching out and pounding the ground in a proud procession, heads held high, necks gracefully arched, feathers on their fetlocks as graceful and curly as their flowing manes. They truly seemed to float along the lanes of the village, so beautiful was their conformation.

Vander rode one while leading the other to the meadow, at a swift pace most of the way with slowing only once or twice to let onlookers have an eyeful. These beautiful horses were the envy of the entire village. The sound of their hooves on the lane sometimes made Piper sad as she fondly remembered the two horses her family had kept when her mother was alive. Inka and Vilho were their names, and they had carried her father and his wares from village to village in the heat of summer and the snows of winter, surefooted and loyal, wanting only to please. Piper and Marek would take turns brushing their manes, picking briars and burrs from their tails, and fetching them water, hay, and sometimes a handful of oats, so that their father could sit and watch his wife sip broth or pray with her that God would spare her and allow her to watch her children grow.

Piper's father could be heard from out in the stable yard, singing softly at her bedside, a sad sweet song about a girl who caught a young man's eye at a village dance. But far from his home, he had tried hard to find her in someone else and spent his life searching and searching. When the songs were done and the summer's harvest was put up in the lofts to keep, Piper's mother's time on earth ran out like a dropped coin on a floorboard, rolling, teetering, circling, and finally tipping, rattling as it finds a place to rest. It was a cool evening in October when the last breath escaped her parched lips, her hand falling from her bosom to her husband's lap, eyes rolling heavenward.

These were the darkest of days. Little Marek would not be comforted, would not be quieted. He cried and screamed and pounded his fists on the bed where his mother once lay, accusing his father of putting her in the dirt. This little lost boy wanted to spend his days at the mound of rocks where his mother was laid to rest but his father forbade him, sometimes striking him out of frustration and ordering Piper to lock him in the chicken coop. Knowing what her mother would think about this, she instead would take him gently by the hand and walk with him down to the harbor and there they practiced skipping stones.

But times were hard and when the snows blanketed their village much sooner than usual, Piper's father, having so little money put by, was forced to trade the horses that winter for food and clothing for his children. He never told a soul, but he was tormented by the idea that he might have to use the horses themselves for sustenance and never wanted to be faced with such a choice, such a betrayal. He felt it was better to trade them while they were still well cared for. They had indeed served him nobly for more than twelve years. And when the early yellow and purple crocuses pushed their way through the soft and melting snow, Piper and her father and brother bade farewell to their home and prayed as they traveled long and far into their future that sadness and despair would not greet them wherever they may land.

Piper was a girl through and through and was given to fits of passion and impatience. She wanted to follow Vander and ask him about his horses and if the stories about where they came from were true. She didn't like the fact that Lyska thought she was worthy of a boy like Vander. She realized, though, that she was a disheveled and dirty mess. She could not run to the meadow pretending to chase a butterfly, and just happen upon Vander on his way home. She wished with all her might that she had a mother who could set things straight for her, too. Instead, Piper was faced with something she was loathe to do: wait patiently.

When she saw him next, Vander was offering to help her skip stones and that had not gone as she might have liked. But days later, Piper saw an opportunity to get a closer look at Vander's horses in the meadow behind her lane. She climbed a tree and jumped onto a giant boulder that looked out over the meadow. Pieferet and Henk grazed on the darker green clover, never far from one another, avoiding the milkweed and sumac that had sprung up in the late summer meadow. She was settling herself on the warm rock as she had done dozens of times before when hiding from her brother and her chores, wanting only a little time alone with her thoughts. Out of the corner of her eye she caught a glimpse of a silky gull feather on the edge of the boulder, fluttering in a light breeze that threatened to blow it away. She knew she could reach it, and so she stretched out her hand and, leaning a bit too far, tumbled to the ground, scraping her knee on the way down.

She hit the lush pasture without a sound, and it took her a few moments to realize that not only had she fallen far, but her knee was gushing bright blood, the skin having given way in a sickening tear, loose edges of flesh suddenly a bright crimson. She cried out for her mother, whom she always tried hard not to think or talk about. Her father was always so sad when Marek asked about Mere, and Piper made a promise to herself that she would not cause her father pain in that way. She never spoke of her mother, not to her father and not to Marek. What made her cry out to her mother who had been dead and buried for so many years now? Why would she not call for Marek or her father? She wanted her mother, needed her. She realized at a very tender age that mothers can never be replaced; she understood, too, that those who still have their mothers don't know the meaning of loneliness.

Her knee hurt, but there was a greater hurt that she had been hiding for so very long. Most nights, she lay on her bed of goose down and straw in the loft next to Marek, swallowing tears and screams in the night, denying that her mother was truly gone forever, while below her, by the fire, her father prayed aloud that his wife was resting at last and that God would give him the strength and the wisdom to do right by his children. Piper screamed for her mother; she screamed so that her father would not have to cry, screamed so that Marek would not call her "Mere" by mistake when his eyes were heavy with sleep. She cried that her mother would comfort her from her place in Heaven. She hollered over and over, not believing that it was her own voice she heard in her ears, so angry and raw.

"Maman! Maman! Maaaaaamaaan! I need you, where are you? Please! Please come back! Why did you leave me here?"

She sobbed and prayed that somehow God would let her mother down from Heaven. Just this once. She promised that she would never ask for anything else so important ever again if God would just let her mother hold her and whisper that it will be all right. If God could do anything, as she had been taught, why couldn't He do this? She fell back exhausted against the boulder, chest heaving, and stared with utter hatred at an ant crawling up her shin toward her bloody knee. She flicked it away and hoped the ant would suffer terribly before it died. She closed her eyes and hoped that when she opened them her mother would be there. After taking several deep, whimpering breaths, she slowly opened her teary eyes and, sniffling, looked up.

A hand was reaching down toward hers. She thought she must be dreaming. Blinking, her eyes searched upward, the sun shining in them making it difficult to see who was there. And then she heard the most beautiful voice say, "Give me your hand." As she shifted her weight up onto her good knee, she could see that it was Vander, his smile a beautiful sight that calmed her, his blue eyes searching hers. And as she touched his warm hand for the first of a thousand times, she was filled with a warm feeling of absolute love and light.

7

IT WASN'T UNTIL MID-MAY that Paul formally asked Piper if they were in a committed relationship. And it wasn't until late May that she said no. The dates they had been on were easy and comfortable. No one beside Sharon knew they were seeing each other outside of work; though they spent a lot of the week working together on different policies, Piper kept him at arm's length. Paul always needed some clarification on one thing or twelve others and from no one except the tall brunette he couldn't stop thinking about.

"No, we're not in a relationship." Piper felt for the first time in her life that she didn't need to explain herself and utter all kinds of apologies and sentiments about not mixing business with pleasure and so forth. It was also a first for Paul in that no one had ever refused a date with him; not in his adult life anyway. He seemed to Piper to be a genuinely nice guy, and very easy on the eyes she had to admit to Sharon, but she was determined to keep things professional, for now anyway. Finding herself in a bit of a mental fog recently and not really able to explain why, she just wanted life to be easy; for her, relationships didn't fit in that category.

She was exceptionally good at her job; even on an off-day, she was outselling anyone in the equine division, giving the impression that she was a completely put-together professional woman. On the inside, however, she sometimes felt lonely; but knew being alone must have a purpose. She trusted that it had a purpose.

Truth be told, her personal life was a mystery to most. On her desk sat a small photograph of her at six, sandwiched between her mother and father, her tiny teeth gleaming save for the one missing. Her pink tongue peeked out from the space it left. In another photograph, larger and in a beautiful dark mahogany frame, was Victory, carefully braided and tacked up for a hunter class at a local show. His eyes were open wide—the whites screaming caution, ears forward and neck craning around to look at the camera. To a trained eye, it was obvious he was posturing, protecting the girl holding his reins, standing at his shoulder, with her back to the camera. On Piper's back, the placard read "9," the number which always brought her luck and blue ribbons. Aside from these photos, a desk calendar, and telephone, her desk was clear.

The calendar, she was mindful, was there for anyone to view and so had only written-in business-related appointments and messages. The occasional "V" was scribbled over and over as a result of either a phone call that dragged on and on or perhaps during the occasional mid-afternoon lull when Piper took the opportunity to sit with a cup of tea and stare out her office window, daydreaming. She dreamed of a time when she might ride again. Really ride. Not just the occasional hack through the open fields of a friend's farm or the infrequent hunter pace she was invited to ride. But really ride, out in the state forests, the old logging roads, railroad beds, and down to the shore well after Labor Day when the beaches would be empty.

She loved the call of the gulls and lure of the waves and the feeling of the salty wind sweeping all the cobwebs from her mind and sending adrenaline crashing through her veins, making her heart beat to the rhythm of Victory's stride. To Piper, there was no sound as inviting or as exhilarating as that of hooves pounding on sand, faster and faster until the three-beat of a canter turned into a four-beat gallop. Her dad used to trailer Victory to Nantasket Beach in the old red Shoop he bartered from a man who needed a flagstone walkway installed. Piper wished away the summer for just this time, this one day each year. Horses were only allowed on the beach when the summer crowds had migrated back to school and work for another nine months, leaving the shoreline empty save for the few joggers and kite-flying children. Her mom would come along for the ride and bring a lunch for them all, including Victory.

Neither of her parents rode, but they certainly felt a deep appreciation for this animal and the wonders he had done for Piper when she was a little girl and talked nonstop of a little boy who would visit her in the night when she was trying to sleep. The doctors all agreed that it was no more than an imaginary friend, harmless and, in fact, the sign of a bright child. They tried to reassure them that Piper was a perfectly normal girl with a very healthy imagination, but Piper's mother was unsettled by it, especially when she heard more than a few one-sided conversations through the closed bedroom door. It was equally unsettling that her daughter knew the names of flowers that certainly did not grow in their yard, neither parent having much of a green thumb. Where would she have learned all these names? How did she know so much about horses? Surely not from the Golden Books on her bedroom bookshelf. Who did she think she was talking to? And why, during these one-sided conversations, did she talk of her mother's death? Piper never heard her mother's terrified voice, or saw the look on her father's face as he tried to hide his concern as his wife sobbed and insisted that there was something wrong with their little girl.

The doctors suggested a hobby or activity that might tucker their six-year-old out and give her something to focus on. Gymnastics didn't hold Piper's attention and swimming was something fun she enjoyed with friends only during the summer months. Piano was far too boring, and Piper adamantly refused to practice. It wasn't until she took her first riding lesson on a dapple gray horse named London Bridge that she felt more than comfortable, more than home. A year later, her parents had tired of the constant whining and pleading, and the never-ending trips to the barn where their daughter wanted to spend all of her time. They were told by parents of other horse-obsessed girls that this was the norm, and, eventually, she would grow out of it. But Piper's parents were worried about her, insisting in her steadfastness that she needed to be at the barn directly after school and not coming home until exhaustion demanded that she do so. On weekends, it was unheard of for her to rise, dress, and arrive at the barn later than 7 a.m. and rare if she returned home earlier than 6 p.m. This worried her mother a bit, but knowing it made her daughter happy, she went along with it, visiting the barn often to be sure that Piper wasn't working too hard. Her schoolwork, rather than slipping, improved, bolstering her mother's belief that it was, in fact, what she needed. But when Piper was at home she was restless, unfocused, wanting only to go back to clean a few stalls, sweep the hayloft, and breathe in the atmosphere that only a barn has. Eventually, her mother and father decided that they ought to build a small barn with a paddock for Victory out behind the house. At least that way, they would have their daughter at home with them.

Piper was startled by the phone and sat up straight, focused her tired eyes, and answered it.

"Piper, it's me. I'm running out for coffee; want to take a walk with me?" It was Paul and to hear his cheerful voice one would not guess that he had just the day before been turned down for a date by a woman who he had been thinking about nonstop for the last few months.

She smiled as she said, "Sure, I'll meet you downstairs." When she got off the elevator of the Prudential building, she felt familiar butterflies in her stomach much like she had when she knew she would soon see Darrick. She missed him, or rather, missed how he made her feel and sometimes wondered if she had made a huge mistake by breaking up with him. Dating since then had not gone well and she missed that connection she had felt with Darrick, that closeness, familiarity. On the one hand, she really longed for that, and on the other, she was incredibly glad to be free of it. She just figured that everything happens for a reason and if she just let things flow the way they do, then it was just going to have to be good enough for her. When she stepped off the elevator in her gray skirt, white cami, thin pink sweater, and heels, the sunlight coming through the lobby windows shone directly into her eyes, blinding her and making her squint, wrinkle her nose, and walk cautiously forward. Paul was waiting for her at the front door and enjoyed the fact that she couldn't yet see him. He liked to watch her when she didn't know he was watching.

He found her more than beautiful. Paul felt that if she would just give him the chance, he could make her happy. What he really loved about her was that she sometimes seemed to be unaware of the way people noticed her. Men and women alike turned their heads, if even just slightly, to catch a glimpse of the taller-than-average, nicely dressed woman who sort of floated as she walked. When she saw Paul at last, she smiled a warm, genuine smile and said, "Looks like the sun decided it would come out after all."

He replied with, "It saw you coming."

She smiled. *How corny, but cute just the same.* Her impulsiveness getting the better of her, as it had since she decided to be born into an ice storm one January night, she decided right then that she could let her guard down with him—take a chance. *What the hell.* Feeling more alive now as they stepped onto the sidewalk and into the warm sun, she turned to Paul.

"On second thought, maybe it wouldn't be out of the realm of possibility that we are in some sort of relationship." He smiled a beautiful, broad smile, the kind that made his skin crinkle at the corners of his dark eyes. "Really," he said through the smile. And just then, as they turned in the direction of the coffee shop, she stopped and took a deep breath. She said quietly, "Do you smell that? I smell something sweet. Lavender, I think."

Paul shook his head. "No. Maybe it's your perfume."

8

SOME BELIEVE THAT LIFE is nothing more than a series of random events that lead a person from one end of his or her life to the other with tragedy, controversy, and joy dotting the fabric, creating the landscape. Others believe that life is a carefully embroidered plan with intricate messages hidden among the details of a baby's tiny fingernail, a puppy's ceaseless love, a husband's knowing and steady patience, a mother's fear-driven religion. Others believe that one's own destiny lies in free choice.

Piper didn't know where she fell on this continuum. She was too busy to really ponder such things anymore. She loved writing, and music often inspired her to do so. Life had moved her forward, as it does, time not waiting for anyone. She was enjoying herself much more in her mid-thirties than she had at any other time she could remember. Since that beautiful cloudless June day she married Paul on the shoreline in Gloucester at thirty-four, life had been a constantly changing and evolving process. No longer did she have time to contemplate the mysteries of the universe, wonder where life would take her, sit and cry, and write her poetry. She had a good friend in Paul, and he trusted her with his thoughts and dreams. Their arguments rarely passed quarrel stage, and when they did, it was about something that was worthy of the energy. She really hadn't believed she would ever meet anyone who made her heart skip a beat the way it had with Darrick. Life has a way of surprising you, she figured, and sometimes the surprises weren't all that bad.

They packed up their respective apartments and, along with Viceroy, settled in a town called Feeding Hills; although she had been born and raised in Massachusetts, she had not been aware that this little farm town exists in the Commonwealth. It was closer to New York so that Paul could visit with his family more easily, but it was still inside a two-hour drive to Piper's parents. The land they purchased was inexpensive, considering the area where she had been living most of her adult life. Purchasing forty-three acres was a dream come true for them both, and knowing there wasn't a neighborhood of new homes and cul-de-sacs within quite a few miles made it all the sweeter. Most of the acreage was abandoned pastureland, which unfortunately had become worth much more as real estate. On the outskirts of the pasture was a thick tree line of old growth hardwoods. It was in these woods that Piper discovered on their walk-through with the realtor the most wonderful selling feature available on the market: a meadow! It was just shy of three acres, but it was what she had always dreamed of having. It was lined with a stone wall, and the gate was still there, though barely. It was a simple gate made of thin branches, tied long ago with rawhide, which had long since rotted, leaving the branches askew.

She turned to Paul and grabbed the lapels of his navy wool pea coat. "Honey, this is the place I have always dreamed of, this meadow ... I want this one!"

The agent winked at Paul, laughed at Piper, looking much the way she did when she was a little girl begging her dad for a pony. Paul wished he could capture the look in her eyes—the excitement there. He rolled his eyes, feigning boredom. Piper playfully slapped his arm and pouted until he threw his arms open and said, "I love it, too! Tell the man we'll take it. We'll take two if he's got another!"

And so it was that Piper and Paul found the place they would call home, paying a little over two hundred ten thousand dollars for a piece of land that would have cost millions just one hundred fifty miles east.

They purchased house plans online and had a local

builder construct it for them. They chose a small, three-bedroom colonial, gray with black shutters and a cranberry door, quintessentially New England. They were very conservative with the upgrades but did splurge on an enormous fieldstone fireplace in front of which they spent most of their evenings: talking, reading, dreaming aloud. The barn, however, was not such a simple endeavor. It had to be researched, designed, and built by a contractor who specialized not only in reproduction homes but also in equestrian women with exacting demands.

"It has to look old, like it's been here for centuries," she told him. She wanted a simple stone and wooden barn like the ones that dotted the countryside in Southern France where they had spent their honeymoon. She felt so content there, like she belonged—a rarity for her. She wanted four stalls and a feed room that could double as a tack room if need be. However, she preferred to keep her tack in the house where she could smell the leather, which was aromatherapy in its finest form. She wanted rain barrels to collect water for the barnyard and didn't want electricity run to the barn, much to the chagrin of Paul who thought this had nothing to do with budget.

They certainly could more than afford some of life's finer things now, having done well since they started their own equine insurance agency a couple of years prior. Paul realized that Piper's desires ran deeper than most people's, and he loved her with such ferocity that he would certainly go along with her desires to have a very primitive stable; but he insisted on electricity. He knew he would regret not arguing that point the first time *he* had to carry hot water from the house to melt the ice in the water trough. The barn plans took time and patience which had never been Piper's strong suit. It took over a year to build because, as it began to take shape, there were other elements added such as the stone wall in front with an archway that framed the barn itself and, of course, the second story hayloft and cupola which Piper thought would make a wonderful place for Paul to tinker with his collection of model trains.

Paul had some ideas, too, that were not exactly welcome; but he had learned over the years how to appeal to Piper and calmly stand his ground. When she had time to mull them over, she liked most of his ideas, although she was not quick to admit it. She could be stubborn, but she loved her husband and knew that she had some giving to do to keep the balance. The idea that needed no hashing over, no dialogue at all, was the one that had the contractor laughing, thinking that it was a joke; but realizing his mistake, he apologized. Eventually though, he, too, thought it was quite unique. Paul wanted a wine cellar added onto the back of the barn, accessible through a thick Gothic style white-oak door with hand-forged wrought-iron hinges and handle. That door, said the contractor, would be heavier than any horse they might hope to keep out of that room!

As it was all being put together, Piper and Paul decided that they should begin the landscaping to complete the look they were reaching for. They planted Pink Rambler roses that would eventually cover the side of the barn with the help of a trellis. Around the roses, they placed several hardy lavender plants. For the archway, two trumpet vines were started which, before long, had wound their way all around the stone. They worked tirelessly every evening throughout the summer months into the fall, wanting to do all the work they could themselves. They purchased a chainsaw and began clearing a path through the wood line to the meadow's gate. Taking down only brush and saplings, they created a gently winding trail through the giant oaks and black walnuts. Piper took several pictures to send to her in-laws as proof that their son was actually capable of performing manual labor.

Paul's parents had raised him to be a good student and eventually it had paid off well at Syracuse and then in the insurance field. His father had been a laborer his entire life as his father before him had been. And he felt that if his son could develop his mind, he wouldn't have to wear out his knees and back by age fifty and still have fifteen years of work ahead of him. His mother loved the idea that her son was trying something new and loving each and every day with his new wife. She uploaded the pictures and sent them to her sister and Paul's brothers in California.

Paul's mother hadn't liked his first wife one bit and was relieved when she met Piper for the first time. As soon as she stepped into her future mother-in-law's kitchen, Piper's eyes widened, as she took a deep breath, smelling the apple pie that was baking in her honor. Like a child whose pure emotion bubbles over, as yet unhampered by social norms, she threw her arms around the cook. Paul's mother had not expected such openness; before the visit with Piper, she had been recalling the demeanor of Paul's cold ex-wife. Stunned for only a split second, she quickly reached up and hugged the girl who towered over her, and felt a warmth and happiness she imagined long ago that she might someday share with her own daughter. Behind them, Paul stood holding a large bouquet of "purple spikes," as he called them, for his mother. From that day forward, Paul knew this was the woman he was meant to be with for the rest of his life.

Paul had never tried his hand at gardening before he met his wife, but he was simply amazed at how many plants she had on the deck of her tiny apartment in Marblehead. He had no idea you could grow an entire garden in 5 gallon buckets, pots, and in bags of potting soil. She had a whole vegetable garden, save for corn, which she had tried once but it blocked too much sun from all the other plants. She had tomatoes in pots, cucumbers, and beans climbing the trellis which leaned against the building. Basil, oregano, sage, and lavender each resided in their own bag of soil, holes punched in the bottoms to let the water drain. In terra cotta planters lining the railing of the deck, she had the most beautiful array of petunias, baby's breath, impatiens, vinca vine, and Portulacas that cascaded down over the edge of the deck. Many days when she was watering and deadheading, weeding and dreaming, she would pluck a shiny basil leaf. Crushing it and smelling the scent brought her back to her grandmother's kitchen where there was nothing but love and garlic. "Two things you can't have too much of," her grandmother used to say.

Paul was more than eager to learn the basics and even took notes, which Piper found annoying yet endearing. She started him with some small sunflowers and nasturtium which she knew anyone could grow. She thought it was funny that, when he would arrive for a date, the first thing he did after kissing her hello was to go out onto the deck and check on his flowers. And now that they had so much acreage, Paul was getting excited about what they might be able to do with it.

When it came time to look for her first horse in over a decade, she knew immediately what to look for. Nothing would do but a Friesian. She had dreamed of owning one of these Dutch warmbloods for a long time and had come across several for sale on different assignments throughout the years. But these animals did not come cheap. Her clients who owned them bought directly from breeders in Holland. She thought she may have to purchase a foal and wait several years before being able to train and ride it; even still, the babies sometimes come with $30,000 price tags. But it wasn't at all about the money.

For Piper, these horses had something other horses didn't. She couldn't explain it, but figured that most Friesian owners couldn't. That didn't make them crazy or inarticulate, hardly. At last year's Equine Affaire, as they were standing in the breed pavilion, a Friesian was led past them heading out to the arena for a clinic on natural horsemanship. Piper tried only once to explain to Paul what she felt when she was around these animals.

"Honey, it's so hard to put into words, but it's like watching a Thoroughbred race. It's exciting—it's what they're bred to do. Oldenburgs, Hanoverians, Trakehners—they dominate the dressage arena and cross-country events, right? But Friesians ... they touch my soul. They have such a fierce elegance, bold dignity, and a loyalty unmatched by any other breed of horse."

She was trying to explain this part, but he was laughing at her, though not in a cruel way. It's just that she had a way of cracking him up when she got passionate about something. She had a vein in her forehead that stuck out a little when she was angry or excited, and her husband knew from experience that when he saw the vein, he was about to be yelled at or lose his wife to the couch for a night or two; or more likely she was going to say something so profound and so beautiful that it would bring him to tears.

Paul suggested that they look around. "Maybe we should just think about it for a while. We said we wanted a few horses. Do you really think we can afford more than one at thirty grand a pop?"

"No, I guess not," she said.

He saw the hurt in her eyes. She was not an extravagant spender and never had been. In fact, one of the things Paul loved about her was how she could stretch a dollar into next week if she had to, and even if she didn't. Then he dropped the bomb on her while giving her a look he knew made her weak in the knees.

"Piper, I thought we were going to talk about starting a family soon. What happened to that idea?"

Now she looked down at her work boots, covered in dust and wood shavings. She said, "You're right. I'm a dreamer, I guess. I don't know what's going on sometimes ..." her voice trailed off. "I'm sorry, sweets, I guess I got a little carried away."

He took her hand and kissed her forehead. "I'm the one who's sorry. I hate when I have to be the grown up. It's a tough job, but someone has to do it."

She poked him hard in the ribs and said, "That's okay, pal. You can make it up to me later."

He raised his eyebrows and looked her up and down.

She said, "Yeah, right, and then you woke up, buddy. I meant you could buy me some fried dough and a beer."

Paul laughed his laugh, the one that came from deep down and meant that he was really taken by surprise. "Oh, how classy, my dear."

This time she raised her eyebrows and looked him up and down, and said, "Well, I'm sure it'll be better than what you had in mind."

He laughed again and said, "Touché, my love, touché." He took her hand in his, and as they strolled through the aisles, picking on each other, they made everyone in earshot laugh as they passed the stalls that held every breed of horse imaginable from the miniature donkeys to the eighteen-plus hand Shires.

When they returned home that night, Viceroy was unsettled, fidgety, and would not stop his pacing. Paul took him outside, but he wanted to come right back in. He barked and spun in a couple of circles, then finally quieted down but wanted to be with Paul wherever he went.

Piper shrugged it off and said, "Huh, there's your son right there. Are you happy?"

Paul scooped up the dog and held him like an infant. "Yes, I am, and I'm quite proud, too. He looks just like your mother, don't you think?"

This time it was Piper who couldn't stop the laugh if she had tried. Paul dramatically turned his back on her and said, "Now if you'll excuse me, I have to put my son to bed." He walked up the stairs singing Harry Chapin's "Cat's in the Cradle."

Piper just shook her head and said a silent prayer, thanking God for sending her a man who knew just how to deal with her and her crazy dreams. She loved Paul, and she really was so grateful to have him. She knew she was in a good place in life and reminded herself to appreciate the things she had and not let the things she didn't have ruin her mood. *Why then, am I not completely content?*

Just then she had her first scent-ache in almost two years. It was different this time, not lavender and burnt raisins, but something she couldn't place at first. She closed her eyes to focus on just the scent. Salt air. It gave her goosebumps, and she shivered. She missed living by the sea and made a mental note to get back to the coast and visit Sharon and some of her other former colleagues in the city. Then maybe she could swing by her parents' house for a visit. But for right now, she decided to put some water in the kettle for tea.

She went into the laundry room off the kitchen and took out of the dryer a pair of yoga pants and a sweatshirt, fished out a pair of Paul's wool socks, and closed the dryer. As she stood back up, the scent-ache came back. Salt air and a glimpse of something. *But what?* she wondered. She closed her eyes again and tried to concentrate. Nothing. She thought it was strange that she was never able to describe this strange occurrence to anyone she met and also that it had been so long since the last one. The kettle was whistling and she hurried to the stove. She laughed to herself that she wouldn't want to "wake the baby." She made herself a cup of rote Röte Grütze with a teaspoon of sugar instead of tea, thinking she could do without the caffeine.

She thought about heading up to her office to check her e-mail, but decided against it because she had promised herself that if she was going to do the majority of her work from home, she didn't want to get into the habit of working on weekends and holidays. And if she opened her e-mail, the next thing she would be doing would be work related. She had learned long ago that work was work, and it would still be there tomorrow; you were never finished. She wanted to keep her schedule the way it had been when she worked for someone else. So instead of heading upstairs, she sat down on the sofa and turned on the television. She smirked and remembered her father saying that no matter how many cable channels you get, sometimes there is just nothing on. That seemed to be the case tonight as she scrolled through the offerings and stopped at MTV. Sometimes, she thought, they still actually play music on that channel.

She pulled the burgundy throw from the back of the cool leather sofa and wrapped it around her. The video playing was black and white, and she thought the guy singing was pretty good-looking in that way only rock stars are. She didn't know the song or the band, but it was a sad song and she really liked it. There was a soothing quality to his voice, and even though he was covered with tattoos, something she would never consider for herself, she turned up the volume and put down the remote. She was mesmerized by the lyrics, his voice, and the video itself. She leaned forward a little to be sure she'd be able to see whose song it was when the words came on the screen.

"H.I.M" was written there, but she had never heard of them. She made a mental note to look them up online the next morning and wished she could hear the song again, it was so beautiful.

Turning off the TV, she got up and grabbed a note pad from the kitchen and a pen. She sat down and looked at the blank page, and, as she had so many times before, she just wrote what was there. When she was a little girl, her mom would buy her little games and activities to keep her busy when they took long car rides. Her favorite was the pad of paper with the "magic pen" that would reveal "invisible" messages on your paper. This way of writing reminded her of that pad of paper in that her pen just sort of revealed words she didn't know she had in her.

> This place
> I feel it
> Once my home my comfort
> Now a stranger to me
> I fit in your arms
> The light so clean
> Young eyes, aged visions
> Generations call to me
> Days never ending
> One into another
> Drawing on my time
> My purpose revealing itself
> Doors closing fast
> This training ground
> How far I ran
> Knowledge erasing wisdom
> Turning my back on the past
> Laughing at time
> Winnowing my way into yesterday
> Through this window
> Pain and joy as one
> The cruelty of birth

Where are you
My love, my joy
Memories painfully sweet
Rivers of gray I wear
Skin dry as flint
The light is fading
Sage cut and burned
Take me home once more
In a cradle far away
Young eyes, aged visions

When she was finished, she looked down at the words and suddenly realized how tired she was. *What does any of this mean? Does it have to have a meaning? Why do I write at all?* These thoughts were swimming in her mind when she finally fell asleep, unaware of the weightless hand resting on her shoulder.

When she awoke the next morning, she assumed it was Paul who had underlined "My love, my joy." Piper smiled and got ready for the day. The scent of lavender lingered behind her nose for hours.

9

YEARS HAVE A WAY OF SLIPPING by unnoticed, seeming shorter and faster as one gets older. Paul explained this to his wife one day as they were weeding the multiple flower beds they had cultivated over the three years they had lived on their farm.

"Isn't it funny how, when you're five years old, a year takes forever to go by? I think it's because it's a huge chunk of your life—a fifth of it, when you think about it."

Piper looked up from under her Red Sox cap and smirked. "Your brilliant way with numbers is what made me fall in love with you, ya know."

He tossed a handful of weeds at her, hitting her in the face by mistake. She coughed dramatically and spit on the ground. Not one to sit idly by and be assaulted, she grabbed a handful of dark soil and ran after Paul who knew he had it coming. She knew she couldn't catch him, so she pretended to trip and twist her ankle. Paul doubled back, brow furrowed, concern on his face. That's just one of the many reasons she loved him so much—he actually hurt when she did.

He knelt down and said, "Honey, are you okay? Let me see."

She looked up at him, smiled, and shoved the handful of sweet dirt down his white t-shirt, patting his chest several times to rub it in, thinking it was his week to do the laundry anyway. Then she pulled him down onto the ground next to her. "Yes, I'm fine thanks, and you?" she answered. They looked at each other and giggled like kids.

He looked into her eyes and said, "You might not like this but I'll say it anyway. Hell, I'm a mess already, how much worse could it get?"

She gave him her "*You must be kidding, right?*" look, but he continued. "You get more and more beautiful as you get older."

She looked back at her husband and tilted her face up to the sun, closed her eyes, and let the light color the inside of her eyelids red. She could hear everything around her, but the sound she loved the most was her husband's voice, and closing her eyes allowed her to block out everything but him. He could still make her heart skip a beat. He leaned over and hugged her next to the dahlia and gladiolus bed, the one Piper had decided would be her cutting garden. After it began to bloom, though, Paul teased her because she couldn't bring herself to cut any of the flowers. The profusion of pinks, yellows, peaches, and whites that set them ablaze was dramatic; she loved to sit in the Adirondack chairs they had bought at the Brimfield Fair before they were married, and let herself get lost in her thoughts staring at them. She hugged him back and said, "I love you, sweets."

When she opened her eyes, she didn't see Paul at first. The sun was in her eyes and was so bright she had to close her eyes again. When she reopened them she saw a man with light hair and eyes that mimicked the sky. His sad, sweet smile struck her heart and made it thump hard in her chest. She wanted to close her eyes and concentrate on the scent-ache but was afraid he'd disappear. *What is it? Who are you?* Her body tingled and she knew if she looked at her arms they would be covered in goosebumps.

He was there for a fraction of a second, just long enough to register and when she blinked he was gone.

Paul was there, smiling. She winked before she kissed him.

"What would I ever do without you?" she asked.

"Well, for starters, you'd have to find someone else to pick on. After that, I guess you'd have to clean the stalls yourself and carry hay bales and grain bags and water buckets and ...."

Piper rolled her eyes as she got up off the ground. "Blah, blah, blah ... did you say something, dear?"

He smacked her backside and stood up, too, holding his lower back. She said, "Well, at least your gray is distinguishing." She had one hand on her hip and was looking him up and down, frowning.

He winked at her, knowing well she found him attractive; she was just in one of her goofy, playful moods that meant she was happy and not worried about a thing. He loved that he could provide a good life for her and that she was content. She was truly the best thing that had ever happened to him. They walked back toward the barn with their tools and bountiful harvest of weeds. Paul slowed, turned and said, "Piper, honey, may we talk about something?" Most people get a little nervous when their significant other starts a conversation with such a line, but she knew better. Though they joked a lot with one another, all it took was a question like this to let the other know it was time to move on to a more serious subject.

"Mm-hhmm," she answered.

He motioned with his hand for her to come closer. She put her armload of shovels, rakes, and gloves down. He turned her around, stood close behind her, and pointed out to the fields for her to see. "What do you think of this idea?" She loved the fact that Paul had become more the dreamer than she had ever been. He said it was something about the land, the vastness, the space, the potential, and the way the sun lit up the fields. "I have been talking with some people and doing a little research ... and I was thinking, well ... what do you think of starting a vineyard?"

She took a breath, not wanting to react. She took a deeper breath, held it for a few seconds before letting it out. She turned around to face him and kissed his scruffy cheek. "You're crazy, that's what I think." But then she saw the look on his face and was reminded that he was, through and through, a business man. She had turned him into a horseman and a gardener, but in his heart, he was always looking for the next big project. She loved his ambition and was rarely disappointed in his ventures.

Together they had built a successful and lucrative equine insurance company that brought business from all over New England, and because of it, they could afford to explore just about any investment they wanted. She looked deep into his eyes and asked, "You're serious, right?"

He nodded and smiled.

"Well, I guess ... then ... umm, I guess we check it out?" she said.

He hugged her and picked her up off the ground.

"You're still crazy, though," she said.

"Crazy about you," he whispered in her ear.

She kissed the side of his neck and inhaled the smell of his skin she loved so much. To her it was home. When she hugged her husband, she fit right into the crook of his shoulder and when she turned her head, she was right where she belonged. No other place felt so safe or so right to Piper. *But why does it feel like something, or is it someone, is missing?* She would die for Paul, and she knew he would do the same. It made her think of a few lines from one of her favorite songs, "When Love and Death Embrace." When she listened to it, she understood it on a spiritual level. It was one of the songs Paul teased her about, calling her a closet Goth girl.

"Who listens to Finnish rock bands ... besides you, I mean?"

She and Paul were the envy of a lot of her friends. They had such a way with each other that even passersby would notice their obvious affinity for one another. One thing Piper never got used to was having a man approach her and flirt openly in a grocery store or a coffee shop. It actually made her really upset. Her thoughts would spin and she would think, *How dare you disrespect my husband like that?* On the occasions that she told him about these advances, he would smile at her indignation and say, "Honey, it's okay. It's you I trust, so I know I don't have anything to worry about. But just in case, I'll do the shopping from now on." She loved the way he could make her feel better by making light of things, and it was true: he did trust her one hundred percent.

"Okay, Mr. Vintner, tell me this grand plan of yours. How are we going to fund this bad boy?" This was Piper's way of letting Paul know that she did indeed think this was a crazy idea, but she was more than willing to hear his ideas.

Paul responded with a deep breath and a raised eyebrow as if to suggest she might not want to hear the entire plan all at once. He said, "Well, I was thinking we could go out for a bite to eat and hash it over together. I don't want you to think I have it all mapped out without you or anything."

She looked knowingly at him and winked. "Uh-huh, you want me to believe that you haven't figured out where every penny will come from? Come on, Mister, give me a little credit here."

He smiled and said, "I just thought we could go out tonight and discuss it over a nice bottle of wine and a couple of steaks; but if you want to stay home and eat leftovers, you go right ahead. I'm still having my steak."

She cracked up and said, "Oh no, if you're having steak, I am, too. And you're paying, my friend."

Just then, the horses began calling to them from the meadow in the woods, letting them know that they were hungry.

"I'll feed the kids, you go wash up; you're such a slob," she said playfully, smirking at his soiled shirt.

When she was a few feet from the barn, the smell of the pine shavings, hay, and horses flooded her senses, and she felt happy. Really happy. She had everything she could ever want except the one thing they truly were missing: babies. She pushed the thought from her mind as quickly as it had entered. There was no need to ruin a perfectly nice Saturday with the despairing thought of being childless her entire life. She grabbed the grain scoop inside the feed room and called to the horses that she was coming. Opening the grain and inhaling the scent of molasses always had an immediate effect on her. It calmed and comforted her. She dropped the scoop inside and dug her fingers through the heavy, sticky grain. Scooping it into the feed buckets, she remembered how her grandmother mixed ingredients.

"You don't need measuring cups, Sweetheart. Just a handful of this and a pinch of that. See? Like me."

Piper mixed the sweet feed with the pellets, added a handful of oats. She liked her horses to have a bit of get-up-and-go. She took the grain buckets and hung them in the stalls. Back into the feed room, she cut open a new bale of hay, the sweet scent reaching her nose and making her smile. There was nothing like the smell of fresh hay that was cut at the right time and properly dried. She shook out two flakes of hay for each horse, because although they had grazed all day in the meadow, they would soon need more.

She walked out of the barn, stopped to grab a couple of lead ropes, but thought better of it. She knew she didn't need them. She walked quickly along the trail through the woods to the meadow gate which she and Paul had fashioned after one they saw in an old Grimm fairytale book they found in Brimfield. It had wide boards that were cut into an arch, the ends held onto the granite gate posts with iron hinges. They had made the handle from a draft horseshoe.

The horses were pacing behind the gate, timekeepers if any animal were. Valo, the alpha male, whinnied to her, the first at the gate. She loved this horse almost as much as she had loved Victory. Pure muscle, he was a beautifully built Baroque-type Friesian, 17.2 hands at the withers. She named him for the singer she admired most, the one Paul teased her about. He once told her that she was born in the wrong century, and if she wanted to be with a man who had long hair, well, she should buy him some Rogaine. Paul surprised her with Valo for their wedding anniversary. Shortly thereafter, he developed a bad case of buyer's remorse when Piper started spending hours and hours in the barn and the fields with this new horse. The laundry piled up, and the dishes didn't get washed for days. At that time, they had two horses, but Paul knew that she really longed for a Friesian, and he had to admit that once you rode one, nothing else would do. He consoled himself, sometimes quite loudly, with the fact that she was cheating on him with a horse and not another man.

She unlatched the gate and pushed the horses back with mere gestures. She asked for space with only her hands and three sixteen-hundred-pound animals stepped back in unison. She opened the gate, walked through and greeted each one as she closed the gate behind her. Valo stood his ground, not stepping any further than she insisted. Dragon hung back a little until she held her hand out and offered him a few raisins from her pocket. He was a stunning black Percheron-Thoroughbred cross that Paul took along on drag hunts and hunter paces. He took care of Paul and seemed to know that he was not a very experienced rider. Standing next to Dragon was Oliver, a distinguished and proud Oldenburg gelding who was given to Piper by a client who no longer had use for him.

Piper loved all her animals, but Valo without question captured her heart. His mane hung past his shoulder at its long point, his forelock covering one eye completely. Her girlfriends would often comment that women would kill for hair as curly and as beautiful as her horse's. *Cowboy Magic and a Miller beer,* she would think but had learned over the years to keep these little bits of wisdom to herself, knowing that even though she was perceived by others as elegant and sophisticated, on the inside, she was a farm girl through and through.

Valo stamped the ground with one foreleg, the feathers rippling as he did, and reminded Piper why she had come to the meadow. Again she gestured to them to give her space, and they heeded, knowing that dinner would only be served once they obeyed. She opened the gate, walked through, and clucked her tongue to signal that they, too, could step through. She stood aside and watched as they broke instantly into a canter, heads tossing, tails in the air. This was their routine, and they knew it well. Valo would enter his stall first, then Dragon, and Oliver would pull the end, the pecking order seldom challenged. Their stalls were their refuge, and dinner was always there before they came in from the meadow. She needn't hurry to close their doors; they were content to be in for the night.

She stopped before latching the gate, the sunlight falling

at an angle making her want to linger here in this quiet place. There was something special about this meadow, something deeply comforting. She knew it the moment she had seen it the day they drove out from Marblehead to walk the land. She scanned the stone walls at the perimeter, hoping to see the fox kits that were born a couple of months prior, but they weren't there. She did, however, see a big, round skunk scuttling along the edge of the eastern side of the pasture.

She recalled the night Viceroy had come back from the meadow late one evening, smelling so horrible from his encounter with a skunk that they simply couldn't allow him into the house. Paul lovingly bathed him in a galvanized bucket they had used the previous Memorial Day to hold ice for their annual barbecue. He used everything from tomato juice to baking soda and vinegar until Piper asked, "Do you think you've marinated the dog long enough? I'll light the grill." The dog had to, for the first time in his life, sleep in the shed. Piper made a little bed out of rags and old bed sheets to make him comfortable and apologized profusely when he whined, but she explained to him there was no way she could let him stay in the house smelling like that. He looked at her in a way that made her feel she was betraying him. She reminded herself that he was, in fact, a dog and would survive the night, although the yelping emanating from the back yard that night made her wonder.

She smiled, remembering that night and how Paul was so sweet with him, bathing him, and giving him sound advice for the next time he was out wandering in the field and picking up dangerous women. The man certainly did have a sense of humor. And she remembered how she had commented to him that he would make a wonderful dad one day. Again, she pushed the thought from her mind and closed the gate.

Walking back toward the barn, she was filled with a sense of excitement and anticipation. Not much time went by without either she or her husband feeling the need to try something different, to spread their wings a little. She knew that he must have done a lot of research and talked to more than a few people, and she was looking forward to hearing what he had learned. Paul was a great teacher, though she an impatient student; together they had a way of making things work. To her the idea of a vineyard was romantic, and she pictured her and her parents and in-laws taking turns stomping grapes in huge wooden barrels. This image made her giggle out loud and shake her head. Through the corner of her eye, she saw movement in the woods. She turned and saw only trees, leaves just beginning to change color. She had the feeling that someone was watching her, or rather watching over her and she turned back toward the barn breathing in the cooling air and letting it give her a second wind. She shivered but she knew she wasn't cold. She turned back toward the house. *I hope I'm not getting sick.* She shook off the thought and turned back toward the tree line.

Piper.

"What?"

She turned to the house and back to the barn and then the trees again. "Paul?" She realized it wasn't Paul's voice but couldn't think who else it could be. No intonation, no gender. Just her name.

She picked up her pace a little, not afraid but wanting a shower. Another shiver. She took a deep breath.

She was going to dinner with her best friend, her husband, the love of her life, and, hand in hand, they were going to start a new adventure.

10

So IT WAS THAT PIPER'S father agreed to let Vander take his only daughter's hand in marriage.

"She's my girl, my angel. I have given her everything I have but ..." He looked into Vander's eyes and knew. He drew a deep breath and worked at holding back his emotions, tears. "I have given her everything I have, including my sadness and fear. Don't give her everything. Only give her happiness. Promise me that."

Vander never took his eyes off Piper's father. "I promise. She will only know happiness and love."

And on a beautiful, warm morning of Piper's seventeenth summer and Vander's nineteenth, they wed in the village center. In the weeks leading up to the ceremony the women of the community put their petty differences aside. The gossip didn't flow so urgently from one garden to the next. A perceived snub at the market was now seen in a different light—perhaps the scale was not very accurate—a simple oversight. Seeing a neighbor's husband stumbling home after a night at the tavern was something to giggle quietly at, not draw attention to. The women came together to help this motherless girl prepare for the day that she and her betrothed would become one and move outside the village to the house that Vander had built with the help of his father and brothers.

Flowers from most of the village gardens lined the steps to the church, the aisle a bed unto itself with roses of red, yellow, and white, tulips, irises, daffodils, and armloads of dried lavender. The scent of heaven greeted guests as they hurried inside the stone church to bear witness to this highly anticipated gathering. The planned feast had been talked about for weeks. If there were ever two people God intended to be with one another, it was Piper and Vander, their bond pure and genuine. Their love was timeless.

Ever since the celebration of spring by the shore the previous year, the wedding preparations had been set into motion, causing a ruckus among the women in the village, all of whom wanted to be the one to help this girl prepare for womanhood. It is this maternal instinct that has pulled women through the ages with pride, strength, and character in a way that defies explanation. Womanhood propels a girl into a perpetual spiral of mysteries, commitment, love, hope, and heartache. Knowing the bond shared between a mother and daughter, the elder women, some motherless at their own weddings, knew how empty Piper must feel inside. Preparing for such a monumental event without her mother at her side to stitch her dress, braid her hair, and explain the ways of men and their needs was a time of sadness mixed with joy.

Her father was a heartbroken man, providing for his family and for years toiling endless hours building furniture for the wealthy in lands he would never visit. Alone without his love, he seemed to crumble unto himself, waking as the sun's first rays fell through his window onto his pillow. He returned as they began to fade, leaving only darkness to comfort his aching heart. He had never spoken directly of his wife to his children after her passing so many years before; but in his mind, each day that passed, was one fewer that he would have to live without her and brought him one day closer to seeing her again. All joy had seemingly been erased from his world. Vander, son of Philip the great warrior, was going to spend his life taking care of Piper, providing for her in so many ways that her parents never could. This, at least, comforted him. He sat at the front of the church, with Marek, now a young man, by his side.

The nervous groom stood at the altar wearing his father's

black wedding coat, his brothers at his side, who were smiling and chiding him about how his life would never be the same. His mother sat across from Piper's father, watching, waiting in vain for him to return her gaze so that she could share her happiness with him. When she realized that he was deep in sad thought, she turned her gaze instead to her sons, so handsome and strong like their father who quietly stood beside them.

As the ceremony began, Piper appeared in the doorway of the church, an angelic vision, making several villagers gasp, her long dark hair pulled back in a braid and tied with grapevines as was the tradition. The vine signified a long family history and a bond that is not easily severed, all traces of fruit removed so as not to appear presumptuous that God would bless the bride with children. Her traditional dress, sewn by seven women, reached the floor and thankfully covered her feet as she had nothing appropriate to wear on them. Piper would gladly be barefoot for the rest of her life, having only her mother's old shoes that were now tattered and worn so thin she could feel the smallest pebbles as she walked along the lanes. In her arms, she bore the most beautiful array of flowers: pink tulips, grape hyacinths and yellow daffodils: all grown in the small garden outside her family's home.

She watched her father turn slowly in his seat, and, for the first time in her life, she saw that he was not only her father, the man who fed her and put a roof over her head, but he was also a person. She saw a sad and lonely man whose wife left him to raise two children alone in a small house at the end of a lane in the solitude of a village filled with strangers. She felt tears spring to her eyes and threaten to fall down her glowing cheeks. Her father looked pale, and she could see that he was fighting back tears himself. She would never know that her father was reliving his own wedding day, the happiest hours of his life. She also never knew how much she resembled her mother and how this was, at the same time, a great blessing and terrible curse on her father.

He looked away and Piper's gaze fell on Marek, her little brother who now towered over her. How proud she was of him, apprenticing with their father, working hard and bringing home wages that helped to purchase bed linens and cooking wares for his sister's new home, a home she had yet to see. He and his father had built a houseful of furniture for Vander and Piper over the past year and had not spoken a word about it to anyone, hoping to surprise them later that evening. Marek, too, looked sad to be losing his sister who had been a mother to him most of his life. His only memories of their mother were of her lying on the bed, skin yellow and eyes fighting to stay open. He sometimes heard her in the night, softly calling his name over and over. But having only ever heard his mother's hoarse whisper, he did not know it was her calling to him through his thin dreams. Nonetheless, he had an ache in his heart that could only be lessened by his sister's unconditional love. And now she, too, was leaving him. A sad river flowed down his cheeks, each tear dripping quietly from his chin and soaking the collar of his borrowed coat. What was going to become of him, he wondered, and what of his father when it was time for him to take a bride?

As Piper neared the altar, her eyes fixed firmly on Vander whose own eyes began to blink back tears. He shifted his weight nervously back and forth, letting each foot rest only for an instant. His oldest brother reached out and steadied him as if he were a panicky horse about to bolt. Vander, in turn, startled out of his trance, stood upright and stone still. This made the guests laugh, as they sympathized with his nervous anticipation.

The vows spoken that day late in the planting season were sown deep in the hearts of the bride and groom. Never would there be a day when they did not hold true to their words. A love like theirs needed defending; but in the hearts of the people of this village, there was little doubt that there would be much in the way of a challenge. Vander had eyes for no one except his beautiful bride, and Piper was born to be with him. There was little else to be said about this matter.

"I will love you until the last of my breath I do take
I will defend you in the darkest hours of your days

You will be in my care and my heart forevermore
You will sleep soundly in the night as I watch over you
Our lives will entwine and bear the fruits of our love
I will toil every day to bring peace to our home
And every night when I close my eyes
I will know that I have done my best for you."

With these words, a kiss, and a simple ring, Vander and Piper turned to face their guests as man and wife. On their faces was written a story so beautiful and so serene that even the most cynical of guests had to wipe a tear from their eye, some pretending to be only swatting a fly. The church was brimming with energy as the sunlight slanted through the narrow windows, bathing in light the flowers whose only purpose in this world was to adorn the union of these two souls.

This day would be talked about for weeks like many of the larger weddings that occasionally took place in this corner of the world. And soon everyone would go back to their everyday rhythms of life: farming, fishing, cooking, washing, raising, slaughtering, sowing, reaping, birthing, and dying. Life moves along, and the seasons blend quickly from one to another, bringing new challenges to overcome, tears of bitterness, bolts of anger, and sometimes joy beyond telling. The same story would then be retold many times in the generations to follow, for reasons unforeseen on this beautiful, perfect day.

As the newlywed couple stepped from the tiny church out into the brightness of day, Philip's two proud horses called to them as if to say, "Now then, good enough, let's move along: there's clover to be had in the trough at home." Philip jumped up into the cart with which he usually transported freshly caught fish and it usually smelled accordingly. For this special day, though, he had spent the entire morning scrubbing it with a hog bristle brush, hot water boiled in the hearth and Castile soap. The bed of the cart was lined with the sweetest lavender, clover, and roses. Amèlie had fashioned streaming bows out of the finest ribbon to be had in the valley. Even the horses had been prepared for this blessed event. Vander's brothers had bathed them the previous evening with a mixture of glycerin soap and ale, their manes flowing and shiny, the likes not seen on many a village animal. Their tails seemed to be made of silk, hanging to their fetlocks and blending with the thick feathers that trailed the ground. These animals were given to the couple later that evening as a wedding gift not only because of the love and affection they shared for them, but also because a pretty penny could be had with them at stud.

Vander, who now stood over six feet tall, lifted his new bride up into the back of the cart and hopped in beside her, smiling at his mother whose tears continued to flow as she blew her son and new daughter kiss after kiss. Her older boys flanked her and laughed at her silliness, telling her not to be sad, that he was going to be home every day looking for his midday meal and a story from his Mére. The onlookers laughed at this and shook their heads at the three tall blonde brothers whom they had watched grow over the years into these fine men.

Philip clucked his tongue, asking the horses to move forward, lifting the reins and letting them drop gently onto their backs. Without hesitation, they pushed into their yokes and effortlessly moved the cart forward, breaking from a trot to an eye-catching canter, with manes, tails, and feathers flying out behind them in a show of elegant power. The guests shouted out their blessings to this beautiful young couple who would, no one doubted, live happily and long. They watched as the cart rattled down the lane toward the south end of the village where smoke rose toward the sky, promising a delicious meal and an evening not soon to be forgotten.

Excitement filled the air as the feast that afternoon commenced, with the sun sitting in the western sky, in the meadow now cleared of cows, horses, and sheep. Two of the fattest hogs had been slaughtered the day before the wedding and were now cooking over a smoldering fire along with the last of the previous harvest's root vegetables. The smell of pork, sage, thyme, carrots, turnips, and potatoes that rose into the air was enough to make the mouths of the pickiest children water. Baskets of warm breads were brought from the oven at the center of the village and barrels of wine were rolled out for the long night ahead. Empty milk pails were filled with freshly churned sweet butter. Makeshift tables were fashioned from empty ale barrels and old barn board, covered with white linens. Chairs, blankets, violins, and song books were brought from homes as were gifts for the bride. Seventeen cakes were baked, one for every year of the bride's life, sliced and filled with the berries the bride and groom so loved. Mixed with sugar, fresh cream and sliced almonds spread out over the warm cake halves, the berries turned the prettiest shade of purple. Several loving hands reassembled the layers and drizzled the delicacies with burned sugar strands, honey, and violet petals. These were the envy of all brides whose weddings preceded this one, as the ingredients alone would have set their families back a season or two. But this village knew a love story when it saw one, and everyone wanted a hand in its writing.

Piper and Vander walked slowly hand in hand through the tall grass as they shared secret whispers about their life and dreams, and also at the fact that more than a few of their dining guests had not made it to the church but certainly weren't going to miss the free meal! The bride's father, now in a lighter mood and loosened by the wine, picked up a violin for the first time since his wife passed and played a lively tune that started everyone's heart pumping, shouts filling the air. Girls of all ages gathered in the center of the ring of tables and danced hand in hand in a circle, their dresses and flower-adorned hair flowing in a vision of innocence and beauty. The boys of all ages hung back, hands only leaving trouser pockets to playfully punch one another. Dares were made with the nod of a head in the direction of the girls until one brave six-year-old ran into the center tripping three of the revelers. Hoots and shouts filled the air as older boys swooped in to scoop up the interloper out of harm's way. Before long, the girls were grabbing the boys' arms, forcing them to dance, too.

The meal was ready when the groom poked at the roasted pig and its eyes fell into the ashes. Cheers rose up and stomachs growled in anticipation. The butcher who donated his services this day showed off his knife skills, making quick work of carving up huge wooden bowls of perfectly smoked, fragrant, moist pork. Amèlie stood close by and used two large wooden grain scoops to place the roasted vegetables on top of the meat before her sons whisked them away to the tables filled with hungry guests. When the bowls emptied, they were brought back to the spit and refilled time and again.

The wine flowed, and the stories began, and, before the sun reached the horizon, Vander called for a bonfire. Boys, men, and a few little girls went along the edge of the meadow picking up fallen branches and dragged them to the meadow's center. Red embers from the cooking fire were shoveled on top of the wood and fanned, bringing them back to life. Soon there was a fire that warmed the cool spring evening and guests now relaxed after their bountiful meal, moving their chairs closer to one another. Long-standing feuds were forgotten, bitter words washed down with yet more wine, and petty matters vanished, their ridiculousness brought to light by merriment and glowing flames. It was times like this that made people remember that whatever life brings their way, good, horrible, or something between, they were all in this life together.

The violins and bows were gathered up and into the night air sweet songs sprang effortlessly from finely tuned strings. It was as if God had lovingly opened his arms and gently placed his angels right there in the meadow to serenade the bride and groom. Piper bit her bottom lip as she remembered her mother and how she used to play for her when she was young. She closed her eyes and wished that her mother could be here to share this evening with her; how different her life might have been if only her mother could have stayed even just a little longer. Hot tears streamed down her cheeks, as one of the women who had hours before braided her hair, now sang.

My true love stay with me
Quietly hold my fears as
I boldly defend your name
And I will hold yours

Whatever you for me
I'll do the same
Walk softly on the memories
Of those who tread nigh before
Remember not the sadness and bitter pain
Just that I love you and that alone
Will see us through the rain

The sadness Piper felt seemed somehow beautiful to her, even necessary. She suddenly made sense of the fact that parents don't live forever and that she was lucky to have her mother for the time she was allowed, as Marek had less than half that. She knew that someday the man she had depended on for everything these seventeen years would be the one leaning on her for steadiness, for care, and for compassion. And some day her children would do the same for her. She was grateful for all of it.

These thoughts were deeply comforting to her as she looked around and saw the glowing faces of young children cradled in their mothers' arms, some still so small that they fit perfectly on a shoulder or in the crook of an arm. She always admired the maternal way women had of handling their babes. She saw the way they rocked and swayed them as they strolled through the marketplace, juggling baskets and toddlers, purchasing goods and holding conversations, their hands seemingly having a mind of their own. She would often giggle as a savvy child would take advantage of his mother's distraction and begin to wander away to peek under a table or reach for a sweet only to have his mother's knowing grasp bring him right back to her hip. How did mothers do it? And how did they keep their wits about them while they managed so many chores, husband, and children? She didn't know, but, at the same time, she was looking forward to finding out.

She looked at her husband with eyes wet and lips stained wine red. She whispered, "Tonight I am your wife. I never thought I could be this happy."

To this, Vander returned the gaze and, as if he had read

her thoughts, said, "Tonight you are my wife, my heart of hearts and soon, God willing, you will be the mother of my children."

At this they both blushed and agreed that they didn't want to have to wait for the celebration to be over so that they could be alone. Philip asked to dance with his new daughter and taking her arm, led her a few steps away from the fire. Guests moved around so as to get a better view. The singing could be heard for miles, and grouchy villagers and those too old or too ill to attend softened at the sound.

Age quickly melts away when the long-forgotten scent of a mother's perfume or the tune a father whistles when he talks of his days as a soldier surprises us, no matter how many years have passed since the last time we encountered it. Senses can transcend decades, centuries, transporting us to that one moment in time that was so blissful, so sweet that it is forever branded on our hearts. Lying dormant for years by work, disappointment, sour relations, illness, and heartbreak, a scent can instantly pervade our soul and transform us into that child sitting quietly by the river fishing with his father, or into the little girl learning to bake her first pie at her grandmother's side, a woman birthing her first child, a father giving his daughter's hand in marriage, a soldier holding the hand of a dying brother. These are moments that define our lives and give us something with which to gauge all the days between them.

For many this gathering, this celebration brought back a flood of memories both fond and bitter. Mistakes made are now are seen as learning curves: battles fought, now seen as mere disagreements; disappointment, now believed to be for the better, God's plan being without fault.

After a few more dances, the bride and groom slipped away as was the custom, running into their future hand in hand, the two of them forging ahead alone with the blessings of their family and friends still warm on their cheeks, laughter and song still nestled in their ears and a passionate fire alight in their full hearts.

Running from the meadow to Vander's parents' home

had them out of breath and dizzy from the wine. They had to stop twice to catch their breath before reaching the barn. Intending only to ride one of the horses out to their new home site, they were shocked to discover the ribbons that had been on their bridal carriage were now around the necks of both animals. There was a letter nailed to the inside of the barn door now dimly illuminated by the lantern Vander lit and held up at shoulder height. The horses blinked sleepily while he read the note aloud:

Son,

I am more proud of you than words could tell. Take them both; they would be lost without each other and without you. Make your wife as proud.

Yours,

Father

Piper reached up and wiped the tears from her love's eyes, smiling at his expression. It was one of true gratitude and surprise, he never expecting anything from anyone. He held her close and kissed the top of her head and whispered, "We are going to have a beautiful life together."

She nodded her head against his chest and breathed in the scent of his skin, the straw, and the horses. They turned to their steeds and smiled as they reached for the saddles and bridles. Pieferet and Henk seemed a bit confused by all this, first the ribbons and now being taken out well after the workday was over. But they would do anything for Vander, and deep in his heart, he knew that each would lay down his life to protect him if need be. Tacked up, they were every bit the riding horse as they were work horse in harness. As they were led from the barn, Vander snuffed out the lantern light and closed the heavy doors behind him, wondering what his father would do without his partners. A sense of sorrow filled him as he imagined his father having so much love for him that he would sacrifice so much.

Piper reached up for a handful of mane and reins in her left hand and waited for Vander to hold her shin and give her a leg up. She gathered her dress around her and sat her horse like she always did, like a boy. She never liked riding with both legs on one side of a horse. Her husband loved that she didn't care what others thought of her: she was a woman with a mind of her own. He brought his left foot up into the stirrup iron, and with a slight hop, he pulled himself straight up and swung his other leg over his horse's back and looked at the homestead with different eyes. How hard his father and mother must have worked to build this farm. The patience and money and time, the labor and love it must have taken. He knew that he and his wife would do the same, and a sense of excitement raced through his veins as he spun his horse around to face west, toward his future.

He looked over at Piper who was quietly braiding a section of Pieferet's mane, waiting as her husband said a silent good-bye to his boyhood in the moonlight of a perfect spring evening. Together they cantered along the moonlit lanes that led them out to the pastures beyond the village toward their new home.

11

S HE COULDN'T WAIT for the plane to land. It had been seven
years since they had been to France on their honeymoon
and Paul's promise to make this trip an even better one had
her wondering just what he had up his sleeve. She turned in
her seat and looked at her handsome husband whose hair was
just starting to gray the slightest bit. He wore it well, and she
thought then that she had never loved him more than she did
at that moment. But then, she had moments just like this quite
often.

He looked at her and smiled. "What's up, beautiful?"

She smiled and gently dismissed his question by resting
her head on his shoulder and said, "I can't wait to see the inn
and meet this guy."

"Me too, sweetie."

After an extensive search, Paul had found an investor in
southern France who was willing to meet with them and possibly fund their vineyard. Piper loved the synchronicity that
he was from Italy and happened to share the last name of several of her mother's relatives. Alfred Porrazzo was from the
Abruzzi region and had moved to France after a university trip
in his early twenties during which he met his wife, Kay.
Together, they worked her parents' vineyard, raised their family
there, and eventually took over when her parents could no
longer run the business. Now in their seventies, they no longer
saw new vintners as competition; rather, they viewed them as
keepers of tradition. They, too, were very much looking forward

to this visit from the young couple from Massachusetts. Most inquiries for capital were from California, and over the decades, "Freddy" had grown tired of the fame and fortune seekers.

As the plane landed, Piper felt a little light-headed and had to sit for a few minutes while the rest of the passengers left the plane. Paul asked the flight attendant for some water, but Piper waved it away, insisting that she just needed a moment. He sat next to her and rubbed her back while she sat with her head in her hands, eyes closed. This was more than her typical scent-ache. She felt like she might vomit but she didn't want to startle Paul by trying to explain any of it. She had never been able to clearly communicate these sensations to Paul. He would only laugh and tell her she certainly was an imaginative one, but that's why he loved her. It used to bother her that he poked fun at her, but as she grew older, it in fact, helped her to just ignore some of these strange occurrences and simply regard them as temporary little hiccups that happened from time to time. But this time she couldn't ignore it, whatever it was.

She stood up and stepped out into the aisle of the plane, eyes wide, waiting for the darkness to lift. When it did, the look on Paul's face frightened her more than a little.

"What?" she asked.

"Honey, are you okay? You're really pale," he said.

She took a deep breath. "Yeah, I'm fine, just a little tired. That was a long flight."

The visions came fast and hit her like sleet in the face, sharp and unrelenting: A child's hand, blackened and limp, a golden medallion clutched in dirt-covered, shaking hands, a woman on the ground, sobbing, a little girl at her side. *Whose hands?! Whose child?!*

Paul grabbed their bags from the overhead compartment and led her down the aisle toward the exit. As she neared the front of the plane, the pilot poked his head out to wish them a relaxing visit. Piper glanced up at him and was struck by his piercing blue eyes. He smiled and nodded in her direction, then looked away as he rubbed his nose nervously. As he did, she smelled salt air, straw, and roses. Her head was spinning and she wanted nothing more than to sit down and rest. Paul felt her swaying and slipped his arm around her waist and held her tight. The two flight attendants looked at her with concern and asked if they should call for medical assistance; but the pilot never stopped smiling. If Piper hadn't been so intent on getting off the plane, she would have noticed the tears in his eyes that betrayed his shy smile.

When they reached the inn, Piper was feeling much better, somehow refreshed; but Paul said that they were staying put and insisted on ordering in. He called down to the kitchen and ordered dinner which they enjoyed out on the terrace by a sparkling fountain. Paul reached across the table and took his wife's hand. "You gave me a little scare back there, Lady."

She smiled and giggled the way she did when he said things like that.

"Sorry, Honey. I was just a little dizzy. No big deal. I'm fine now."

He paused and tilted his head a little bit, which reminded her of Viceroy when he heard a curious noise. On her husband, the expression meant, "Are you sure?" She took a sip of her wine and said, "What? You don't believe me?"

He looked at her. "Well, it's just that you were pale as a ghost and quite frankly it looked like you were seeing one to boot." She remembered the scent-ache and realized that if the expression on her face had reflected how she felt at that moment, then yes, she could see how her husband thought she was terrified. She had been. The visuals came so fast and so furious that she couldn't comprehend them. They were a blur. She remembered, though, that as they flew through her mind, she felt like these were actual memories. The pictures that normally accompanied these sensations were like bits of a dream, something that hadn't really happened to her. But this time it was different. She had heard of flashbacks before, but Piper knew that people who experienced those sorts of things usually had either used hallucinogenic drugs or had been through an extremely traumatic experience. But neither of those things applied to her, and she was just having a hard time shaking the feeling that these were memories.

She ate her salad and raw oysters and relaxed with the sound of the fountain. She drank all of her wine and then excused herself from the table. "I think I'll lie down for a little bit, Honey. Then maybe we can take a walk, what do you say?"

Paul looked up at his wife as she stood in front of him. "Sure, Babe. Yell if you need me. I'm going to call Freddy now and set a time for tomorrow. Okay?"

She smiled at him and nodded. He furrowed his brow, stood up, and put his arms around her slender waist. "You're not getting cold feet on me are you?"

She stepped back and took his hands in hers. "Paul, look at me. I told you before I am in this a hundred percent, Sweetheart. I'm not getting cold feel. I'm just feeling a little under the weather. I promise; that's all it is." She stepped closer and let go of his hands.

He folded her into his chest and he took a deep breath and kissed the warm skin on the side of her neck. He could feel her pulse and loved the very life blood that ran through her veins. He felt a sudden stab of sorrow for not being able to start a family with her. They had been trying for a while but each month brought disappointment. She didn't like to talk about it and he wasn't going to mention it now, especially with her not feeling well.

Back in the room, Piper took a hot shower, letting the water scorch her white skin and turn it bright pink. She didn't feel tired as much as mentally exhausted. In the weeks leading up to their trip, there had been several clients whose horses had been injured in "accidents"; the adjusters she hired per diem were not available, which was often the case, and which necessitated that she investigate the accidents on her own. The phone calls from the vets were eerily the same: "Suspicious wounds," "Unlikely injury," "Strangest thing I've ever seen." Piper had been in the business long enough to know trouble when it dialed her phone. These situations weren't rare in her field, but each one turned her stomach just the same. *How could someone wound their own horse or someone else's for the money?* She didn't know of a more loyal animal, except for maybe a family's dog. She couldn't imagine that someone with a heart could intentionally pick up a syringe of snake venom and inject it into the legs of a horse so that it wouldn't be able to compete in an upcoming competition and likely need to be put down. And what goes through a person's mind as she offers a handful of yew berries to an aged horse, which for years had served as companion and trusted mount, now viewed as nothing more than an eating machine worth a lot more if dead? These phone calls from the equine vets shook her up and made her want to get out of the business altogether.

But most of the time the job wasn't stressful; in fact, she found it very invigorating and loved how every day was different. It was far from ever being boring. She scrambled prior to the trip to France to get an agent from her old office to take her calls for her while she was away. And her own animals, well, she absolutely hated leaving; but she had entrusted them to their neighbor to the south. He was a gentle, older farmer who had owned Belgian draft horses his entire life. When she asked if he could feed and water her horses and dog, his eyes brightened and he tugged on his beard. "Oh, I'd love to, sweetheart. That Friesian you got there sure is a looker."

He was a lonely man whose wife had passed away two years prior, and he used every reason he could come up with to wander over and see what the young couple had done to the property that had been in his family for over 150 years. At first Paul thought he was going to make a pest of himself, but Piper gently reminded him each time he mentioned it that the man was all alone. Soon, though, Paul came to realize that the guy was just trying to be helpful. He shared with them pictures of the old homestead and his family throughout the many generations who had worked the land that Piper and Paul now owned. They had him over for Sunday dinner once a month and Paul found himself taking the long way home on more than a few occasions to stop in and check on the old guy. Piper felt more than comfortable with her animals in his care. She reminded herself to look for a gift to bring back to him as a thank you.

She lay on the bed not feeling tired, but not wanting to sit outside and talk, either. Sometimes she just needed to be alone, which was nothing new. She always made time for herself each day: riding, listening to music that inspired her and, of course, her writing. Paul could easily spend every waking moment with her and never get sick of her company, but he had learned that she was a much happier woman when she had some space.

She got up, rummaged through her purse on the bureau and pulled out her iPod and a piece of her favorite clove gum. She lay back down and turned on her music—the band that Paul teased her about. She loved Ville's voice and found his music comforting, meaningful in a way that she couldn't explain. Paul said the only reason she liked him was that both his first and last names began with "V."

She closed her eyes and let the music fill her heart. She was going through something lately but she couldn't quite put her finger on it. She felt like she should be happy but somehow wasn't quite there. What was missing, she wondered and instantly stopped herself. She knew and Paul knew. They wanted a baby. She rolled onto her side and let the tears come. It had been so long since she had cried, but between the stress of being away from home and all of her responsibilities, while not feeling well, and taking this giant step, this financial risk with the vineyard, was too much. She let herself cry, a luxury she usually denied herself.

The tears stung this time, not as much a relief as they usually were. These angry tears swelled into waves of resentment pulsing through her veins, and she didn't know why. She curled the pillow over the back of her head and held it so that the ear buds of her iPod sank so deeply into her ears that it hurt, the music filling her head and drowning her thoughts. After a while she tried to relax and released the pillow, letting it uncurl gently onto the bed. She lay there eyes wide, chest still hiccupping with unrelenting sobs. It wasn't the first time she had wondered if she would be childless her whole life and how it would feel to watch her friends' children grow, marry, and make her friends grandparents someday. Her horses and dog, and of course Paul, were her life; the animals had filled an important void even when she was a child. But now? Now it just wasn't enough, and she always felt that she was disappointing Paul, who grew up with siblings and wanted a big family. Over the Fourth of July weekend, his entire family came out to the farm and had a grand time. On one of her many trips into the house to get more napkins, lemonade, salsa, and batteries for her camera, she spied Paul at the grill on the deck as his brothers played softball with their kids. He looked so happy watching them; yet, at the same time, there was a look of longing on his face and she could have sworn the reason he rubbed his eyes was not because smoke got into them. She asked him later that night about how he felt having everyone here at the farm. He cocked his head and furrowed his brow and asked, "What do you mean?"

She had said, rather curtly, "What do you mean what do I mean? I just want to know how you felt seeing this place filled with kids and ...." Her voice betrayed her bitchiness and the tears rimmed her lids, making Paul's heart ache.

He pulled her close, and pressed his warm lips onto her forehead. He said, "Sweetheart, you know I love having everyone here. It's awesome to have the family all together and see the kids getting bigger and watching them become their own people, ya know?"

She nodded her head against his chin. "I know you're disappointed, Paul, and I'm just sorry that I can't seem to give you a family."

He pushed her back gently yet a bit abruptly in order to get her attention. His expression was stern bordering on angry. "Do *not* say that. Piper, honey; we've been through this. It's not your fault or my fault or anyone's. All the doctors say the same thing—there is absolutely no medical reason that we shouldn't be able to conceive a baby. Remember?"

She remembered. She remembered the stress, the tears,

the tests, the appointments, the phone calls, and the endless books on infertility. They both knew it all too well. She also remembered how loving and gentle her husband had been to her, not pressuring her, and always reassuring her that his life was full with her, that she was all he needed, and too, that he loved the trying part anyhow.

What she never told Paul, though, was that she had gone to a psychic. In fact she told no one, not even Sharon. The woman seemed normal enough and Piper was a little surprised by it. She didn't expect a crystal ball per se, but perhaps a purple head scarf or at least a woman in her 60s. This woman was late 20s tops, and dressed in jeans and a cute top from American Eagle. She was even more surprised when the woman gave her details that no one could know, like what she had had for breakfast that day and that she cut her knee shaving that morning.

Piper asked, "Will I have children?" This was the only question she had for the woman, but she let the reader first tell her what was there, to see if she could trust her answer. The woman closed her eyes for a moment and when she opened them she looked over Piper's shoulder and said, "Well, it's not clear, but you could. If... you see, sometimes people have a block—an energetic block that keeps them from receiving what they consciously want. I can help you. I can help you clear your block but we'll have to set up a time for that. I only do readings here. But you could come to my apartment where I do clearings and can take the time to explain it more to you."

Piper was already reaching for her purse before the woman was finished. "How much is it? For today, how much?" The woman looked upset like she wanted to say more but Piper had no patience. She tossed three 20-dollar bills on the table and said, "Thank-you." The woman looked at her and asked what scent Piper was wearing. Piper straightened her tall frame and tossed her hair over her shoulder.

"Umm, I don't know. I didn't put on perfume this morning. Maybe it's my shampoo." The woman looked at her with an expression that read: Stay. There's more to discuss. Piper ignored it, and walked quickly out the door of The Tea House on Tremont

Street, hoping no one she knew would see her.

Now, here in this beautiful inn in the south of France, she lay cold and brokenhearted to think that maybe this vineyard idea was Paul's way of putting all of his attention and resources into something that would live on after he was gone, like children they'd never have.

She pulled the covers up over her head and felt a chill run through her as she pressed her hand to her forehead and realized she was sweating. She thought she might be sick to her stomach and wished she hadn't had so much wine. She sat up, getting ready to sprint to the bathroom if need be. She tossed the iPod off the bed and closed her eyes. The scent with which she was familiar, but couldn't put a name on, flooded her. Familiar, but somehow this time foreboding. What's wrong with me? What's happening to me? She wished she were at home with Viceroy sitting on her feet on the couch while she wrote her poetry, with Paul working on the computer upstairs giving her time to be alone. He loved her so, but she knew that he couldn't help her. She needed to work through her feelings and come to grips with her reality. She was an educated woman pushing forty, married to a great guy, lived in a beautiful home, owned a lucrative business doing what she loved while getting paid for it, and she was childless.

Her dinner came up then without warning. She sprinted but didn't even come close to making it to the bathroom. Instead, she tripped on the jeans, sweater, and boots she had been wearing earlier, which lay in a heap at the foot of the bed. She hit the ground hard and the wine, salad, and very expensive oysters were once again in front of her looking not that different from when they went in earlier that evening. She pulled herself up, locking her elbows so that her arms were supporting her, legs out behind her, torso twisted sideways, resting on her hip. She stayed as still as she could for a moment to make sure there wouldn't be anything more coming up. But her stomach clenched again and up came a little more, mostly bile and acid this time. She wiped her mouth with the back of her hand and pushed her long hair back, wishing she were home.

She stood up slowly, feeling much better. Before she could take a step toward the bathroom to find something to use to clean up the mess, though, she felt a warm trickle down her thighs. She looked down and saw bright red blood there. *My period—that figures*, she thought. *It's late again but it's here, mocking me, reminding me every month that this cycle is like all the others— useless.* It made her feel less and less like a woman each time. But by the time she reached the bathroom, the trickle had become a painful torrent of dark red. She held her arms over her abdomen, leaning forward and grimacing in pain. "Jesus!" she cried out with fear as she crumpled to the floor in front of the toilet. The cramping was intense, and she thought she might faint from the stabbing pain. She heard Paul coming and didn't want him to panic. She looked around the bathroom and into the bedroom and realized that even if she had ten minutes she wouldn't be able to clean up everything and hide from her husband that she was unwell. Just as she finished this thought, Paul came through the door and stopped. She wanted to call out to him to give her a few minutes, but he cried her name and rushed straight to the bathroom.

"Piper! What? What happened, what's wrong? Where is this blood coming from? Are you hurt?"

She let him finish the battery of questions as she simply didn't have the strength to try keeping him calm. She looked up at him, saw his distress, and tried to force a smile which quickly reduced her to tears. Paul crouched down and touched his wife's face with such tenderness and love that it set off another cascade of emotions. Tears, sobs, apologies. He scooped her up and carried her to the bed, grabbed the phone by the bedside and called the innkeeper, his breath coming in spurts as he gulped air.

"My wife—needs an ambulance—she's bleeding. I don't know what's wrong. We need help—please—right away."

Piper lay back and bit down hard on the back of her hand to keep from screaming. The pain was too intense, and she knew something was wrong.

At the hospital, a kindly nurse stood at Piper's bedside and tried to smile down at her. She knew this poor woman was distraught and in pain. She felt for her, as she herself had suffered two miscarriages. "How are you feeling, madam?" she

96

asked. Piper stared at her and managed in a weak and raspy voice to ask where her husband was. Paul was out in the hall with the doctor who had treated her in the emergency room.

"It appears your wife was only about six weeks along, monsieur. She mentioned that she tripped and fell and sometimes, well, that is all it takes. There is no reason that you cannot try again in the next cycle. God bless you and your wife."

And with that, the doctor patted Paul's arm and walked away. Paul was utterly stunned. Only six weeks. Only. He bit his lip, trying unsuccessfully to hold back the tears. Six weeks. He thought back, a month and a half ago ... which night was it? Which night had they conceived their baby after years of trying, years of praying, of crying, of disappointment? He didn't know how he could possibly walk into that room in which his tortured wife lay and not fall apart. This time it was Paul who needed some time, some space. He walked down the hall in search of a quiet place to think.

He found the hospital's chapel and opened the door. He was enveloped instantly by the comforting hush of the tiny room. It felt right, like coming home. He kneeled in the first pew and bowed his head. He cried and he prayed and when he was finished he asked God for one favor: "Please God, give me strength to lend to Piper." He sat for a few moments with his eyes closed and just let the atmosphere soak into his thirsty skin. He knew God was not an angry God, not a selfish one. He knew that everything had a purpose and that there was a reason for everything. However, right now, he just wanted comfort for himself, but mostly for his wife. He bit his lip, hoping to hold back more tears, but they wouldn't obey. Why was this happening? *Were they really meant to be without children?* His shoulders shuddered as he remembered how, on their honeymoon, they talked about being careful, not wanting to get pregnant right away. They wanted to enjoy their time together for a few years before starting a family. He thought now how presumptuous they had been, how arrogant. He felt like a failure and a weak husband sitting there in the warmth of the chapel when he should be with Piper.

He gathered his thoughts, wiped his eyes, said a last prayer, and stood. The room swayed a little, and he cleared his throat to break the silence. He straightened up and walked quickly from the chapel into the rude florescence of the hospital hallway.

When he reached his wife's room, he paused and drew a deep breath, knowing that he owed it to Piper to be strong. She had saved him from his post-divorce misery and had given him a chance at the relationship he had always dreamed of finding. He quietly walked into the room, only to find her asleep. He felt a wave of relief as he had no idea what he was going to say to her. He bent down over his love and kissed her clammy forehead. "I love you, Sweets," he whispered in her ear. She stirred but Paul's whisper was no match for the nurse's sedative. Holding her hand, he softly recounted for her the history of their relationship. Starting with her beautiful face on the insurance company's website, their first meeting in Sharon's office in Boston, his asking her out, her turning him down, her coming to her senses, their first date. He told her about how nervous he had been when he proposed to her and that even though he knew they were meant to be together, he was afraid that she might turn him down again. He spoke softly as he recalled her walking down the aisle toward him at their wedding, and how absolutely beautiful she had looked that day and every day. His voice cracked and again the tears fell.

"Oh Piper, I'd be so lost without you; you're my whole world, Sweetheart. I'm so sorry. If we didn't come on this trip ... maybe ... maybe the ... the baby ... oh God, the baby ... I am so sorry. Piper, I love you so much. You are my everything."

She heard him walk into the room. She'd know his walk anywhere, the way he scuffed one shoe every other step. She sometimes teased him about it, telling him that his horses made less noise. She felt his warm hand on her cheek, gently soothing invisible scars, like waves reclaiming the sea's abundance of broken shells and leaving the surf once again smooth and untouched. How he loved her with his ancient heart. She lay in the hospital bed, resting, recovering and listening to the

PIPER, ONCE & AGAIN

voice that was a salve on her soul. Wanting only to open her eyes and see his, to tell him that everything would be all right as long as she had him to lean on, Piper fought against the medication. But it was no use, and so she lay still and listened.

Piper, my heart of hearts, don't be sad. I am here with you, always. Take my hand and feel me here. I promised I would never leave your side and I haven't. Not when you were little and not now. Do you remember when you were nine, and Tommy Milliken pushed you into the cafeteria tables and you bit your lip and your shirt reddened with blood—you were scared, but I was there. I held your shaking hands. When you found Victory lying in his stall that summer morning thrashing at the walls, colic twisting his gut and you thought you'd lose him, I was there. I was the breeze on your neck, the nudge on your arm. When you left Darrick behind that day in his car, I was there – the child who held the door to your apartment and smiled at you. It was me my love. I am all around you. Death does not erase love, and life does not erase death. It's how God wants it. I am Valo when he calls to you from the meadow and Viceroy, too, when he steals your slippers. I am the crocuses in your dooryard showing you that the winter is gone, and I am the bluebird who sings in the summer afternoon. I am words on your pages. I am yours and you are mine. God promised. Your heart may break, Piper, and your path may change, but I will be there. I will never leave you. Look for me. Learn your lessons, Love, so we may come together again. Not now, not this life, my heart. Learn patience, and if you listen through the noise and you search through the fog and feel through your numbness, you will hear me and I will help you. Rest now, Piper, and don't be afraid. It is only one life and there is so much more. I have been waiting a long time, and I will wait the rest of your days. Take my hand, Piper, and don't let go. He softly sang the bittersweet song that melted away the centuries:

Tämä ikivanha lupaus
Suurin koskaan tiedä - henki puhelut
Ja kuuntelen sinua
Sinun siniset silmät paloi
minun muisti elämien sitten
Odotan sinua
Etsi sinua valossa

Salvia, rovio, jäätyneiden järvien
Odotan sinua
Minä odotan sinua
Vuosisatojen avautua ja minä
odotan sinua
Odottaa sinua valo

When she opened her eyes, Paul was sitting in a chair at her bedside, asleep. She watched him for a few moments before reaching out and stroking his hair. He bolted upright.

"Piper," he blurted out.

"Shhh, it's okay, I'm okay," she told him. He leaned over the side of her bed and kissed her mouth, and the tears came, hot and fast. They cried and held onto each other like frightened children.

"Honey, I'm so sorry. I'm sorry about the stress and the trip and—."

She put her hand up to his mouth. "Don't Paul. It's not your fault. You didn't do this. It's nobody's fault. It just ... it just wasn't meant to be." His eyes were red and tired, and he blinked back his disbelief.

"I love you," he whispered. "I'll always love you."

She closed her eyes and held her breath, concentrating on the scent-ache. Lavender, strawberries, and freshly washed baby's skin filled the cavity behind her nose and accompanied an image: a white blanket wrapped around a baby in a man's arms, his hands clearly strong and weathered, cradling his only daughter. One hand with a slight scar in the shape of a half-moon caressed a tiny cheek. The image flitted behind her eyes for only a moment, but left her with a feeling of quiet strength.

Paul rested his head on his wife's lap as she stroked his hair and told him that she had a strange dream she couldn't quite remember, but that it was peaceful. She silently wished the nurse would come back and give her another sedative so that she could get back to that serene place where there was no hurt, no mourning, only yesterday.

12

THE SUNLIGHT AT THIS TIME of year was comforting as it streamed through the window and warmed the table on which Piper prepared their meals and where they shared their plans for the days and weeks and months that flew by. She loved this sunlit corner more than any other part of their home except for their small bedchamber, of course. Her life had changed so much in the previous year that it was unrecognizable from the time prior to her marriage to Vander. They had been living in their new home for only three months when she began to feel a bit queasy and unsteady on her feet. Vander was so busy in the fields, and she didn't want to worry him. She suspected that she might be with child, but she had heard countless stories of the superstitions surrounding the first three months of pregnancy. She didn't even allow herself to stop and think about it as she was too busy to really slow down. This ill feeling was with her when she woke and came and went throughout the day. It was the worst when she was cooking, especially when she smelled chicken roasting, something she normally relished. She let her hand touch her lower belly when she knew she was alone, excited at the thought that there might be a new life inside her.

Being without a mother to confide in was painful for her, but certainly not a new feeling. She knew she could talk with her mother-in-law, but it was a long ride to the village, and she didn't feel well enough for it. Her blood had not flowed for many weeks, and she knew enough to know that this could indicate pregnancy. She was never one to keep track of these things; she just knew that it had been a while since she scrubbed blood from her bed linens with the coldest hand-numbing water drawn from the well.

Piper often woke to Vander's handsome face staring at her. On a particularly warm June morning, soon after she began to suspect she might be pregnant, he reached out and stroked her cheek. She blinked and when he came into focus, she saw tears in his eyes. Startled, she opened her own eyes wide, but he quickly assured her that everything was fine.

"You are so beautiful. Sometimes I watch you sleep ... Just now you ... you looked so peaceful."

She closed her eyes again and moved closer to him. Her head rested on his broad chest. She reached for the medallion resting there. She had saved the money she earned selling flowers in the market for almost an entire year for his wedding gift. He promised he would never remove it, in return for a promise from her that someday she would bury him with it. This thought made her sad and comforted at the same time. The gold coin glistened in the early light of their room, her finger tracing the V that stood out in its center. She had an elderly goldsmith in a village to the east fashion it for her with the bits of gold she purchased from him each week. She would never know that the kindly man and his wife needed to add several grams of their own stock to make a coin large enough to make a medallion worthy of a wedding gift. They knew that to truly give from one's heart meant you needn't receive acknowledgement for the act.

Vander held her close and asked her if she thought maybe they would soon have a child. She laughed, lifting her head to look at him quizzically. "Why do you ask, Vander?"

"I just have a feeling. You have a look about you ... and ... it's just a feeling," he answered, with a shy and boyish shake of his head, his straw-colored hair falling over his eyes. She pushed it back with a gentle hand. She loved that he looked almost the same as the day he came to her rescue in the meadow when they were mere children.

"What do you think it will be?" she teased.

"I am certain it will be either a boy or a girl," he teased right back. He loved to make her laugh. He would, for all the time they would be together, always be able to drag a smile from her when she woke up in a bad mood during the months the rains lasted too long, or the winter's cold made keeping warm difficult.

Just then the horses started to call from the stable which got the sheep bleating, which in turn signaled the goats to butt their heads against the wooden trough. Everyone was hungry, and romance had no place in a stable yard. Vander laughed and said, "Well, at least we will be used to early feedings when the babies do come."

Piper giggled and pulled the linens back. She sat up and felt nauseous again. She held her belly as she got out of bed and looked at her husband. "Maybe sooner than later, my love."

He smiled at her and a heart full of love jumped in his chest. She was the very sunlight to him, the lifeblood by which his own depended. Would he ever have to endure life without her? The thought chilled him as he silently hoped not, as he was certain he could not. He blew her a kiss from across their small bedchamber and finished pulling on his boots. He headed out to feed the animals and to begin a day that would last until the sun set in the western sky, reminding him that sleep was a necessity whether he liked it or not.

Piper busied herself early by dressing, sweeping the floors, and feeding the hens that roosted in the tree at the south side of their house. She came back into the house and lit a fire in the small stove Vander had given to her as a wedding gift. He had traveled for three days to the city to purchase it, causing the young women of the village to whisper (some more loudly than others) that he was getting cold feet, what else could explain his absence so close to the wedding? No one was more surprised than Piper to see the black iron box in their new home. *How hard had he worked to earn enough money to purchase such a luxury?* She put water in the kettle, placed it on the stove, and reached for the ends of the previous day's bread. She sliced them thinly and added a helping of milk and butter to soften them, and tossed in just a pinch of sugar. She mixed this together in a small pot on the stove and kept it warm until Vander came back in the house for a quick breakfast before heading out to the fields. Hands never idle, she worked one chore into another, reaching for her kettle again. From the rafter, she took two sprigs of lavender and placed them into a small glass jar, added the honey she bought at market the week before, and replaced the lid. She smiled at the thought of the wonderful cakes this mixture would make for Vander's coming birthday. When he came back in, he was holding his hat in his hands, the hat filled with berries and grapes for his wife to add to the day's meals. She celebrated this as a gift, her hands rising to her chest in surprise.

"So many!" she exclaimed.

"It's been a strong season; God willing next year will be, too," he said.

She took a few of the blackberries and raspberries and topped their breakfast with them and added another tiny pinch of sugar on top. They sat together, and though Vander was ravenous as usual, Piper only picked at her food, her stomach turning with the thought of actually putting it into her mouth. She managed to eat just a bit, with Vander searching her face, hoping to see that she was all right. His nervous smile was far from the comfort it was intended to be. She just tried to avoid his gaze as she walked about the house, fussing with nothing and everything.

Before he left for the bulk of the day's work, he reached around his wife from behind and placed his large and gentle hands on her belly as she stood at the window. She jumped out of surprise, then softened, leaning her head back onto his chest. He bent down and kissed the side of her neck, reminding her that it was his favorite place to be, right in the hollow of her collar bone where he could feel her pulse against his cheek. She reached with one arm around the back of his neck and stroked his hair, whispering that she couldn't wait to see their child in his arms.

Vander, with a start, left in a hurry as he realized he had lingered longer than usual and there was much to do to ready the farm for the imminent harvest.

The days at the farm were busy for Piper. After mixing her dough for the day's bread, she set it to rise on the still-warm oven, covering it with her apron. She headed out the front door to her garden which was set in front of the house away from their voracious animals. A lattice-work fence fashioned the branches surrounding her carrots, potatoes, leeks, onions, tomatoes, garlic, and cabbage. She spent the morning pulling weeds and checking for signs of rabbits and other intruders. The early September sun warmed her arms and neck and made her happy. She hummed as she left the garden and walked to the stable yard to give the uprooted sweet clover to the newly weaned lambs. She loved their little faces, and it sometimes made her sad to think that they were born only to serve people. She consoled herself with the fact that she and Vander had no plans to slaughter and eat their sheep. They wanted only their milk and wool. The adorable pink piglets on the other hand ... she stopped herself because lately the oddest ideas could bring tears she didn't understand. She stood with her face to the sun and let it warm her, comfort her, and she wished the nausea would pass. Shielding her eyes from the sun, she looked out to the fields, trying to catch a glimpse of Vander and the horses working the new plot he was hoping to plant with a late crop of root vegetables to sell at market. She couldn't see over the rise beyond the meadow where he likely was, and so decided she had better put together a midday meal for him. She thought the walk out to the fields might do her some good. She walked back toward the house singing a haunting song from her sad childhood. It made her think of her mother lying sick on her bed, her father trying to pray the disease from her wasting body. And this time the tears did come, cleansing the sadness from her past, and leaving her feeling refreshed and ready for whatever lay ahead.

Tämä ikivanha lupaus
Suurin koskaan tiedä - henki puhelut
Ja kuuntelen sinua
Sinun siniset silmät paloi
Minun muisti elämien sitten
Odotan sinua
Etsi sinua valossa
Salvia, rovio, jäätyneiden järvien
Odotan sinua
Minä odotan sinua
Vuosisatojen avautua ja minä
Odotan sinua
Odottaa sinua valo

She gathered together some cheese, grapes, wine, and a jug of water fresh from the well, and put them in the basket she usually took to market on Saturdays. On her way back outside, she stopped in the dooryard and picked a few of her favorite gladiolus stems and tucked them into the basket, their pink blossoms adorning this sweet gesture with the romance that was interrupted earlier that morning.

She opened the wooden gate at the back of the stable yard and stepped through quickly so as not to let the kids out, remembering how hard it had been to herd them back in just a few days ago. Loose livestock draws wolves from the deep woods surrounding their many fields and they could not afford to put their livelihood in harm's way. In the beginning, Piper had often voiced her concern with living so far from the village, but trusted Vander's good sense; slowly she had realized how wonderful it was to have this place to themselves. She lifted her dress and stepped high through the tall grass until she reached the path Vander's cart created with its heavy wooden wheels. She took a deep breath and listened to the birdsongs in the fields. She walked along slowly, knowing that she was early with the midday meal and didn't want to interrupt her husband's work. He was determined to make the farm a lucrative business for them, something so many told him was impossible because most families grew almost everything they needed themselves. He planned to someday have enough produce to sell at the markets in the city, an idea that most people raised an eyebrow at, the city being days away.

It had been a long while since she had come out this far. Vander did most of the farming himself, his brothers and father occasionally coming out to help fix a broken wheel spoke or to look at a stone-bruised hoof. She would like to ride out here in the pasture with Vander, but lately what had been the daily routine when they were children seemed now to be a frivolous use of time. As she reached the rise, the stone wall looking much taller than it had from the stable yard, she could hear Vander talking to the horses, telling them that it was almost time for a break and a cool drink at the brook. They snorted as if to say, "Almost time? I'm tired," but they were in their prime, and Vander would never work them hard enough to even challenge their stamina. Each horse was immensely powerful, and together they were an incredible team of muscle and loyalty.

The scent of lavender reached Piper's nose, and she inhaled deeply, wondering where it was coming from. She had planted a few young plants that spring, which she had traded for some goat milk at the market; but those were acres away in her dooryard. As she drew closer to the stone wall at the top of the hill, she began to see purple, lots of purple. She took a few more steps and gasped. Her hand loosened its grip, and she dropped her basket, spilling the water all over her husband's food. She didn't notice. As far as her eyes could reach was a sea of lavender. Her breath caught in her chest, her heart leapt and fluttered at the sight. Waves of purple crested and rolled in the warm breeze. Her mind shouted questions as she stood motionless. *Why hasn't he told me about this? What is he planning to do with so much lavender?* She loved the color, so pure, and the fragrance was unmatched in its ability to soothe and calm.

"Piper!" Vander's voice was excited and surprised, reaching her ears, but she didn't hear him. She was in shock. He steadied his team, wrapping the reins around the brake on his cart and asking them to stand. He jogged up the hill and swung one leg over the stone wall and then the other. "Piper, I wanted to surprise you. Uh ... are you ... surprised? Piper?"

She couldn't take her eyes off of the sea of ethereal purple so immense that she was having a hard time comprehending its size, let alone its purpose. He placed his hands on her shoulders and said,

"For you, my love. It's all for you."

She slowly tore her gaze from the most gorgeous sight she had ever seen and blinked back tears. She looked up at her husband. From his back pocket he drew a handful of lavender stems and held them out to his wife.

"For you. Everything for you," Vander said, his eyes searching Piper's.

Piper took the bouquet and held it to her heart. She noticed the color closely matched the dress she was wearing. The material for the dress had belonged to her mother but it was never put to use, having been purchased a year before she passed. Now the dress fluttered in the breeze and as Piper looked past her husband's tall frame to the acres beyond, she stifled tears.

"Vander, I don't ... I ... what am I going to do with that much lavender?"

He leaned back and released a hearty laugh of relief. She had a way of making him smile, too. "I mean, these herbs, well, they are going to be sold. In the city, to a perfumery. And the money, well, the money is the part that's for you."

It was her turn to laugh. She knew he was either nervous or drunk when his words made no sense. And as far as she knew he hadn't had any wine that morning. "What do I need money for? We have everything we need when we go to market with the crops and we have more than most. I don't understand."

He took her hand and led her to the stone wall, then bent and scooped her up and stepped over the stone wall with her in his strong arms. She giggled and played with his hair, damp with sweat. He walked slowly through the rows of purple spikes until they were surrounded. Gently lowering himself to his knees, he placed her on the ground between two rows. Together they sat in this sweet-smelling secret ocean so far from anyone they knew, just the two of them. He looked into her eyes and tucked her hair back behind her ears.

"Piper, there's something I never told you, and ... and I thought I never would ... but, well, you're my wife and I want to tell you everything." His voice was serious and low, and it made her realize that no matter what he was about to say, she was going to be all right. They would be all right. "A long time ago, your father ... he pulled me off my father's fish cart one day and pushed me against the wheel when I was helping to unload it at the market. He told me that I had better have good intentions toward his daughter, that she was all that was left of his wife and she deserved a good man. I tried to tell him that I loved you from the first time I saw you that day in the market, how I wanted to be your friend, but I was too shy, and I didn't think you would talk to me. But I was scared. He was so much bigger than me then and his eyes were fierce. He told me that the man his daughter would marry would do more for her than her father ever could. She was not meant to live in poverty; she would have proper shoes and would sleep through the night without night terrors making her call out to her dead mother. She would have a good life, a life he couldn't give her. He told me that if he had more money he would have been able to bring your mother to the city doctors and they might have saved her life. Ever since that day I have tried to show him that I am a hard worker, that my family is decent and honest. I wanted him to know that I would take care of his daughter until the day I die." Tears were streaming down his cheeks leaving little rivers of clean skin in their path, dirty droplets falling onto the powdery earth below.

Piper gently wiped his dirty face and kissed his dry, hot lips. She rose to her knees and held her love's head to her bosom. She didn't know she could love someone so much. All around them the lavender swayed gently back and forth in a rhythm not unlike the rhythm of life itself: sometimes giving, sometimes taking away.

13

TWO DAYS IN THE Hospital de la Timone in Marseille was more than Piper could bear; so, at the end of the second day, she asked to be discharged. The doctor and nurses all told her she really ought to stay and rest, that she had lost a lot of blood. One joked that Americans were always in such a hurry and she wondered aloud where they were always in a hurry to get to. Piper ignored the remarks and stated simply, "We're here on business, and I cannot stay another day."

The nurse turned her back to Piper and said over her shoulder, "Madam, hasn't your mother ever told you that patience is a virtue?"

Piper looked at the redheaded nurse with disgust and replied, "I'm not feeling very virtuous today."

With that, the nurse excused herself, and Piper was alone in the room with the afternoon sun glinting through the window and falling in long rectangles across her bed. She pulled back the sheets and swung her long legs over the side of the bed and let her feet feel the cold vinyl floor. She stood up, and feeling a little shaky, grabbed the bed rail and steadied herself. She looked for her clothes and shoes and hurried into the bathroom before anyone else could come in and slow down her progress. In the bathroom, she washed her face with Castile soap and cool water. She looked deep into her eyes in the small mirror over the sink and noticed a hint of wrinkles around her tired eyes. She brushed her hair hastily, not making much improvement but feeling the need to try anyway. She dressed quickly and went back out to the small hospital room that now felt like a cell. Once she was intent on doing something, not much could stop her. She rummaged through her purse, found her cell phone, and dialed Paul. There was no service. *Of course.* She dialed the nurse's station from the phone by her bed and asked how to dial out. With a shaking hand she punched the numbers, keeping time with her racing heart.

"Honey, I need to leave now. Will you come get me?" she asked breathlessly.

"Hi Sweets, I'm with Mr. Porrazzo at his vineyard, remember?"

She sucked in air that seemed to weigh a ton.

"Oh, I forgot," she said, deflated. "I ... I want to leave now. I'll just call a cab and...." Her voice trailed off as tears threatened to fall.

"Piper, no. The doctor said you should be there for at least one or two more days. Don't you think you should stay? What's wrong, are you okay?"

"No. I'm leaving." For the first time since she met Paul, she hung up without saying good-bye and I love you. She tossed her phone back into her purse, gathered her belongings, and hurried through the door. She left behind in the wastebasket a crumpled piece of paper on which she had scribbled the night before when the painkillers had worn off and she couldn't sleep.

> *I wait here for time to unravel its truth*
> *And deliver me into your arms again*
> *You call to me through the rain*
> *The cold breath of night on my skin*
> *Many times the end promised me peace*
> *My thirst for your voice unrelenting*
> *Why won't you come to me in this place*
> *Lessons to be learned and promises to keep*
> *My lifeblood flows and begets not life but pain*
> *My love, come for me and fill my empty heart.*

When she arrived at the inn, Piper took a hot bath and scrubbed her skin until it was raw. She soaked and cried and prayed. When she was finished, she toweled off, put on one of Paul's Aerosmith t-shirts and ran a comb through her hair. She looked for her iPod, but not finding it, decided she wanted to feel the pain this time and let it work its way through her like a bitter pill. Her pain turned quickly to anger. *Why would God do this to me? To us? Aren't we decent, hardworking people? Wouldn't we make loving, responsible parents? What is the purpose of life without children to pass your values, love and history on to? Why did this have to happen now?* If they had stayed home, she thought, she would still be pregnant and would have soon known about it. How excited she would have been to see the look on her husband's face when she told him the news he had waited years to hear. With her tears and energy spent, she stared at the wall as she lay curled up on her side, clutching her pillow. She heard her phone ring, but she didn't even consider getting up to answer it. She knew it would be Paul but didn't want his sympathy or his apologies. She wanted to be alone; in her solitude, she felt whole, the feeling familiar and comforting. She wished she had her notebook but realized she had left it at the hospital in her haste to leave. She exhaled deeply and scolded herself aloud, "When will you learn to take a breath and be patient?"

Deciding then that tea might make her feel a little better she shrugged off the feeling that she deserved punishing. She called the innkeeper's office and asked if someone could bring her some tea with honey. While she waited, she combed her drying hair and sprayed it with a glossy humectant to keep it from getting unruly. She stared at herself in the mirror and felt a strange sensation. *Who am I?* She'd often joked with Paul when he cooked for her or picked up his own dirty underwear and socks. "Who are you," she would joke, "and what have you done with my husband?" But this time she was not in a joking mood. *Who am I and what does this journey mean, this life?*

As she stared into the glass, her vision blurred with tears and, before she could blink, glimpsed out of the corner of one eye the figure of a smiling boy holding his cupped hands up to her as though he wanted to show her something. In his small hands she saw for the briefest moment a tiny gleaming pearl. Startled, she blinked and spun around. Nothing. *Great,* she thought, *now I've lost my mind.* She took in a deep breath and let it out slowly. She brushed at what she thought must be a fly in the room with her. It was still there, and she brushed at it again. Still there. Exasperated, she left the bathroom to answer the door. Her tea had arrived.

It was late in the evening when Paul arrived back at the inn. Piper was sleeping on the chair in which she'd had her tea, her feet resting on the ottoman, a blanket around her shoulders. Paul kneeled next to her and shook her shoulder. "I'm back, Honey."

She stirred and opened her eyes. Her anger still brimming, she stared at her husband but didn't speak. He knew the look all too well and knew that she never communicated effectively when she was in this state, so he decided to wash up and give her space. She could smell what must have been a delicious dinner on his breath as he quickly kissed her furrowed brow. *He was enjoying himself while I was lying in that god awful hospital bed,* she thought.

She got up from the chair and walked quietly to the closet where her clothes hung. Pulling on a pair of jeans and thin red sweater and then slipping into her shoes, she snuck out of the room before Paul finished brushing his teeth. She still wanted to be alone with her thoughts and her anger. When she felt like this her sharp tongue seemed to have a mind of its own, and she didn't want to hurt Paul. He was hurting, too, she knew; but to keep his appointment with Freddy at the vineyard after what had happened seemed a bit cold if not cruel. It wasn't like Paul.

Piper welcomed the cool night air and let it fill her lungs and feed her blood. She felt wide awake and wanted nothing more than to be at home getting ready to ride out to the pond and watch the ducks come in for their noisy landing. She closed her eyes and pictured her house, her barn, her horses, and couldn't wait for the next few days to pass her by so that she could be there, right where she belonged. France was beautiful, but the way that she was feeling right now, and the things that had occurred since she landed, left her feeling more than a little homesick; but not quite displaced.

Paul heard the door close and stuck his head into the bedroom, glancing around to see if Piper really had just walked out into the night. He stood shaking his head and thought about going after her, but quickly thought better of it. His wife was not the kind of woman who wanted to be chased after when she stormed out. When she was that heated, she truly meant to be by herself, inside herself. She once confided in Paul that sometimes she had lied to him when they were dating about having other plans. These were times that she simply wanted to be alone, to listen to her music, and to write whatever was on her mind. He suggested that maybe she was a little depressed, to which she responded, "Don't flatter yourself." He never challenged her on this point ever again. She was a deeply thoughtful person who could handle a lot of stress effortlessly to a point; but when she reached her limit, she crashed.

Walking purposefully down the crushed gravel drive of the inn, despite having no idea where she was going to wind up, suddenly invigorated Piper. The brisk night air felt good and she loved the feeling of adrenaline rushing through her veins. She remembered there being a tavern at the end of the road that Paul had said they ought to try before they left. She thought to herself, *Yes, I will try it before I leave.* She walked faster and faster and finally broke into a run, the wind pushing her hair from her face and making her clean skin feel young and new. As she reached the door of the tavern she slowed just enough to catch her breath. The lights glowed inside, and she could see through the window that it was quite crowded. She smiled when she saw the door handle was a draft horseshoe. She pulled hard on the thick, heavy, wooden door and was met with the faces of strangers, music, and the scent of cigar smoke, something she secretly loved. Her father and grandfather both smoked and the scent of tobacco reminded her of Christmas Eve, the whole family around the table sharing the seven fishes, pasta, stories of generations past. Some of Piper's fondest memories were of the times when the conversation between her great aunts went from the size of the meatballs in the Wedding Soup to the outrage of the price of chicken breast at the grocery store. It was only on this night that anyone was allowed to smoke indoors. Her grandmother said it took the next 364 days to get the smell out of her house. *I miss you, Noni,* she whispered and drew in breath through her nose, knowing the scent of anisette was not at the tavern.

Feeling completely anonymous, she smiled as she approached the bar and caught the eye of the bartender who did a double take, causing several patrons to turn in the direction of his gaze. A few men looked her up and down, causing their dates to scowl in return. Piper's cheeks were pink from her run and the fresh air had given her shiny black hair a wispy fullness, lending her a bit of a wild look, something she normally tried to avoid but tonight didn't mind one bit. *No one knows me here. I can be who and whatever I want.*

"I'll have a scotch, please." She ordered with a sense of urgency and deliberateness that Paul would have been surprised at had he been at her side. Realizing then that she had not been in a bar without Paul since they began dating ten years before, had her feeling a bit guilty. "Whatever," she muttered to herself as the young man approached with her drink. She took the glass directly from the bartender's hand and as she looked at his hand, she was struck with the feeling of déjà vu, something she'd heard other people talk about. She had never experienced it previously, but now likened it to her scent-aches. She seemed to know that he would rub his nose nervously when she thanked him for the drink. She stared for only a moment at his beautiful shy eyes. Then she tipped the glass up and let the liquid fire numb her grieving insides. An elderly gentleman nodded at her ambition and stood up to offer her his seat which she gladly accepted. She hadn't eaten in almost forty-eight hours and was suddenly ravenous. She asked the bartender if there was a menu she could look at.

"Well, madam, it's a little late so I will check to see what we have. This is okay?" She nodded and added, "And I'll have another scotch when you get back."

He smiled and dropped his gaze to the bar top before departing. The man who gave up his seat asked if she was on holiday. "No, not really," she replied. "I'm here," she hesitated, "just visiting ... on business, sort of." The alcohol had gone straight from her lips to her brain it seemed, and the man looked at her with a mix of amusement and understanding.

He put his hands into his trouser pockets and said, "We all need a place we can go to just escape, right?" She nodded her appreciation, but before she could ask if he lived in the area, he was gone. The bartender came back and informed her that there was plenty of fish and a few Cornish hens left, and she could have either served with potatoes or rice or both, whatever she wanted. She looked at him for a moment and felt like she knew him, or wanted to know him, or maybe she just wanted that scotch.

"I'll have the hen, my friend, and some rice would be great."

He nodded, and called through the kitchen door to the chef to make the lady a nice dish fit for a queen. She smiled at him, and this time he smiled back. Piper hadn't the faintest idea why, but she felt that this man could easily be one of those people that once they walk into your life, they never leave. *It's just the liquor, Piper*, she reminded herself and turned her attention to the other side of the bar. There were couples sitting so close they were wasting bar stools, hands in places they shouldn't be in public. The smoke in the air was so thick that it hung like a semi-private screen for those who were too drunk to realize they were actually in public view. She thought to herself that she was glad she had skipped out on all the bar-hopping her friends had done in college. She loved going out, but only with someone special, not just for the sake of sitting around having men undress her with their lewd intentions. But now, thousands of miles from herself and her home, she felt a sort of freedom she had never before felt. What was to stop her from being someone else right now? Nobody knew her here, and in two short days, she'd be on a plane headed back to Massachusetts and her life with Paul on their farm. She would never see any of these people again, much less have to answer to any of them.

After she finished her second scotch, another man approached her and asked if he might join her for a drink.

"Sure," she said, not feeling one bit out of line. "I'm Piper by the way."

She reached out to shake his hand and had the conscious thought that she was not at work and didn't need to be so forward.

She drew in a deep breath and this time she didn't experience the anisette but a sweet mixture of cinnamon and cloves and something familiar and pungent. Ugh, she thought ... burnt raisins.

"Piper? Really. Truly?" The handsome gray-haired gentleman's eyes brightened and she visibly noticed his pupils enlarge as he scanned hers.

"My great-great grandmother was Piper. It's such an unusual name; you don't hear it often," he said, and nodded.

Piper reached for her third Scotch a few seconds after it arrived, like a quiet guest who doesn't want to interrupt, but everyone notices. As she took a slower sip this time, she saw in her mind's eye a pregnant young woman juggling a toddler and an armful of packages for an elderly woman who sat at a table, smiling, taking in the scene.

When she returned the glass to the bar top she looked at the man who was studying her face intently.

"Wow, your great-great grandmother?" She looked back at her drink and was glad to see most of it was still in the glass. She reminded herself to slow down.

"Yes, Madam. She lived to see her ninth great-great grandchild born when she was ninety-six years old."

"Wow, that's ... that's incredible, what a full life. God bless her. I should hope to be so lucky."

She looked around then to see the smoke begin to dissipate. Patrons were either beginning to come to their senses and go home or had become hopelessly lost in the restrooms fumbling with buttons and zippers.

"Where are you from?" asked the stranger who pulled up a stool next to the beautiful woman who had at least three inches on him.

"The States. Massachusetts to be exact," she replied.

"Ahh, you derelicts, throwing all that good tea into the harbor, starting all kinds of trouble."

"Yeah, that's us, troublemakers according to the history books. But well-behaved people rarely make a lasting impression, don't you know?"

He laughed heartily in agreement as the bartender winked at him and served them each a glass of house wine. She was feeling good now, but deep down she knew she was just trying to numb the pain she knew she would feel all too soon. "So, your family has been here for a long time I'm guessing?"

"Yes, as long as France has been France; mostly farmers and tradesmen, some fishermen, too." He laughed quietly, enjoying this rare moment of anonymity. He found it utterly refreshing to go unrecognized and couldn't remember the last time he had had a conversation with a stranger that didn't have to do with business. As Piper saw her dinner coming, she wished she could be alone so that she wouldn't have to eat while being mindful of others. She was hungry and already had had too much to drink.

"I have a farm, too, back home. Horses for now, but my husband and I are trying to start a vineyard. That's why we're here ... doing some research."

"A vineyard; how very ambitious, my dear," he replied, and hoped he didn't sound arrogant.

"It's my husband's dream, I guess you could say. And since we don't have children—" She couldn't believe she had just blurted that out but given the double scotch and the three sips of the best red wine she'd ever tasted, she was even more surprised that she wasn't sobbing and telling this man all her woes. "I mean, since we don't have children yet, this is something we'd like to put our efforts into for now." She noticed the man was tilting his head as she spoke.

He noticed her noticing him and said, "Sorry, Madam, but there's something about you that is very familiar, but I cannot say what it is."

"Really?" she asked and turned toward her dinner.

He looked at her apologetically and said, "Well, then, I will leave you to your dinner and I must say it was a true pleasure to have made your acquaintance." She felt badly about having made it so obvious she wanted to be by herself.

"Oh, yes, thank you."

She moved to stick out her hand but this time stopped herself.

"It was very nice talking with you, Mr. .... ." She hated when she painted herself into a corner like that.

"Pecheur, Claude Pecheur." He filled in the blank for her, then gently reached out to her hand on the bar top. He raised her hand in his. She was struck by the name and even as he gently kissed her hand and nodded his good-bye, Piper was aware that she was frozen in disbelief.

The man left without another word and for a moment she saw cobblestone streets and heard hooves as they struck the hard surface—a sound she always found exhilarating. Remembering how hungry she still was, she turned back to her waiting hen and rice, and looked up at the bartender as if for an explanation.

He smiled, eyebrows raised at her as if to say, "Yes, you heard correctly."

She smiled back and wondered if she would have acted the same way had she known she was talking to one of the world's most powerful men in the perfume industry. She shrugged her shoulders slightly and started eating the most delicious meal she could remember ever eating.

When the scotch began to wear off and the bones of the poor little hen sat naked on the plate with not so much as a bit of skin or grain of rice to keep it company, Piper felt that she had stayed away long enough. She reached for the euros she had hastily shoved into the pocket of her jeans earlier but the bartender stopped her.

"No Madam. Monsieur Pecheur owns this tavern and wishes only that you enjoyed your meal and the atmosphere tonight. There is no charge (*my love*)."

She sat up and tilted her head. *Did he call me love? Or did I just imagine it?* He looked somehow boyish and ducked his head as he turned away from her, rubbing his nose nervously.

She wanted to touch him.

Plain and simple, she wanted to touch him. Not in a sexual way, but in the way that she couldn't resist touching a puppy or a newborn foal. She only wanted to feel his hand, his arm, his warm skin next to hers. There was something about him that was so familiar but she knew, too, that even though the alcohol was wearing off, she was very sensitive and emotional when she drank. She knew then that she ought to be heading back to Paul, to reality, to her life as she had left it a few hours before. Knowing that waking up the next morning was going to be unpleasant, she wanted just this one last indulgence. She stood up slowly from her seat and left twenty euros tucked under the plate for him.

Looking up to wish him a good night she was surprised to find he was gone and she realized that he must have gone back to the kitchen. She raised her eyebrows, tucked her hair behind her ears, and turned for the door. She immediately bumped into the young man she had just been looking for.

"Oh!" she exclaimed as her hand flew nervously to her throat.

"Pardon, Madam, I did not mean to startle you."

She looked up into his shy blue eyes.

"That's okay, I didn't know you were there," she said, feeling childish somehow.

I will always be here.

"I will see you to the door, Madam."

He held out his arm to escort her. As she hooked hers through his, she was instantly flooded with pure love and light.

14

AS THE MONTHS PASSED and her belly swelled, Piper felt more and more content and settled into her life with Vander. With the harvest of wheat, squash, onions, garlic, and corn having been put up in the lofts and the surplus sold in the village of their youth, and with winter quickly approaching, they were finally able to spend more time together getting ready for the arrival of their first child. Piper calculated that they would officially be parents by the middle of April. Her father visited more often now, knowing that his daughter was happy and content and that Vander was the husband he had promised to be.

On one visit during late autumn, Piper's father came to help Vander build a cradle for his first grandchild. As he stepped through the door for the first time in over a month, he looked at Piper with pure love and admiration. She looked at him sheepishly, but when she saw the expression on his face, she hurried into his open arms. She drew a deep breath and smelled the wood shavings that seemed to always be a part of her father.

"I missed you so much, Père. Next time you come here, please make sure Marek comes with you."

He looked down at his only daughter and smiled. "I can't believe you are going to be a mother soon. Your mother would ..." His voice caught in his throat but then he continued. "A father couldn't be more proud." He looked at Vander and nodded his silent approval.

"Hello, Père," Vander said and quickly came to shake his

hand. Piper stepped back and looked at the two men her heart adored. She didn't think she could feel safer or more loved than she did with her father and husband standing there in her house. She imagined the only thing better would be to have her mother and Marek here with them.

Her father spoke up. "How did your harvest look, Vander?"

"Very strong, and, God willing, next year will be as good."

His father-in-law nodded. "Yes, God willing and only if." He clapped Vander on the back. "Let's get to work. Your child will need a place to sleep soon." And with that they walked out toward the barn.

Piper watched through the small window near her hearth as they stepped through the gate into the stable yard, and her breath caught in her throat as her father scooped up one of the barn kittens and nuzzled it. She couldn't remember her father ever seeming happy since her mother had passed from this life. She was glad to see him smile, relax, and be excited about his grandchild. She turned back to the vegetables she had been washing and cutting for the stew they would have for their evening meal. She carefully finished cutting the potatoes, carrots, and leeks, and tossed them into the cast iron pot on her stove top. To it, she added the large pieces of salted beef her father had brought from the market and a little black pepper. After adding more wood to the fire, she turned her attention to her knitting. She had been knitting a blanket for the baby but was not pleased with the way it was coming along. She had no mother to teach her the things a young woman needs to know as she is growing up. Vander's mother was a wonderful substitute, if there can be such a thing, teaching her the basics of knitting, sewing, pregnancy, and what to expect of childbirth and baby care. Piper was very nervous about the birth, especially since her closest neighbor to the north had died in childbirth a month prior. As soon as she was certain she was with child, she asked her mother-in-law if she would help at the birth. With tears in her gray eyes, Amélie said she would be honored to help. "I only wish that your mother could be here, too, love," she told Piper.

To this Piper responded, "God gave me one mother for the first years of my life and then called her home. I was angry at Him for this until I realized that you would be my mother from then on. I will always miss my Mère, and I will always love her. But now I have you and I am thankful for that."

As she knitted, she periodically stopped to gauge her progress, often pulling the yarn apart to knit again. She stopped suddenly when she felt her baby fluttering inside her. She wished Vander were close by as he loved to feel the baby when it moved. Putting her needles and yarn aside she looked at her belly, swollen and full of life. Tears threatened to flow until she reminded herself that this was a happy occasion and demanded the tears stay put. The thought that perhaps her mother was there with her in spirit comforted her.

She got up from her chair at the table and stirred the stew. She noticed the sun sitting in the western sky and thought how short the days seemed this time of year. She hurried to the door and picked up the bucket of cracked corn from the stool near the door and stepped outside to feed her hens. The cold air greeted her, and she stepped back for a moment. She took her wool cloak off the peg by the door and wrapped herself in it. Out in the cloudless evening, she looked up at the stars and wondered for the first time in her life how long she would be on earth. She wondered if she would outlive Vander and have to live out her days alone or if he would be the one to mourn her. *Which one is worse?* She shrugged and thought it was morbid, but hoped anyway that they could die together and not have to miss one another for even a season.

That thought dismissed the matter from her mind altogether as she tossed the corn to the hungry hens, who soon would need to roost in the barn to keep from freezing. She noticed one of the hens had a broken leg and wondered how it had happened. The hen, she thought, would make a wonderful meal when Marek came to visit. Her brother hadn't come around much lately and she wondered why. Vander had hired him to help with the farm when they were first married but he abruptly stopped coming after only three weeks. Vander explained that her brother found working with their father and working the farm too much on him. But Piper didn't fully believe it as her father had told her that Marek did not work with him at all when he was working the farm. She didn't challenge her husband about this, though. Piper felt that Vander would not lie to her, and so she decided it was better left between the men. She missed her brother, but he was not the same brother she remembered growing up with. He was a handful of mischief then, but given the fact that he was without a mother, and his father was not much more than a provider of meals, his behavior was always deemed acceptable. Until, that is, he grew into a young man.

The villagers often regarded Marek as different and not wholly trustworthy. His quiet way was often perceived as stealth and he was blamed for more than a few missing hens and broken windows. He was an excellent craftsman like his father, but had few social skills, and he often scared girls he showed interest in. Marek was handsome in a dark way, his hair unruly and longer than that of most respectable men. He was very tall and muscular like their father. She was proud of him and knew that he would be all right if only he could meet a girl and settle down, have a family. She knew that would make him happy. Piper made a mental note to tell her father to let Marek know that he was welcome to visit any time for a meal and that he could stay for a while and help her with the winter chores before the baby came.

It was late in the evening before the men came into the house for their dinner. Piper served them steaming bowls of stew, thick slices of bread, and wine. She nibbled on some cheese and bread and sipped some broth as she had eaten her own meal hours before.

Vander took his wife's hand and said, "The cradle is coming along and even though we still have a lot of work to do, it's really taking shape. I hope you'll like it, Piper."

She looked proudly at her husband and said, "Of course I will like it. How lucky our baby is to have a father and grandfather so talented and kind."

He laughed. "Your father has the talent; I just do as I'm told." They all laughed then, the three of them at the table, two candles lighting the small room.

When it was time for sleep, Piper's father climbed to the loft and called goodnight to the expecting parents. They wished him a good night's sleep and teased him about the kitten he seemed to have adopted who rested curled up, purring on his shoulder and didn't budge until morning.

Piper and Vander climbed into bed in their bedchamber and held each other tightly, knowing that a love like theirs was not to be taken for granted, and that there is no guarantee how long they might have one another. They knew they were lucky and that God had smiled down on them.

"I never want to know what life would be like without you," she whispered in his ear.

"You will never be without me, Love. Not in this life or in any other."

She ruffled his hair, "What? What did you say, Vander?"

"Shhh ... go to sleep. The morning will be here soon. Just know that there will never be a time that you won't feel my love. You are my every good thing."

15

WAKING TO THE CALLS OF Valo, Dragon, and Oliver from the barn was a salve on her heart. She missed them so and had wanted to visit them the night before when they arrived home from the airport, but felt it better not to disturb them so late. Viceroy was, however, a different story. He heard the Volvo pull into the drive and was so excited when they stepped into the house that his little heart was like a humming-bird's wings, beating so fast it was just a hum. He jumped and whined and spun in circles until Paul bent down and scooped him up, holding him tight. Piper kissed his little face and tugged on his warm ears.

"I missed you little guy. Have you been keeping an eye on the place, you little bugger?"

He seemed to know what she said, tilting his head and squirming in Paul's arms. He slept between them that night, a rare treat they just couldn't deny him. How he ended up under the covers at the foot of the bed by morning, they didn't know, but he managed it. And happy as a pig in mud as Piper's dad always said.

Piper rolled onto her side, feeling for Paul but he wasn't there, his side of the bed cold. She pulled herself up, feeling rested and happy to be home. Stepping out of bed, and stretching her tall frame backward, Piper felt her muscles come alive. Knowing she would be busy catching up on work for the next week or so, she promised herself this one day to do what she loved most. She pulled on a pair of navy breeches and her favorite old Les Misérables t-shirt which had a couple of tiny holes and bore hoof-oil stains. She pulled her hair back into a flowing black ponytail and brushed her teeth. Her skin was clear and looked somehow refreshed this morning. Her mother always said that happiness does wonders for the skin. She smiled and raised one brow. She made a mental note to call her parents. *Maybe later today,* she thought. Wanting to keep her skin looking young as long as possible, she washed her face and dotted on a citrus-scented moisturizer.

She trotted down the stairs. "Good morning sweets," she said when she saw her husband, his five o'clock shadow having evolved into a beard.

"Hi, Darlin', want some coffee?"

"No, thanks, I want to feed the guys so I can ride in a little bit," she said, heading for the mudroom.

"I took care of them, Hon."

She stopped and turned, seeing her husband with two mugs of coffee in his hands, waiting for her and making her heart skip a beat. "You're the best; did I ever tell you?" she said without looking him in the eye.

He rolled his eyes toward the ceiling dramatically. "Umm, no. No, you never have," he teased.

"Oh, well you are." She took the mug from him and sat in the breakfast nook to have her coffee. She sat with her foot tapping, shifting in her seat, not really wanting to be indoors but also not wanting the cold interchange with Paul to continue.

"So, do you want to talk about anything?"

He had tried to ask this on the flight home but knew it wasn't fair to either of them or anyone else on the plane if an argument broke out at 30,000 feet with nowhere to go.

"No, not really. Do you?"

Her voice was cool, which was a pleasant improvement over the last couple of days.

"Yes, I do. I think you owe me an explanation. Don't you?"

He looked directly into her eyes so that she would not avert his gaze. She didn't usually back down in a staring contest.

"What would you like me to explain?"

She raised her brows and tilted her head mockingly and silently reminded herself that she had nothing to hide.

"Well, for starters, where were you the night after you left the inn? I was worried and you didn't bring your phone so I couldn't even reach you."

She sat up straight, ready for battle. Placing the mug of bitter-tasting coffee on the table a little too hard got her heart beating faster, and she scolded him for treating her like a child.

"I just went out for something to eat since you had already eaten with your *investor friends*."

She knew she sounded childlike but didn't much care. *I don't need this right now, not from my husband.*

"And you know, leaving me in the hospital so you could keep your precious meeting really pissed me off, if you must know."

He looked at her with a look that said *come on now*.

"What?" she said and shook her head.

"You know we only had a few days there, and Mr. Porrazzo is a busy man. He couldn't change our appointment. You know that, Piper, honey."

"Don't 'honey' me," she said as she got up, took her mug to the sink and poured it out slowly, making sure he knew what she was doing. She walked quickly to the mudroom and pulled on her field boots with the hooks that hung on the wall. She wasn't sure there was much else in life that gave her the same feeling as well-worn riding boots did: comfort, second skin, anticipation, purpose, joy.

She reached for her helmet and stopped. "Screw it," she muttered under her breath as she made her escape and slammed the door behind her, leaving Viceroy and Paul looking at each other in confusion.

As she neared the barn, the scent of the horses and shavings filled her, and she could feel her heart slow. All three horses looked up from their morning hay. Valo's nostrils flared, and he whinnied a surprisingly loud, *Hello, and where have you been?*

She smiled and said, "I missed you, too, all of you." She

went into the feed room and grabbed some Rounders for each of them. She offered one crunchy apple cinnamon treat to Oliver, one to Dragon, and two to Valo, never hiding her obvious favoritism. She slipped his halter over his ears and clipped the throatlatch, slid his door open, and stepped back. He wasted no time in stepping out of his stall into the aisle and halting at the crossties. Her friends all laughed when she used the crossties because they knew that he would just as soon stand for her as long as she wanted him to. She quickly ran a soft brush over his sleek coat, checked his hooves for small rocks, and decided they did not need picking. She carefully sprayed horrible-smelling insect repellent over his body, making sure not to miss his belly and ears, to avoid him being ambushed by deer flies.

She didn't want to be in the barn if Paul decided to bring his questions out here to her sanctuary. She quickly tossed a navy quilted saddle pad onto his back and followed it with the beautiful black stock saddle that Paul had presented to her the day Valo arrived. It had been custom-made for Valo in Holland and fit him perfectly like her boots fit her. Tightening his girth and patting his neck, she decided she was really angry with Paul. *How dare he? Was he questioning my integrity, my fidelity?* She slipped reins over her horse's neck and held the snaffle bit under his mouth, which he opened without hesitation and let the metal glide gently in over his tongue, avoiding his teeth. She pushed the headstall over his giant ears and fixed his forelock so that it flowed gently over one eye and hung past his muzzle. She fastened the throatlatch.

"Come on, walk on." He turned and followed her, only one stride behind. She needn't lead him with reins; he wasn't going anywhere she wasn't. By stopping and turning toward him, she silently asked him to stand. After lowering her stirrups on each side, she came back to his left. She gathered the reins in her left hand, lifted her foot up to the stirrup iron, bounced twice on her right foot and hoisted herself up, gently swinging her leg over his back, settling into the saddle. She drew a deep breath and closed her eyes.

Home.

She took another, deeper breath and decided not to turn toward the house in case she saw Paul coming out to the barn. She didn't want to see him. Gathered reins in hand, she squeezed her legs against Valo's side and instantly felt a calming reassurance that she was where she was meant to be. She rode through the woods, past the meadow, and out to the pasture that would soon be tilled under in preparation for the first planting of grapevines. Valo snorted as he warmed up and she could feel his muscles tense as he anticipated her letting him go. She smiled to no one and leaned forward, loosening her reins and grabbing a fistful of mane. Valo tossed his head and lunged forward, his stride having unbelievable scope.

They covered a hundred feet in a matter of seconds, his hooves pounding the ground sending quail fluttering into the morning air. She stood in her stirrups, her upper body poised over his neck, her hands giving and taking as horse and rider as one thundered through the field. She could feel the power beneath her and knew that he had more to give. She clucked her tongue and squeezed her legs against him again. His ears flicked back for a moment showing that he was listening and then pulled against the reins as if to answer with "Really? More? No problem." He shifted into a higher gear and was soon in a full gallop. Piper thought for the briefest moment how stupid it was to leave her helmet behind, but she really could have cared less this morning.

She gently pulled on her left rein and turned him toward the center of the field, and, as they approached, she sat back and let him know she wanted him to slow. She loved the feeling of pulling up a horse and falling into that perfect collected canter that made the rest of the world stand still. He broke to a trot and she posted for a few strides, and sat back, asking him to halt. The wind kicked up a bit and sent her ponytail up and over her head, Valo's mane mimicking it but on a much grander scale. She released her grip on the reins, letting them fall and get lost in his thick mane. Taking her feet out of the stirrups and letting them dangle felt good. She leaned far back in the saddle and stretched her arms up over her head feeling the soreness in her neck and shoulders loosen.

"The outside of a horse is good for the inside of a man," she said, quoting Ben Franklin. Valo stood still and snorted as if to say, "Come on, I'm not tired, that was fun." Feeling the slightest bit bad about having bitten her husband's head off and wasting his terrible coffee, she decided she must apologize when she got back. But she wasn't in a hurry to eat crow, so she once more gathered her reins, lifted her knees until her toes found their stirrups and soon they were again flying over the ground, the wind roaring in her ears, blocking out all the sorrow, the anger, the despair.

She lived to ride and hoped that there would never be a day that she was too old to get into the saddle. Paul once suggested that if that were ever the case, he would buy her a carriage and she could learn to drive her horses. The look she responded with cemented in his mind that he should never broach that subject ever again, leaving him to wonder if he would ever understand women.

When they reached the edge of the field, she decided they ought to take the trail out to Mr. Boudreau's house and thank him for taking care of her animals. The head of the trail was crisscrossed with two fallen branches, and as they approached, Valo's ears flicked backward once more, listening, waiting for his cue. Piper leaned forward and loosened the reins a bit and felt him once more shift into overdrive. He cleared the jump with several feet to spare, all of his finely-toned muscles launching them into the air. She smiled, thinking how she'd been told time and again, "Friesians don't jump." She said out loud to no one, "This one does," and patted his thick, arched neck as they cantered up the hill and deeper into the woods. When they slowed, she gave him his head, letting the reins fall gently onto his mane. He knew the way. She listened to the sounds of the woods: twigs snapping under hooves, squirrels scurrying from branch to branch, birdsong, the groaning of leather. She let her feet dangle below the stirrups again and wished she had left her saddle at home.

Suddenly, Valo lifted his head high, planted his front

hooves firmly on the ground, and pulled up short, his muscles tensing. She looked around nervously, as he wasn't one to spook easily.

"Hoooo," she said in a low voice, quietly reaching for her reins just in case he decided to spin and bolt. She scratched his withers knowing this calmed him.

"Easy buddy, there's nothing there, walk on." For the first time since she owned him, he refused her commands. She clucked her tongue and gave him a reassuring squeeze with her legs to move him forward. His breathing quickened as he lowered his head, nostrils flaring. He let out a squeal and lashed out with one foreleg. He took one small step backward, spun, and reared. His 1600 pounds of muscle came down hard and jolted Piper, but she sat firmly and calmly, now glad to have her saddle beneath her and now wishing that she had her helmet, too. She instinctively found her stirrups again and pulled him around in a circle to avoid plunging back down the steep hill they'd just come up.

"Hoooo, easy Valo; there's nothing there," she said, but, at the same time, she wasn't so sure. She decided it best to dismount and lead him if he was that frightened. She swung her right leg over the front of her saddle and slid down all 17.2 hands to the ground. He immediately craned his neck as if to see why on earth she had done that and to say, "Aren't we getting out of here?"

This time she lifted the reins over his head and tried to lead him forward. He shifted his weight onto his hindquarters and pulled his head straight up, the whites of his eyes clearly begging her not to force him, as if she really could. She caught the scent of burning wood mingled with something sickening; she had a glimpse of dirt falling onto a small white blanket; sadness and a chill ran through her. She shivered in the warm air and drew a deep breath, trying to steady herself and her horse, who she knew, could easily drag her wherever he felt the need, a horse's self-preservation was no match for even the best training.

As quickly as the scent-ache came, it was gone, and Piper

noticed Valo visibly relax, chew on his bit as horses do when they are comfortable, with his ears pointing in no particular direction, his head low by her side. She asked him, "Are you done with this nonsense?" not really believing it to be any such thing.

It occurred to her then that scent-aches had never happened to her around her horses. She wondered if Valo had picked up on it, too, or just felt a change in her and reacted to it. She shrugged the thought off and remounted, thinking that at least one of her legs was getting a good workout. Knowing that horses have memories better than even the most deeply scorned woman, she felt the need to force him to walk past the spot at which he had first faltered, so that the next time they reached this spot he wouldn't spook just because it was what he had done on this ride. He lowered his head as they approached and walked right on past the soil and leaves he had just moments before kicked up. She rode on down the trail toward Mr. Boudreau's house but decided she wouldn't stop today. She had forgotten his gift at the house in her haste to escape the quarrel that had ignited in the breakfast nook. She turned Valo out to the road and took the long way home, trotting most of way, loving the sound of horseshoes on pavement, slowing only a few times to let onlookers get an eyeful.

16

ER BELLY WAS SO BIG and she so uncomfortable, that getting out of bed was just too difficult. Vander brought her the tea she had brewed earlier that day and some day-old bread but she refused to eat.

"My Love, you need to eat, for the baby."

She gave him a look that made him close his mouth, put the bread and tea aside, and let her be. He went out to feed the animals for the evening, noticing that the light hadn't faded even at this late hour. Spring was fast approaching, and soon the planting season would be here. And so would their baby, finally.

Piper stuffed Vander's pillow on top of hers which was propping her up in the bed. She rubbed her belly and wondered if she was going to be able to get this baby out of her, as it seemed utterly impossible. The baby moved inside her, and she marveled at what must have been its head pressing so hard against her insides that her entire belly shifted in one direction. She drew in a sharp breath; then, pressing back, she pleaded with her baby to take a nap, for she was tired and wanted rest. She sipped the tea but left the bread untouched, her appetite having disappeared earlier in the week when the pains started.

She was scared and wanted her mother-in-law to be with her, but she wasn't feeling well and didn't want to bring the sickness to her son's home. She said that as soon as she was feeling well, she would pack some clothing and come to stay until the baby arrived. Piper was terrified that the baby would come before then, but on this day, she didn't much care who was or wasn't there; she wanted this baby in her arms, not her belly. Her back ached, she couldn't sleep, and she knew she was being unkind to Vander with her remarks and her foul mood. Her mother-in-law had told her months before that all of this was to be expected and that she shouldn't feel badly for telling the man who put her in this state exactly how it felt to bear his child. Piper smiled when she remembered this conversation. It was a milestone in her life as it marked the first time she shared a bond with another woman simply because she was a woman.

Piper closed her eyes and thought about her own mother and how she wished she could be with her now; she needed her so. Imagining how her mother felt at this stage of pregnancy made her feel courageous and fully capable of doing what God designed her body to do. When she was young and her mother was still well, she had told Piper of her grandmother and her grandmother before her and how life goes on and changes, and how girls grow into women, have babies of their own, and then one day they go back to Heaven to watch over all of their grandchildren and great-grandchildren. This made little sense to a six-year-old who couldn't imagine her mother ever leaving her to go up into the sky and leave her with only a father and brother, not knowing that in just two years it would be her reality. But now, as she prepared to give birth herself, she could see with great clarity that she belonged to all the women who came before her, and that she was simply doing what they had done—bring their children into the world.

Imagining them watching over her gave her strength and vigor. She rolled her swollen body off the bed, and brought her empty tea cup and bread out to the hearth where Vander had left her a handful of purple and yellow crocuses in a glass of water. She smiled when she heard him approach the dooryard: the hens, like guard dogs, squawked and scrambled whenever someone was near. The look of surprise on his face to see his wife up and about was enough to put her in a better, lighter mood.

"Thank you for the flowers," she said and smiled.

He nodded and looked at her protruding belly with nervous wonder.

As she stepped toward him, she felt a warm gush of water soak her legs, and she stopped, frightened by the suddenness of it. Vander's face went white, and he, too, froze in place. With much anxiety she looked down at the water on the floor and lifted her nightdress as if to see where it could possibly be coming from. She looked slowly back up at her pale husband.

"Go! Get your mother, now! Now Vander, ride as fast as you can, I need her!"

Vander stood for what seemed like years to Piper before he could comprehend what this all meant. "The baby?" he asked still clearly in shock.

"Yes! The baby is coming, hurry!"

Vander hurried out the door and into the darkening night toward the stable yard. He hitched his team up with confused fingers, seemingly having forgotten how to do what they'd done effortlessly for years.

When the horses thundered past the house, Piper shouted from the door yard, "Hurry, Vander, there's not much time."

He didn't hear or see her, being focused on the path ahead, and the long ride to the village. A few strides into the woods, he began to wonder if maybe he should go back and do whatever needed doing himself. But quickly he realized that he knew nothing about birthing babies. Since he was a child, he had helped the ewes and the sows and the mares plenty of times, but this was his wife and his firstborn child. He was certain his mother could take care of everything if only he could get her there in time.

His horses' stamina was never a concern to Vander, be it out in the fields, the forests, or at the shore. What concerned him now was the lack of light in the woods. He knew the short trail well, as did his animals; but there always seemed to be an obstacle that needed clearing. Branches fell, and rocks were washed free from hillsides. He prayed aloud that God would deliver him to his mother safely so that she could deliver his child.

When finally he arrived at his boyhood home, he was out of breath, having held it through most of the ride. The horses hadn't yet completely halted when he jumped off the cart and fell forward to the ground. Landing in a painful heap, he yelled to his parents. "Mère! Père! The baby! The baby is on its way! Mère! Piper needs you, Mère!"

His father opened the door with a look of concern and surprise as he caught his stumbling son by the shoulders. "Garcon, calm down, it'll be fine. I'll get your Mère."

"Hurry, Père, there's not much time!" He jumped back into the cart and pulled his horses around, wanting to offer them water but knowing that they still had the ride back and he couldn't give them water while they were lathered and hot. He steadied them, and when his parents approached, he reached down and hauled his mother up into the bed of the cart, her nose red from sneezing, but her smile relaying her excitement.

Next Vander reached for his father's arm and realized then that his father was not the young sinewy and agile man he grew up with. Philip's arms were thin and soft, and, when Vander pulled him into the cart, he heard his father groan with pain. "Père?" he asked.

"Oh, I'm, fine, son, just getting on in years is all."

Vander swallowed hard and realized what was about to happen. He was going to be a father, like his father, and his father before him. The night air stung his eyes as he called to his faithful team to get on, to take them home, their only light the blessed full moon guiding them into their future.

Shortly after Vander vanished from sight, Piper put some water on the hearth to boil as her mother-in-law had months before instructed her. Then she went to the bedchamber to try to calm herself. She looked at the bed linens and wondered if they would ever look the same after the birth. Just then the pains began, making her lean forward, holding her belly and crying out into the empty night.

"God help me. Mère, what do I do? I need you!" She lay on the bed as the pain passed, making her feel calmer.

"Oh, now, little one, hold on, please. Wait for your father and grandmother."

A few minutes later, the pain returned to sear her insides again and later that night she would try deciding which was worse, the pain or the fear of being alone.

The pains crashed and retreated in waves as she lay sweating on the bed in the mid-April night. She prayed aloud to every saint she knew and asked God's forgiveness for all the transgressions she could remember from childhood right up to giving her husband a nasty glance when he told her she must eat for the baby's sake.

"St. Christopher, help Vander come back safely and quickly. Mother Mary, I need you. Please take this pain from me! St. Monica! Help me!"

She wanted to make a deal with God if He would just listen to her pleas.

"Please God, let Vander and Mère be here soon. I'll do anything, anything you want. I'll give my children the best life I can; I will be generous in the market and give extra to those in need."

She took a sharp breath as the pains came and a guttural scream escaped her, so primal and fierce that it scared her.

"I'll learn to be patient, I promise. This time I mean to do it, to be patient and listen and watch before I act. I promi—"

The pain tore through her and she bit the side of her hand as she bore down and began to push.

"No!!!" she screamed, "Not now, not yet!" She writhed on the bed, twisting and kneading the bed linens in her agony.

As the pains subsided for shorter and shorter intervals, her breath came faster and she could feel her heart beating like the hooves of Vander's horses, louder and faster until finally she realized that's what she was hearing. "Vander, hurry!" she pushed her head back against the pillows and tried to escape from the pain. In through the door came Vander and his parents. She lightened at the familiar sound of Vander dragging one boot heel every other step. She wanted to scream that he ought to be running! He stopped outside the door to the bed-chamber. Vander's mother shoved the men aside and ran to her daughter-in-law, bent and brushed the sweaty hair from her flushed face.

"I'm here, Love. Everything will be fine, don't fret."

"Philip, bring me a knife from the hearth. Vander, the water—now!"

Piper raised herself up on her elbows. "A knife!"

"Oh no, sweet girl. It's for the life cord. It needs to be cut once the baby comes. Lay back."

Another pain came, and Vander nearly dropped the pot of boiling water as he jumped and craned his neck around to see where the blood-boiling scream came from.

"Piper?" his indigo eyes wide. Philip recognized the fear. He thought of the many boy soldiers he had been in battle with—some at his side and some at the other end of his weapon. He put his hand on his son's broad back, assuring him he knew just how he felt.

"It's the way it is, son. She's just doing her job, like the mares in the field and the cats in the loft, and it's not an easy one. You will cherish your wife for her strength and never forget that she endured this for you, for your lineage, your blood."

Vander looked into his father's eyes and for the first time in his life, saw tears there.

"The water, boys, the water, now!" reminded Vander's mother as she looked under the bed linens and assured Piper that it wouldn't be long now. The men stood looking at one another as if they wished she had named the other specifically, each so he would not have to enter the birthing room.

Vander's trance broken by the pitch of his wife's voice and the words that escaped her. "Vander! Now!"

He hurried into the bedchamber with blankets over his shoulder and carrying the pot of steaming water, which he placed on the floorboards at the foot of the bed. He saw blood and the crown of his child's head and everything turned black behind his eyes.

"Philip, come take your son before he falls, and I have three patients to take care of."

Vander righted himself and went back to the hearth, pale, looking like a scolded, exhausted child, but feeling relieved.

With one final push, Piper delivered a scream into the night air and her daughter into her mother-in-law's hands.

"A girl, Piper, a perfect little girl, look." She lifted the baby for Piper to see. She reached out for the newborn, but her mother-in-law said there was still work to be done. After washing the knife in the hot water she cut the cord, tying it off with a piece of boiled yarn. She handed the wailing babe to Philip who smiled down at his granddaughter and wrapped her in a warm blanket. He took her out to the hearth where Vander could be heard crying, holding his long-awaited gift in his arms. Once the afterbirth was delivered whole and Piper was out of danger, Vander brought to her their perfect angel, whom they named for her mother, Peyrinne.

Together the family welcomed their newest edition with much love and hope, and they wished to celebrate. Philip called for a drink to toast the happy occasion and went to the hearth to see what could be found. Vander followed, saying he had saved ingredients from the Christmas celebrations for just this occasion. Into a clean pot he tossed the dried peels of their Christmas oranges, together with almonds, cinnamon, cardamom, and cloves from the market, some water, and lots of red wine. He looked into all the small pottery bowls above the hearth, knocking over more than one, eliciting concerned inquiries from both his mother and wife. With shaking hands he found the proper bowl and smiled at the feel of the soft raisins he had held over from the summer's grapes. He turned the bowl upside down over the pot and when nothing came out, he began to turn it back over to see what the problem was. As he did the sticky mass of raisins tumbled out, most hitting the mark and splashing the potent liquid upwards, sending it spattering onto the stove. Some, however, fell unseen, behind the pot onto the hot surface.

He let the brew simmer as he had been instructed at Christmastime by Piper's father, who had shared this recipe his wife taught him years before. The men stepped out into the chilled air and at the same time exhaled their tension. They both laughed, feeling more relaxed now. They went to the smokehouse to take a hog leg down to cook for the tired and happy family.

When they reentered the warm house the smell of glöggi filled their noses. They each inhaled deeply. Vander frowned.

His wife called from her bed, "What is that horrible smell?" He looked around the stove to see if he could find what was amiss and saw the sticky mass of melted raisins bubbling next to and underneath the pot.

"A few raisins, Love, that's all. I didn't know raisins could smell like that!"

They all giggled at his boyishness as he rubbed his nose nervously.

Philip washed handfuls of potatoes and carrots and placed them in a pan with the hog leg and a few small onions, and set them to cook on the stove next to the winter drink. And into the night they celebrated the birth of Vander and Piper's first child, the child that would forever change the way they looked at the world.

17

"WELL, SWEETHEART, it's almost here." Piper looked at her husband with anticipation.

"I can't believe it. Can you?" he responded.

The vineyard was now in its third season, the five-year-old Vidal vines having been personally delivered by Mr. Porrazzo and his wife, six months after the young couple's visit to France. Piper and Paul used their true first crop as a "starter" with which to learn and experiment. They built a separate barn on the property to house the winery and all their winemaking equipment and office.

She marveled at the accomplishment and likened it to the progress a new foal experiences, but kept this to herself. At first the long legs are wobbly and the baby doesn't know what to do with them. The foal stumbles and shakes but is determined to get it right. Fifteen minutes later the foal is galloping around his or her mother in the field as she stands grazing. Both are just doing what nature tells them they must. And before you know it, the foal is weaned and onto the next stage of life.

"Are you ready for this? I mean really ready?" Piper asked. "I mean, it's been your dream for so long and now it's finally here." He raised an eyebrow.

"Almost here."

She ruffled his hair at the kitchen table.

"You've waited this long, a few weeks won't kill you."

He took her hand and looked at her with a serious expression on his face.

"Honey, I know it's been stressful these past couple of years and I just ... I just want to thank you for your patience and—"

She burst into surprised laughter. "Patience? Did you say you want to thank *me* for my *patience?*"

He rolled his eyes.

"Did I say that?"

She kissed his lips and smiled. "Yes. Yes you did, my dear."

He smiled then. "Well then, you can thank *me* for teaching *you* the lesson of patience."

"Whatever," she said as she got up to clear the dinner dishes away.

Patience was something completely lost on her. It just didn't seem to be in her genetic makeup. It wasn't that she didn't make efforts throughout the years, but she always slipped back to her old ways, taking shortcuts, being a bit impulsive. Paul loved her despite her chronic impatience, saying that it was what made her so "cute," a term she hated. In return, she was so grateful for him, not being able to comprehend how he could have so much patience.

"I've got enough for us both," he would sometimes explain, which left her feeling completely off the hook.

They suffered two more miscarriages over the years, one Paul knew about and one he did not. On a drag hunt one Sunday, Piper rode with the Nashoba Valley Hunt Club, having been invited by one of her long-time clients. She fell hard from Valo's back when an inexperienced rider pulled up her horse hard in front of them. Valo balked at the stone wall, sending Piper over without him. At first she didn't think much of it as she felt certain she hadn't broken anything. She rode the rest of the morning and returned home before the familiar cramping struck her like a bolt from the blue. She made the trip to her obstetrician, calling Paul on his phone and telling him only that she was going to the market to get them some fish for dinner and she might stop at Mr. Boudreau's for coffee. He was so busy pruning the vines in the field she was certain he would lose track of time while she was gone.

At her doctor's office it was confirmed that she had in fact been pregnant and that she had just lost the baby. This being the third time, she was almost used to the stinging disappointment, the pain, the guilt, the fear of being alone in her old age. But having reached her early forties, she decided that she most definitely would remain childless and knew that Paul had already accepted this fact. She decided then and there as she sat in the blue johnny inside the emergency room that she, too, needed to come to grips with that reality. She never spoke of it again with Paul.

The tasting of the first bottling at Black Horse Vineyard was scheduled for November 20th, a Friday night event that they had planned for months. Family and friends all pitched in and printed up formal invitations and placed ads in several New England publications. They worked out all the details through emails and the vineyard's website, and several reporters were invited to cover the story. White lights were strung over the gable end of the two-story barn, and, inside, they twined around the beams on the ceiling. A dozen round tables were covered with elegant linens custom made for the event, with the vineyard's Black Horse silhouette logo on each, and a hundred chairs were scattered throughout the barn. Paul "borrowed" Piper's stereo system from the barn, much to her chagrin. For the prior week and a half she'd had to resort to using her iPod out in the barn doing her chores, ignoring her vibrating cell phone, making a point to let Paul know that she couldn't hear her phone ringing like she could with her normal musical setup.

He was undaunted and spent every evening planning the flow of the event evening. First he would make an announcement to thank everyone who had traveled there to try the area's newest (and best) wine. Then he would thank Piper for her "patience" and graciousness throughout the years and for allowing him to follow his dreams. He would thank his parents and siblings and the Porrazzos for their unending support, and finally, Mr. Boudreaux for his encouragement. And then the wine would flow, hors d'oeuvres would be served, and he could finally relax after years of planning, growing, harvesting, cooking, fermenting, tasting, bottling, testing, designing. He would, at long last, have his "baby," his legacy. He had given up years ago on the idea that he and his wife would become parents. He knew there was always the chance they'd have a "miracle baby" but no longer waited for each cycle to come and bring with it the hope and ultimately the despair it had for years. He left it in God's hands, praying, "Please God, whatever is meant to be, let us do it well, whether it's being parents, vintners, insurance agents, or just your servants, just let us do it well."

He never prayed out loud, as he knew Piper would be upset with the knowledge that he was ready to accept whatever it was God gave to them.

The week leading up to the grand tasting was a tumultuous one. Seemingly, everything that could go wrong, did. The labels for the wine bottles, which they had so feverishly worked on, were not ready yet, the printer from Wellesley having called Piper's phone and left a message on her voicemail which she forgot to check. He had said something about the foil border they chose clogging up his equipment and not being able to have it fixed in time to print their 1,000 labels. The cocktail napkins with their logo had come in but were misprinted, and though they had a chuckle over "Black Whores Vineyard," they knew they absolutely could not be put to use. The matchbooks with the same misprint, however, would be kept for posterity.

The evening of the 19th was a very tense one. Piper explained that she would get the last of the supplies in the morning. Paul would meet with the caterer and the waitresses they had hired to help out that night. Paul asked why she hadn't gone to pick up the labels that day, that a thousand labels was a lot of work if they were going to be placed perfectly.

"Well, we don't need a thousand bottles labeled for tomorrow, Paul, only about two hundred fifty probably. You said so yourself."

He raised one eyebrow.

"I did?"

She raised both brows and responded,

"You said you'd be happy if you sold 250 bottles."

"That's not the point, Sweetheart. That's just not the point."

He stared at her with a stern look which suggested anger was not far behind. What he didn't know was that the new order of labels had not been sent to the same printer and it hadn't been placed until the 18th which was the day before the celebration, and his wife was paying a huge rush order fee because she had not retrieved her voicemail until that morning, thinking the voicemail was Paul wondering when she would be done in the barn, and what was for dinner, etc. The only printer willing to rush the job was in Albany, a two-plus hour drive one way. She didn't want to leave the overnight shipping to chance, and she knew Paul would have absolutely flipped out if he knew his labels were that far away on the eve of his big night. She planned on being up early and out the door by 7a.m., home by noon, and she would have all afternoon to "perfectly place each label" on the bottles for her husband. This was not her dream and she had to admit she was getting a little tired of all she had to do to get it to come to fruition. *You're being selfish and you know it*, she would think and shrug it off with, *So what? He's being selfish by not wanting to talk about adoption or being foster parents, by not talking about anything but his godforsaken grapes!* But she knew, too, that once the big night passed, life might get back to a somewhat normal pace. And besides, she could use the time to herself on the drive, staying out of Paul's way.

Paul couldn't sleep that night; he tossed, turned, tossed again until Piper woke up for the third time. She called up her most patient-sounding tone.

"Why don't you have some chamomile tea? It'll help you sleep."

She reached out, rubbing his back, her eyes not opening.

"No. I was almost asleep until you just said that."

She opened her eyes wide then and wanted to yell at him, but knew it wouldn't help even a little bit. She quietly got up, slid her pillow from her side of the bed and went downstairs to the living room. She closed the blinds and curtains and settled herself on the leather couch; she thought about writing, but knew she really needed to sleep and closed her eyes. The first scent-ache in nearly a year came to her: lavender, a glimpse of rocks piled one on another, freshly turned soil, a deeply sad feeling, panic. She spoke in the quiet room to no one.

"Not now, I don't have time to wonder what that's all about."

When she woke up the next morning and looked around, Piper realized where she was and bolted upright, throwing her blankets to the floor like an angry child, Viceroy jumping and barking in surprise.

"Oh my God! What time is it?" she whispered loudly. She jumped up, looked around and prayed that it was not yet 7 a.m. She tripped over the blanket but righted herself and rushed to the kitchen to see what time it was: 9:47.

"Oh my God," she said again. "I've got to get out of here." She saw a note on the microwave door, *Hi Babe. Sorry about last night. I'll be out at the barn.*

Paul thought she was only going to Wellesley for labels and decided to let her sleep. She raced upstairs, threw on a pair of jeans, a navy sweater and her favorite black leather clogs. She ran back downstairs, heart thumping, and grabbed her purse and keys and was out the door only six minutes after she awoke. She sped down the driveway and out toward the turnpike. By her calculations, she would be home before 3:30 and she would just have to deal with Paul's questions later. Her cell phone buzzed in her pocket when she passed Exit 2, but she ignored it, figuring it was Paul wanting to know if she had left for Wellesley yet. She stepped on the accelerator and hoped that Paul fed the animals that morning.

When she finally arrived at the printer, she tried to compose herself. She looked quickly in the visor mirror, took her hair out of its elastic and shook it out, tossed her keys into her purse and, realizing that she hadn't brushed her teeth, searched for a piece of gum. Her shaking hands spilled the contents of her purse onto the passenger seat.

"Screw it," she said and grabbed her purse by one strap and got out of the car in haste. As the door handle left her hand she caught a glimpse of the keys on the seat. "No! God, no! What the f—?" she said to no one. She tried the handle but knew she had locked it from habit as she had learned to do when her car was cleaned out of change, CDs and a new stereo the year she moved to Marblehead. "Arrgghhh!" was all she could come up with. Her phone buzzed in her pocket; but, again, she ignored it and rushed into the printer's. She hurriedly told the man at the counter her name and order number as she fumbled through her wallet for her AAA card.

"What's wrong?" asked the man at the counter.

"Oh, nothing, just locked my keys in the car. I was hurrying."

"Oh, wish I could help, but the new cars are harder to get into. The old ones were easy: you just needed a coat hanger. AAA's your best bet, young lady. Even the police won't help anymore—'fraid o' lawsuits, ya know." He winked at her, but she had looked away, toward the window.

"An hour?" She spoke slowly and deliberately into the phone, "Is there anyway someone could come sooner than that? *Any way* at all? Okay. Okay. Yup." She hung up and sighed even as the dispatcher was wishing her a nice day.

"There's a breakfast place across the way, great coffee, and they serve breakfast all day."

The man at the counter tried to be helpful, but she was extremely irritated and just nodded, handing him her American Express card.

"Sorry, Miss, we don't accept American Express. Master-Card, Visa, Dis—."

She slid her Discover card on the counter toward him and he could tell she was out of patience. He ran her card, and she signed the receipt in an illegible scrawl, thanked him and left, almost forgetting her package. The man at the counter, once again alone in his store, shook his head and said aloud, "Young kids, always in a hurry."

She took his advice and went across the street to the breakfast spot and ordered coffee and French toast, something she always loved as a kid. Deciding she should check her phone, she saw both messages were from Paul but decided only to listen to them once she got back into her car and onto the turnpike. She tried to eat slowly and relax, knowing that nothing she could do now would help the situation. *I can't believe I am sitting in a diner in New York when I am supposed to be at home in Massachusetts preparing for the biggest night of my husband's life. He's going to kill me.*

When the tow truck pulled up, she quickly paid her bill and ran out the door. The driver looked her up and down and tipped his ball cap backwards so he could scratch his forehead. Rocking back on his heels, hands in his pockets, he asked, "Afternoon, Ma'am, this your car?"

"Yes, I'm in a big hurry, how long will this take?" She knew full well it would only take the guy a couple of minutes at most, but she didn't want the small talk that she knew this guy was capable of.

"Oh, just a minute or two," he said as she tapped her foot, arms crossed. She looked nervously around, wondering how fast she could get back onto the highway. When the man finally had her door open, she jumped in and grabbed her keys.

"Just a second there, ma'am, I need you to sign—" She pretended not to hear him as she shut her door, turned the ignition and tore away from the sidewalk, leaving her AAA card and the confused-looking man behind.

The man from the printing office joined him on the sidewalk, and this time they both scratched their heads.

"Over the phone, she was nice as pie when she ordered her labels, needed them in a hurry, she said. Asked about a hundred questions about the self-stick ones and then ordered plain ones. I couldn't figure it."

The driver looked at him and laughed. "Women, I'll tell ya, can't make up their minds to save their lives. And patience?

Haven't met one with more than a thimbleful."

When she reached the turnpike, she took a deep breath. "Please God, don't let me get pulled over or hit any traffic." She knew that Fridays on the Pike could be horrible, but she felt she had left early enough and pressed the accelerator, feeling the power of the engine throttle her up to 90mph without so much as a hiccup. She gripped the wheel, and then put the radio on, thinking it might calm her and quickly decided it was only going to be a dangerous distraction. She looked around, hoping not to see any troopers waiting for crazy women like herself.

When she saw Exit 2 again, she took a breath and reached for her phone. She flipped it open and saw that Paul had called five times. She dialed her voicemail, pressed her password and held her breath. She skipped the first three messages, having no patience and figuring that she would get all the information she needed in the last message or two.

"Piper, where the hell are you? I called the printer and he said you didn't place a second order with him. Call me and let me know what's going on."

She pressed delete, took a breath and held it.

"I'm starting to get worried here. If you get this message, call me right away, I can't concentrate on anything. You're driving me nuts, Piper. It's 2:25. Bye."

She shut her phone and tossed it on the seat beside her. *Not as bad as I thought.*

"Now if only I can come up with a somewhat solid excuse, he might not want to divorce me after today." She rolled her eyes and exhaled deeply, feeling a little panicked by the darkening sky. *Where does the sunlight go after October?* She pulled into the driveway at 20 mph and slammed the car into park before it had stopped moving, hoping Paul wasn't within earshot. When the car stopped rocking, she grabbed the bag of labels, left her purse and ran into the house. She was relieved that none of the family had shown up yet. Glancing at the clock, she realized that she hadn't even taken a shower yet, cleaned the stalls or the house for that matter, but she felt a surge of adrenaline rush through her from her heart to her fingertips. She had heartburn and a headache but ignored them both and headed for the stairs. Paul stepped out from the laundry room and just stood there with his hands in his pockets.

"Hi," he said, knowing she hadn't yet noticed him.

She screamed and dropped the labels, her hands immediately flying to her throat in a panic.

"Shit! Paul, what the...? You scared the hell out of me."

He raised his brow, never having liked it when she used profanity. He felt it was beneath his elegant and educated wife. "Where on earth have you been? *Do you* even *have* the labels?" He glared at her as if he just caught her with another man.

"Yeah. Right there," she said and pointed to the bag on the floor. Neither of them being able to swallow their anger or frustration, they both stood their ground.

"Whatever," she said under her breath, knowing full well her husband could hear her. She knew, but didn't much care, that this made her sound like a teenager and how that answer bothered Paul to no end. She stepped over the bag in an exaggerated snub and ran up the stairs, peeling her sweater over her head and tossing it into the bedroom as she stopped to check the thermostat, feeling the chill in the house. Paul walked toward the stairs and intended to demand an answer and possibly an apology from her, but when he looked up to his semi-clothed wife, saw her breathtaking figure as she stood briefly in the hall, he was overcome with a sensation of pure love. He felt tears forming behind his eyes as, for the first and last time in his life, he experienced what his wife had tried to explain to him for so long. A scent-ache: burnt raisins and lavender sat not in his nose, but behind it. He saw a glimpse of roses and a black veil, similar to Piper's dressage turnout. He was instantly washed in a warm light that gave him an inner peace he had never before experienced.

18

THE HOT WATER FELT GOOD, and Piper wished she could stay in the shower longer and let the stress of the day wash down the drain. But she shook the thought from her tired mind and jumped out, wrapping a towel around her tall frame, grabbing another for her hair, and froze as she caught the image of Paul out of the corner of her eye. Breath held, heart in her throat, she waited to see why he was just standing in the doorway, arms crossed.

"Piper," he said in an eerily calm voice. She didn't turn or respond, knowing that even though he was not aware of the fiasco she had just been through, he should still be appreciative that she got the labels even if there was only a couple of hours before guests would begin to arrive. She stood, bent at the waist, and towel-dried her hair. When she was finished, she flung her hair back as she stood straight, something Paul normally found irresistibly sexy.

"Piper, do you realize these labels are not self-stick?"

She felt a jolt in the pit of her stomach and was worried her French toast might come up, but instinctively held herself still, not wanting to show surprise. She recalled from somewhere deep in her subconscious that wolves were known to attack one of their own if one shows weakness—a matter or rank or perhaps survival. At a loss for words, she glared at him through the mirror.

Paul glared back. "No answer? That's just beautiful, sweetheart, just *frigging* beautiful," he shouted, getting her back for her uncharacteristic profanity toward him moments before.

"Paul, I'll take care of it. Don't wo—"

He interrupted her even as he stormed out into the master bedroom.

"Take care of it? Take care of it! You've taken care of enough. I'll deal with it. Just like everything else around here!"

He grabbed his keys from the bureau and ran down the stairs. She heard him slam the front door and then Viceroy barking after him from the mudroom, wondering why he hadn't gotten so much as a pat on his loyal little head.

She instantly felt horrible for treating her best friend with contempt when it was she who had screwed up so badly. She wanted to know where he was going and what his plan was to fix the problem was. *Funny,* she thought, *how when he's in my face like that I wish he would just disappear, but when I hear the door shut and the car engine rev, I want nothing more than to make things better, to know that he's okay. I want to know that he's coming back to me.*

She picked up the phone by the bed and dialed his cell. It rang and rang and finally went to voicemail. "Hello, you've reached Paul, leave a message and I'll get back to you as soon as I can. And if this is my beautiful wife, I love you."

That always made her smile.

"Uhh, Paul, honey, I'm so sorry, I know I screwed up. I … I had to go to New York for the labels. I didn't tell you because, (sigh) because I missed the call from the original printer and … it's a long story. I'm sorry. Just call me and let me know you're okay and what you need me to do before everyone gets here. Paul, I … I love you and I'm sorry."

She hung up, hardly feeling relieved, but reaching in that direction anyway. As she turned, she saw that the emerald gown she was planning on wearing for the celebration was carefully hung on her closet door and she began to feel a little excited. She knew they'd get through this and when it was all over, they could laugh about the slipups, the screw-ups and about how funny the story would sound when they told it at Christmas time, and in the future whenever a party needed a good laugh.

Deciding it was too early to get dressed, she pulled on a pair of yoga pants and a sweatshirt. Figuring she had enough time to dry her hair, she went back into the bathroom where, through the steam from her shower, she thought for a split second she saw Paul there. She shook her head, sucked in her breath, and the image was gone. She shook it off, telling herself to calm down, put on some makeup, and blow her hair dry, something she seldom did. When she finished, and hung her wet towels to dry she trotted downstairs and thought to feed the horses early so not to leave it until the last minute, as some people might begin to show up early, particularly Paul's parents. She looked out the window at the gray sky. November was never as beautiful in New England as in September and October. No sign of Paul's car. *Where did he go? Maybe to get some glue for the labels?* Just then Viceroy yelped, and she spun around, frightened in the stillness of the house. He yelped again, and she realized he was still in the mudroom, probably waiting for Paul to come back for him. She admitted to herself that she knew how he felt. "Vice, come on pup. Viceroy. It's okay little guy. He'll be back s—"

A howl this time. It froze Piper in midsentence. She had never heard him howl before. A sudden chill ran down her spine, and she rushed to the mudroom. Viceroy was standing in a puddle of urine. Piper didn't know which surprised her more, the howling or the accident. Certainly neither was the norm for her dog. She jogged to the kitchen for paper towels and some Simple Green, and, when she came back, she heard the sound of tires crunching on the stone-dust drive. "Paul," she breathed, "thank God." She peered through the side light on the doorway and saw a dark car slowly come to a halt on the driveway. She dropped the bottle of cleaner right on top of the already upset dog, making him growl and snap at her dangling hand (another first in a day of beginnings and endings of which she was not yet aware).

She watched the trooper get out of his car, reach back in for his hat and place it squarely on his head. He reached over to the radio sitting on his shoulder, turned his head and spoke into it. A few seconds later he spoke again. He quickly scanned the yard, the garage area and then took a step forward. Piper clawed at her chest. She couldn't breathe, and she could feel her heart pulling and thrusting in the cavity of her chest, blocking all thought and sound. She ran back to the kitchen and tore the phone receiver off the wall. As she dialed Paul's number again, and before she finished, the doorbell rang.

"No!" she screamed and lost her concentration. She hit the call button on the phone, clicked it a second time, and tried to dial again but kept hitting the wrong numbers, her fingers just wouldn't obey. The bell again, this time louder in her ears, calling to her, screaming at her, demanding she pay attention. Viceroy whined and growled and stood his ground at the door, tail tucked between his legs, no hint of his usual friendly curiosity.

Piper walked to the door, not wanting to open it but knowing she must.

"Viceroy! Sit!" She knew he wouldn't but wanted only to try her voice to see if it would even work. Her hand felt so cold and stiff as she turned the doorknob that she wasn't at all sure she would get the door open. Using her whole hand and wrist to manipulate the suddenly slippery bronze, she flung the door open, resulting in a gasp from her and the man on the other side. Looking up as if directly into the sun, with eyes squinting, and anticipating pain, she found herself face to face with a Massachusetts State Trooper. He looked into her eyes for a moment, and then removed his hat. She had seen something similar in a movie before, but she couldn't imagine why this man was removing his hat at her door. Wasn't he just going to ask if that Volvo in the driveway was hers, that he had seen her speeding on the Pike that morning and he had a nice fat speeding ticket for her? *That's all it is,* she tried to convince herself.

"Is this 9 Farmdale Road?"

She nodded like a little child who realizes she is in trouble and must own up.

"What is your husband's name, Ma'am?"

She glanced at his badge as she let "Paul" slip from her lips.

"Ma'am, I deeply regret to inform you that your husband was killed in an automobile accident, a half hour ago."

Numb, she stood stone still and looked at his watery blue eyes.

I know you.

She felt rather than heard this. She tilted her head to the side.

"No, he didn't. He just went to the store, to get some glue for the labels because you see, I screwed up and ordered the wrong ones and ... and ... you see we have a lot of people coming in a little while, and—"

The trooper reached out his hand and touched her arm.

"Ma'am, may I come inside, please?"

She took a step back, right onto Viceroy's paw, and he yelped again. This time he ran to his bed next to Paul's chair in the great room. She jumped, and the trooper's hand tightened on her arm to steady her. Her legs were like dry sand, sifting and shifting and running in all directions. For a brief moment she thought she might pass out—sweaty and hot, but cold at the same time. Darkness, light, fading, brightening, too much too fast. He gently turned her around and steered her into the great room. She steadied herself, wanting to run past him and get into her car to go find Paul, her wonderful, loving husband whom she had been so nasty to just an hour before. She composed herself and sat quietly on the sofa next to this stranger.

"Ma'am is there anyone you'd like me to call? Family, a neighbor, a friend?"

Piper turned toward him and asked if he'd like something to drink, some coffee perhaps.

"I never touch the stuff," he said knowing full well it was not a time for jokes but it was true. He'd much rather have tea with lavender but simply shook his head, smiling, knowing that she was in shock and that he needed to just sit with her until it sunk in. He remembered how, in the academy, his instructors told him he would never get used to this, the worst of all duties.

"I could get you some coffee, though, or water," he offered.

She shook her head.

"My husband will be home shortly. He just ran out to get some glue or something for the labels. Would you like to see them? I just picked them up today. They're for our first bottling."

He just stared at her and shook his head.

They both turned when the front door opened, and saw Paul's parents rushing in, concern on their faces. "Piper, honey, where's Paul? Why are the police here?"

She tried to explain again, about the labels, the glue, her screw-up this morning, the hectic week, her incurable impatience. The trooper introduced himself to Paul's parents. "I'm Sergeant Van der Beck, Massachusetts State Police, and I am here to aid Mrs. ..." *Vander! Come for me, help me, I'm here, I need you my love, my heart!*

Her mind swirled with the smell of fresh soil as it filled her nose. She choked on the memory of a funeral long ago and wondered why it felt so hot in the house all of a sudden. Paul's mother was screaming miles away somewhere, and his father was begging her to stop, that it was going to be all right, they would be all right. She turned toward the kitchen and saw the note on the microwave from this morning. Reality. *Thank God for that.* She went to the note, Paul's flawless handwriting comforting her. *He can't be dead, he had just written her this note hours ago, and people who were about to die did not write on sticky notes and then head outside to the barn where the biggest night of his life was going to happen.* She felt comforted by the little yellow square and turned back toward the three people huddled in her great room. She refused to see the cars coming down the road toward the house. Thoughts swirled and careened in her mind.

People can't be showing up yet, they still had a thousand labels they needed to bottled and the notepads with the reporters hadn't arrived and why was it so cold? The door is coming through the people or the people and their sense are making no words! Everything went blessedly dark just before Piper fell soundlessly to the tile floor.

19

WATCHING HER CHILDREN GROW was a gift Piper never took for granted. Becoming motherless at eight years of age and always wanting her mother near made her appreciate becoming a mother herself. *Would you be proud, Maman?* Even as her eyes brimmed with tears she often felt the whisper of a breeze or a tingling in her shoulder blades that made her feel as though her mother truly were with her. And always with it was the scent of her mother. If someone asked her to describe it, she wouldn't have been able to find the words. How does one describe something so unique and so close to one's heart?

When Peyrinne was in her third summer, Piper and Vander welcomed into their lives not one, but two boys. Philip and Luuk were as alike as twins could be, and as they grew, were never more than an arm's length from one another. Vander delighted in wrestling with them before their evening meal and Piper, at the hearth, often explained to her daughter that boys had a different way of showing love for each other, a very loud way indeed. Peyrinne with her raven black hair and eyes to match, would inevitably snuggle closer with her mother, enjoying the time alone with her.

On an exceptionally warm summer's evening, Vander explained to Piper that there was a man in Paris who had approached him about making him a partner in his new per-fumery.

"Imagine that one day, Piper, we won't have to toil so

hard; that we can just purchase the lavender from a silly young buck who loves plowing the heavy soil and baking himself in the summer heat. And when it's delivered to us, we can pay him a fair wage and still make tenfold that amount by selling the perfume ourselves."

Piper turned to her husband with a look that suggested he may have lost his mind from the heat of the day. "But Vander, the perfumery is paying *you* a good wage, a great wage for the lavender. We don't need more than we have. Do we?"

Vander looked down at his children, playing by the garden fence just beyond the window of the bed chamber. His wife looked to see what had caught his attention. The boys were running after a rabbit, and Peyrinne was, at the top of her voice, encouraging the rabbit to run faster, faster, that her brothers intended to skin him and eat him for dinner. The couple stood side by side at the window and laughed, as the rabbit seemed to take the directive well and made it to the tree line before the boys could catch him.

"I just want the children to have something when I am gone, something they wouldn't have if I ... if I ...." Vander's voice trailed off.

Piper responded, "If you what? If you just worked hard every day like you do, like your father and his father? Do you think something is wrong with that, Love?"

Vander looked beyond her to the empty wall of the bed-chamber. He shook his head slowly and said, "No, I suppose not."

She felt badly that she didn't share his dream, his desire to be more than common folk. She liked the way their life had come together in a way that she had never dreamed. The house, the farm, her babies; she wanted for nothing more but realized that sometimes men with ambition needed more. And she loved her husband so; she just didn't like the idea of moving far from where they had built their lives. The thought of the city frightened her, and she couldn't imagine not having acre after acre of open pasture and their sea of lavender to escape into.

Vander excused himself. "I think I'll take a ride if you don't mind, down to the brook."

She nodded her head and smiled, knowing this was his way of taking a break, of working things through in his mind. She loved him so. "I will bring Pieferet around and then I'll feed the hens." She left the room before he could protest. He was never one to have his wife wait on him. He pulled his weight around the house as well as the rest of the farm.

When she reached the stable, the scent of hay and horse tugged at her and she wished she could ride with her Vander; it had been so long. *With the children always underfoot it's a wonder I get through the day sometimes,* she thought and laughed softly because she wouldn't trade her life for the world. She reached up and took Pieferet by the rope halter. He was beginning to show his age and this made her more than a little sad. She stroked his long thick neck and fingered the silver rivers running through his mane. "Come on my friend, you are going for a run to the brook." He seemed forlorn ever since Henk had died the summer before. Vander did not want to replace him, as there was no replacement for such a fine animal, a loyal friend. But needing a team to pull the plow he traded Pieferet's stud service for a Percheron gelding at the horse fair in the city. Piper slipped the reins over his neck and gently slid the bit into his mouth, talking to him as she always had. "I will have your evening meal ready, Monsieur, when you return."

Taking him loosely by the reins, she led him into the stable yard and waited for her husband, who was now brushing dirt from one of the twin's scraped knees. She reached down and scratched the head of their oldest doe who had just delivered two kids the week before. "Time marches on, doesn't it love?" The goat answered with a switch of her tail and a friendly butting of her head against Piper's thigh.

As Vander approached, Piper noticed his slumped shoulders, the unmistakable look of disappointment on his face and how he dragged his boot heel every other step. He saw her looking and put on the best smile he could find and thanked her for bringing the horse around for him. She stood at the horse's shoulder, the spot she knew he needed to be in order to mount up. He looked at her, confused for a moment, and then realized she had something to say to him.

"What is it Piper?" he asked her.

"Vander, I ... I don't. I don't want you to regret your days when the end comes. I want you to be happy and to follow the path that you find. The one you choose."

He looked at her and noticed the slightest hint of a wrinkle around the eyes he loved so much. He kissed her forehead and stroked her cheek with his weathered hand.

"I won't be long. We're just going to the brook."

Piper stepped away, confused. She thought he would be excited that she was willing to hear more about his plan; but she knew, too, that he needed time to think about what to do next. She watched as he and Pieferet cantered off into the pasture, Vander's face buried in the billowing mane of his horse. She stood watching as the pair became smaller and smaller and finally disappeared from her sight. Leaning against the fence, she recalled the first time she saw him riding down the lane near her home when they were children. He was so small on the giant black horse and yet looked as if he had been there his entire life—wings on Pegasus. His brown trousers were torn and ragged and eventually he tore the pant legs off below the knee, freeing his quickly growing legs. He always rode barefoot, much to his mother's disapproval. Philip would try to comfort his wife by explaining that if one of the horses stepped on his foot, a boot was not going to do him much good anyway. Piper smiled when she remembered these conversations as she and Vander played in the stable yard of his boyhood home. These fond memories seemed a lifetime ago. Peyrinne was now the age Piper had been when she met her husband.

She repeated, this time to no one, "Time surely does march on." She turned toward the house and decided the evening meal could wait a little longer, as she wanted to play with her children before the light faded. She snuck around the back of the house and sprang up from the tall grass behind the garden and sent her two sons bolting and screaming from her, not bothering to look back at the voice that was now giggling at them. She raised her voice so they could hear her, "Boys, it's me, it's Maman. Come play."

They turned and ran at her, saying that they thought she was a wolf coming to eat them.

"I would never let a wolf eat my boys. Never!"

When the twins tackled her, knocking her to the ground, she hugged them close to her, feeling their ribs poking into her sides.

"Ouch!" she said comically. "Doesn't your Maman feed you two?"

"Yes, yes, yes, she feeds us! Don't you know her, she looks just like you."

They rolled around in the grass, tossing leaves and grasshoppers at each other, Piper playing with them the way she had learned to do with Marek long ago. Peyrinne joined them, and the four of them tickled one another until they were all laughing so hard, no one heard Marek's horse as he rode up to the house.

It was Luuk who saw him first.

"Maman! It's Uncle Marek."

He scuttled behind his mother, always wary of the uncle he didn't know well.

"Marek!" Piper called and waved to him. A pang of sadness jumped in her chest as she looked at her disheveled brother. She had hoped he would marry and find happiness, but those things were hard to find when you were always at the bottom of an ale barrel or in a fist fight. As he approached, the children gathered themselves and she instructed the boys to wash up and help her get the evening meal ready. Piper so wished her children could have known that Marek would never hurt them; that he had been small once, just like them, but was so very sad. She hugged her brother tightly and chastised him for not coming around more often. He rubbed his eyes, sniffled, and shoved his hands nervously into his trouser pockets.

"Where is your husband tonight?" Marek asked in a way that was urgent, almost demanding.

"Uhh, he went for a ride, to cool off at the brook. He'll be back soon. We will be eating then. You'll stay won't you?"

He shook his head and looked over his shoulder at the field to see if he could spy Vander returning home.

"Is something wrong, Marek? Your eyes ...."

"No, I just need to ask Vander something. I'll wait for him."

He turned and walked past the house, not seeing the twins peering from behind the curtains at him. He walked out to the stable yard, kicking the goat kids away with his boot as they tried to nuzzle him. *Sadness was always his closest friend.* She turned toward the garden. *And anger a close second. Please, Maman, watch over him.*

She didn't want to go into the house and leave her brother out here alone, but it seemed that was what he wanted. She looked over at the horse he had ridden out to the farm, a flea-bitten gray she had never seen before. He was favoring a hind leg, not putting weight on it. She went to the garden and brought up three large purple carrots, shook the soil from them, and snapped the tops off. Tossing the tops over the fence for the rabbit who had narrowly escaped her boys earlier seemed the kind thing to do. At the well, she washed the roots clean and filled a bucket with fresh cool water. She offered both to the poor old horse who had clearly, or so she hoped, seen better days. His ribs were visible through his dull coat, his eyes sad and watery, flies collecting in their corners. She brushed them away and rubbed the old fellow's neck. He closed his eyes and enjoyed the kindness he rarely received. He took the carrots with his old and worn teeth, and she could see eating was not the pleasure it was for younger, well-cared-for horses.

"It's all right, Love. I'll make you some mash for dinner. Would you like that?" He leaned in as she scratched behind his ears, with the carrots, partially chewed, dropping to the ground. It had been years since someone had treated him as anything more than transportation.

In the house, the chicken and vegetables were cooking,

Peyrinne being a natural at the hearth. Her mother inhaled deeply and nodded her exaggerated approval. "Boys, would you help me get some bran mash for the poor horse your uncle rode here?" They looked up at their mother with concern clearly swimming behind their blue eyes. Their hands fiddled with each other behind their backs, as they squirmed uncomfortably. Piper's dismay was something she didn't hide well, but she didn't want to upset her children any more than they clearly were.

"You don't have to bring it outside, just fetch it for me from the pantry." Relieved, they galloped past the hearth to the small pantry where the dry goods were stored. When they returned to their mother, they each had almost as much of the bran flakes in their hair as they did in the half-filled wooden bucket. Caught by surprise, she laughed heartily at the adorable, yet serious faces staring up at her. She shook their hair out over the bucket, catching the loose flakes as they fell. The boys giggled, loving their mother's sense of humor. She added some warm water from the stove top to make the mash. To it she added more than the customary pinch of sugar, a bit of salt and two handsful of raisins. After mixing it, she asked the boys if they'd like to help. They looked into each other's eyes and with that mysterious way that twins have of communicating, made up their minds to stay put.

When Piper took the mash to the malnourished horse, she could hear loud voices coming from the barn. She froze when she heard Vander shouting. There were very few times she could count when she had heard her husband raise his voice in anger. She slipped the horse's bridle over his ears and let the bit slide out of his mouth so he could eat his dinner.

"No, Marek. I have said it before and this is the last time. No!"

Marek, never being able to hide his feelings of despair, of abandonment, shouted back, "What kind of brother are you, treating me like a stranger?"

Piper shook her head, wishing she could help her brother, but knowing it was never a good idea to interfere with dealings between men. She didn't see Marek often, and when she did, it seemed her memory was kinder to him than he deserved. Each visit was more intense and more often than not ended with Marek departing abruptly, leaving her feeling guilty, somehow responsible for his loneliness.

When the old gray gelding finished his bran mash, Piper slid the bridle back on and wished him a good evening, clearing his eyes of flies once more. She brought the buckets back to the well and set them down, and as she did, Marek stormed through the stable yard gate and left it wide open. The goats and sheep thundered through in a frenzy of bleating and dust and headed for the open pasture. Vander cursed him, but when he saw his wife, tried his best to compose himself.

Piper called to Marek then, her heart sinking to see two of the men she loved most, arguing.

"Come back, Marek. Have a meal with us!"

Her voice cracked as tears of sympathy and despair slid down her cheeks. She went to the barn and filled a bucket with corn and oats and headed to the field with her husband to try to round up the loose animals before darkness fell and brought the wolves from deep in the woods.

20

THE DAYS FOLLOWING Paul's death blended one into another until Piper couldn't tell night from day. She wanted only to be alone on her farm, but family and friends refused to let her stay by herself for more than a day. After a week of nonstop unsolicited concern and pity, she took to lying to each one who called, saying that someone else was staying the night, thereby getting her wish to suffer alone. Curled in her bed under her covers was where she wanted to be unless she was feeding the animals, the only thing she didn't mind doing. But as soon as her chores were done, she went straight back to her bed which still smelled like Paul, his skin, his soap, his aftershave. The tears, sobs, and anger devoured her energy, and despite the endless pans of lasagna, meatballs, salads, and brownies that were brought to her door, she was losing weight. Sleeping in Paul's shirts and boxers comforted her only in that it reminded her of how he loved to see her in his big clothes.

Thanksgiving and Christmas came and went without notice, though New Year's Eve brought a handful of phone calls from well-meaning friends and colleagues; but Piper turned them all down. Curled up in bed with a box of her favorite fried rice she had had delivered, she ignored the next several phone calls that came. *Celebrate? How can I celebrate? And how does the world just continue to do all of these ridiculous, meaningless things? How could I have enjoyed anything at all in life knowing someone was suffering like this? I guess I never knew what this was like?*

She took a mouthful of the now cold, dry rice and decided

it didn't taste very good and that she wasn't very hungry. She lay back on Paul's pillow and tried to feel him around her. She spoke out loud as if someone were there with her.

"Where are you? People say they can feel their loved ones once they are gone. If that's true, where are you, Paul? Show me a sign. Something? Anything."

She looked at the blank television screen and willed it to turn on. Then she looked at the light in the ceiling fan above the bed. "Just a flicker? Please?" With a heavy sigh, she closed her eyes and tried to picture Paul there with her, feel him there. She took a couple of deep breaths and let the stillness of the house surround her, and she focused on every sensation in her body.

Just as she was about to open her eyes, she felt a rising panic in her stomach and thought she might vomit. But bolting upright she realized the feeling was now more in her chest and she grasped her bathrobe. Now further up in her throat she felt as if she could not take another breath. She tried inhaling and began choking, heart racing and terror traipsing through her mind on a galloping horse. *I'm dying. I'm going to die! I'm alone and I'm going to die that way!*

Her mind spun and spun all the while her pulse kept up its frantic dance. She realized she had gotten out of bed and was heading for the stairs. *Why?*

Piper then realized that if she was asking herself rational questions, then she was probably okay. Finally, taking a full breath and feeling the sweat that had announced her first panic attack, she relaxed.

She reached with a shaking hand into the pocket of her robe and pulled out her phone. As she listened to the ringtone on the phone she thanked God for cell phones and pre-programmed numbers.

"Sharon! Hi, umm. I think I just had a heart attack. Or a panic attack. Or something ... not sure what."

Just then, as she turned toward the stairs that would lead to the comfort of her kitchen, she missed the flicker of her nightstand lamp and the scent of Paul's cologne as it circled his pillow.

"No. I don't need an ambulance. I'm okay. No, really. Please, Sharon, don't. I just—"

And then without warning another wave of adrenaline swept up from her stomach to her chest. She dropped her phone and ran to the bathroom. Over the sink, she bent low and splashed cool water on her face as she gasped for air. *My God, what's happening?*

21

"CATHERINE, Honey. It's Mom and Dad. We're here, Cathy. It's going to be okay."

Piper fought to open her eyes but the sedative was still working on her. Who was calling her Catherine, she wondered. No matter. She liked the feeling of warmth and comfort she found only in this in-between state. There was no pain here, only serenity.

Remember, Love, I am here, in the midst. Years mean nothing here, and here there is no sorrow. I have waited so long for you—lifetimes. I would wait an eternity to hold you in my arms again, in the fields of your favorite lavender. To see your hands reaching for mine as we dance between the rows and feel the warmth of the sun on our faces, and to watch the children grow and learn to ride Pieferet. To see all three of them at once on his back is a memory so sweet it begs me to break my ancient promise to be silent. I long to bury my face in your hair and to feel your fingers in mine; if only God would allow it. I know your pain is crushing you, Love, but you will go on and you will live the life God wants you to. We all do. Learning is never easy when it must be done alone. But alone, you will finally learn it. Paul was there to bring you to this point, and a fine job he did. He was born to teach you. Your path is there, my beautiful one; look for it. And look for me. I will never be far. I am the V you assign to all that you love; I am in the songs you feel deep inside. I am the words on your page. Look for me, I am not gone.

"Catherine, can you hear me? Can you open your eyes, honey? Catherine Elizabeth! Open your eyes!"

Piper opened one eye warily. She could only make out her mother's fuzzy figure. She was wearing her customary blazer over a turtleneck and her hand clasped her crucifix necklace. Piper thought to herself. *Are we at church or lunch? Those are the turtleneck/blazer occasions. Where am I? And who is Catherine?*

She let her eye slide shut again and wanted to feel the warm light, but it was gone. And the voice came again.

"Cathy. It's Mom. Can you hear me?"

Now she opened her eyes and squinted at the face looking down at her with a stern yet loving expression.

"Mom," she said, not realizing how much energy one word could use. "Why? Why are you ....?"

"Shhh. It's okay, just rest."

Piper, through the fog of medication and confusion, had one clear and conscious thought: My mother has a way of making me feel guilty, silly, and three years old, all with just the tone of her voice.

Then she heard her father's voice somewhere beyond her mother's shoulder.

"Your mother just wanted you to know we're here. Go back to sleep, Sweetheart."

"Dad, why is Mom calling me ....?"

"Shh, Go back to sleep. We'll be here when you wake up in the morning."

And with permission from the two people who brought her into this life, Piper fell into a dark and dreamless sleep.

When she woke again in the blue light of early morning, the stillness of the hospital gave her the chills. She sat up and looked at the clock across from her bed: 5:49. She reached for the call button on her bed rail. A nurse came in quietly and smiled at Piper like she was a small child.

"Yes?" she asked.

Piper looked in her direction but didn't want to look her in the eye. "I need to leave. I have to feed my animals and ... ."

The nurse looked at her, and with lips pursed, she noted something on the chart in her arms; as if Piper had not just spoken, she said, "Now, I can get you something to help you sleep."

Piper looked at her. "I just woke up. I don't want to sleep anymore."

The nurse turned and said, "I'll get the doctor, sit tight, Hon."

She watched the hands on the clock as they barely moved. After ten minutes passed, there was a knock and the door opened. She closed her eyes and took a deep breath, trying to remind herself to listen and be patient.

"Catherine, this is Dr. Randolph. He's been taking care of you since you came in." It was her mother's voice but for the life of her, Piper couldn't understand why she was calling her Catherine. She shook the man's hand and looked into his small, unfriendly eyes for any clues as to why she would be here in the hospital and feeling so confused. *Did I have an accident? No, Paul had an accident. Paul! Paul, I need you. I am so sorry.*

"Nice to meet you," she responded to his obligatory greeting.

Piper's mother looked pleased to have gotten through to her daughter and to see her awake and alert. "If you'll excuse me, I'm going to go find your father. He's probably in the cafeteria. I'll be right back."

Piper nodded to her frazzled, disheveled mother, feeling badly that she couldn't even remember the last time she had visited with her. *She's starting to look old, really old.*

Dr. Randolph pulled up a chair to her bedside and flipped open her chart. "Okay, let's take a look at your eyes." He pulled out his penlight and asked her to follow it as he traced a figure eight in the space between them.

"Good. Very good." He noted this in the chart.

"Excuse me, Dr. ... Randolph is it?"

Piper was quickly losing what little patience her loss of consciousness might have temporarily bestowed on her.

"Can you explain to me exactly why I'm here?"

The doctor looked at her and sighed, hating this part of his job about as much as Sergeant Van der Beck hated some of his duties.

"Well, you are here right now just for observation. You were brought in on the 31st for a panic attack, by ambulance. Do you remember that night?"

She rested her head back on the pillow and looked up to the ceiling. She nodded and looked back to the short man with the glasses.

"Yes, a little. What day is it?"

He looked at her and answered, "Today's the fourth. Happy belated New Year." He tried to sound cheerful and missed the mark by a mile.

"The fourth? Oh my God! I have to get out of here. My horses, my dog. Oh my God ... ."

The doctor stood now, wanting to prevent her from jumping up which is exactly what Piper was preparing to do. He reached into his pocket, but she lay back, feeling lightheaded and weak.

"Listen now. Everything is taken care of. I heard your parents talking with a friend of yours on the phone—Sharon, I think—something about your neighbor taking care of your pets."

Pets?! This guy is pushing it. But I'm too tired to argue. Why am I so tired?

Her thoughts were swimming and she just wanted to be at home.

"Okay. So if I came in with a panic attack days ago why am I still here and why don't I remember anything after that night?"

She looked at the doctor, squinting. She realized he was a little nervous, a fact she found quite funny.

"Well, you see Catherine, you—"

She shot upright in the bed and pointed at him.

"Catherine? Who is Catherine? My name is Piper. It's Piper for Christ's sake!"

He looked at her with what she thought might be a smirk and asked her if she'd like something that would help her relax.

When she only stared at him, he continued, "Well, yes. We are trying to get to the bottom of that. Your license reads

Piper but your mother insists your name is Catherine. If you want me to call you Piper ...."

She sprung out of the bed then, yelling.

"Get me out of here! I don't know what the hell my mother told you or what's going on but I, Piper, not Catherine, am going home!"

She lunged toward Dr. Randolph, only because he was standing close to the door that she wanted to get through. As she got close enough to see droplets of sweat on his wrinkled brow, he pulled a syringe from his pocket and when he saw his opportunity, stepped forward.

Her weak legs gave out and sent her crumbling to the floor as the doctor ever so gently injected into Piper's arm the sedative that would render her once again completely helpless. As he called for a nurse to come assist him, Piper thought of the Guiding Light, the soap opera she enjoyed with her Grandmother after school when she was in middle school. The dramatic hospital scenes always made her afraid of ever having to go to one. And now she realized that it was far more frightening than the one hour show could ever convey.

The light dimmed in front of her eyes and the last thing she heard was her mother's fading screams.

"Catherine! Catherine? Mother Mary, please save her!"

22

THIS TIME SHE WOKE UP in a smaller room, with only a clock on the wall behind a metal cage. She turned her head and tried to rub her eyes, but she couldn't move her hands.

What the hell? Who tied me down?

"Help! Somebody? Anybody! Is anyone there?"

She heard hurried footsteps and garbled voices in the hall outside the room, and when the door opened, in spilled shouts and cries and harsh fluorescent light.

"Catherine? Or do you prefer Cathy?"

The blonde nurse standing over Piper spoke in a voice she remembered from her sleep.

"Where is Dr. Randolph? Actually, no. I don't care. Where is my father? I want to see my father, please."

Piper's voice began to crack when she thought about her Dad and how she hadn't spent much time with him since she and Paul moved from the coast. *Paul, oh Paul, I miss you, I need you.* Her thoughts were beginning to spin and she could feel that familiar choking sensation rising in her throat again. She pushed it away and tried to breathe deeply to calm herself. The nurse took her pulse and calmly told her that her parents could come during visiting hours which would begin in about a half hour.

Piper felt herself losing her grip as her impatience tugged at her like a child wanting a partner in crime. Begging, seducing. She sighed heavily.

"What's your name?" she asked the nurse quite politely.

"Elise," she responded in a friendly manner.

"Rachel? That's a pretty name."

Piper looked at her with an accusatory glare.

"How would you like it if people called you by a name that's wasn't yours?"

The young nurse shook her head with what Piper understood to be a mix of impatience and pity as she wrote something in the chart at the foot of the bed, the chart Piper would have kicked across the room if her feet had not been bound.

She watched the clock on the wall and when twenty-seven minutes had passed, the door opened and her parents stepped in, cautiously.

"Daddy!" she screamed, like a frightened child.

"Daddy, I ... I want to go home."

Her mother, startled, hung back in the doorway with an expression one might say was doubt mixed with intolerance.

"Hey, Sweet Pea. How ya feelin'?"

His voice was just as it had always sounded, so familiar and comforting. Her dad had been her best friend when she was growing up, always making her feel like the most important person in the world. He understood her and knew what made her tick when so many others hadn't.

"Dad, what's going on, why am I here? Why is everyone calling me Catherine?" She whispered this last question so as not to get her mother riled up or bring back that nurse who *seemed* friendly.

"Listen, honey, you're here because you've been through a really awful time. The accident, Paul's funeral, and, well, you just need some rest. You've lost weight, you were dehydrated and ...."

Piper relaxed then as felt her father was making more sense than anyone else had since she woke up. *Dehydration, weight loss.* These were ideas she could understand and tolerate; they made sense.

"Dad, why am I restrained? Why have I been here for days, and why is everyone calling me Catherine?"

She noticed her father flinch as she said the name.

"Dad?"

She was not going to let him off the hook.

"Dad, what?"

He turned to his wife and nodded. Piper's mother held a tissue in one hand that fluttered nervously near her throat. Reluctantly, she turned and left the room.

In the silence of the room, Piper laid her head back and relaxed her neck, which she until now, hadn't realized had become stiff. She turned her head slightly to look at her father, and saw his exhaustion, his worry, his grief written in the lines of his face. He slowly reached for her hand and as he did, tears silently rolled off his chin and onto his faded Levi's.

"You're my little girl, right?" He asked this and struggled to keep from crumbling.

She nodded, her own eyes now flooding, too. She wanted to wipe her face dry, but her hands were rendered useless by the leather straps.

"This is hard, you know? I ... I don't ... know if I can ... I don't know what to say, what the doctors want me to tell you."

She craned her neck now, lifting it as high as she could and clenched her fists.

"The doctors? Screw the doctors! What the hell do they know about me? Dad, come on, talk to me. Tell me what you have to say. Please! I'm your daughter."

He looked into her dark, watery eyes, the eyes he had so loved since the first time he saw them that cold January night long ago. His baby, his only child. "Honey, the doctors say that you suffered a hell of a blow with all you've been through that ... that you ... it's just that you shouldn't be by yourself right now and—"

She interrupted him for the first time in her life. "Dad! Dad. Listen to me, look at me." She paused until he looked at her again. Not believing what came out of her mouth, she asked, "What's my name, Dad?"

He looked at her, stared into her eyes and said, quietly, "Piper. Piper."

Her heart leapt into her throat, her relief a welcomed

friend. "Thank God!" she said. "So why the hell is Mom and everyone around here calling me Catherine? I don't get it!"

Her father sat back, taking his hand with him.

"Your mother asked everyone to call you Catherine. It's, it's hard to ...."

He rubbed his eyes and stretched back against the seat and looked up at the ceiling as if there might be some help up there.

"Listen, I'm not supposed to discuss any of this with you. I don't want to make anything worse for you. I ...."

She rolled her eyes.

"Dad, I'm tied to a goddamn bed in what I'm guessing is the psych ward of a hospital. I don't see how *you* telling me the truth is going to make things worse. I trust you, only you, Dad."

He took a deep breath and looked at his daughter in the bed, so lost and pale. He had vowed to always protect her, no matter how old she got. Promises to his child were more important than any promise he made to doctors now or in the past. And his wife, well, for once, he thought, she was not going to tell him what he could or couldn't say to his own daughter.

"Okay. I'll tell you everything. What the hell? It's all gone to hell now anyway. It's about time you knew ...."

Piper took a deep breath and told herself to stay calm, to listen and, for once in her life, have patience.

"Do you remember, kiddo, when you were really small? I'm talking four or five years old. Can you remember back that far?"

She nodded, brows furrowed, "I think so. I remember kindergarten, I think. Or maybe first grade?"

He nodded and cleared his throat, something he did when he was nervous. "Do you remember having an imaginary friend, someone you talked to at night?"

She shook her head, "No, not really, I mean, well, vaguely. Why?" Just then she had a scent-ache of lavender and of the seashore. And she was there riding a black horse that looked similar to Valo. *But who was that boy with her?* She took a deep breath and let it come rushing out.

"What about it?" she asked.

"Well, Honey, when you were small, real small, you would talk to someone who wasn't there, and it would really scare the hell out of your poor mother. I mean, she just ... she just about lost it a couple of times there. You would talk about this friend, I can't remember the name. It was a boy, though, strange name. Anyway, you'd talk about him like he was right there in the room with us at the dinner table, or watching TV. I have to say, it was a little strange, but a lot of kids have imaginary friends, especially only children. That's what they said—at first anyhow."

Piper tried to pull herself up, feeling the restraints pulling at her ankles.

"They? Who's they?"

He smiled at her, wanting to keep her calm and feeling sudden relief that he could talk about this for the first time without being scolded or hushed.

"Well, there were a lot of 'theys' back then, ya know? First it was your pediatrician, then the psychologists. But your mother, she wouldn't stop there. She wanted someone to explain everything to her and some of these quacks, they just talk about theories and bullshit. So, anyway, she brought you to a priest, do you remember?"

She shook her head no.

"Yeah, talk about crazy. Your mother didn't tell me she was taking you. The only way I found out was because he called me. Your mother told him you needed an exorcism, that you were possessed. Well, I told your mother then that she had pushed just too far. No child of mine was possessed. I mean I believe that can happen to people, sure, I think it's real. But not you, not my baby girl. I knew there wasn't nothing inside ya that shouldn't be there. I thought maybe, and I know how this sounds, but I thought maybe you were seeing a ghost or something. Maybe you were seeing a spirit and that's who you were talking to. But your mother, she just didn't believe it. The priest agreed with me and that just about did your mother in, said the devil had us both fooled. She just wouldn't let it go, so we brought you to Children's Hospital in the city. And they ran every test you could imagine. And you were a little trooper. You didn't complain once when they poked you with needles for blood or put you in that tube to take the CAT scans. You said your friend, the ghost or ... well, he told you it would be okay—said he was right there with you. Do you remember any of it?"

She shook her head again. No.

"I don't remember any of that, Dad. How old? Four or five did you say?"

"Yup, you were just a little pup, so beautiful. There was something special about you kiddo. I knew it the second the nurse put you in my arms when you were born. You were only a little thing, less than seven pounds, but you sure did fill my heart." He smiled at her and pinched her cheek, wet with tears. "I knew that anything bad I had done in my life, anything I ever did wrong or mean was just gone, right then. It was like God gave me a second chance to make things right, to let me show this little kid how to be a good person, to lead a good life. That's all your mother and I wanted for you. We named you Catherine Elizabeth that night—"

Piper jolted back against the pillow and drew a breath.

"What? What did you say?"

"I said, we named you Catherine Elizabeth."

"No you didn't. I ... I don't ...what? How come I don't remember that name? I grew up as Piper, that's all I can remember."

Her father stood up and went to the door. He opened it slightly, motioning to her that it was okay, he wasn't going anywhere. Seeing that no one was there, he quietly closed it again. He reached into his coat pocket and pulled out his weathered brown wallet. He walked back to his daughter and flipped it open as he had done a thousand times before and took out a picture of her when she was five years old. *Funny how you can remember something so clearly when you see it or smell it, though you hadn't thought of it for thirty years and you never would have until it was right there with you again.* Something pulled at her thoughts then, but her dad pointed at the photo and caught her attention.

The edges of the photo were tattered and wispy, having been handled so many times over the years. He sat back down and looked at the picture for a moment before he continued.

"Honey, you and I are a lot alike, more so than your mother would ever like to admit. You see, she always felt a little left out at home. You were my sunshine, kiddo, and we bonded from day one. But your mother and you ... it was like mixing oil and water. You'd be fine for a while but then you'd be at each other's throats. I don't know, I think sometimes she wasn't meant to be a mother. No, that's not fair," he scolded himself. "She was a good mother. She is a good woman. But she just didn't click with you, do you remember?"

Piper thought about it for a moment.

"Well, yeah, when I was a teenager, but not when I was little."

He rolled his eyes then and rubbed his face hard, turning it white and then red.

"Oh God, this is hard. Agghhhh. You and your mother would argue over this little friend, name started with a 'V,' I think, I can't remember. Anyway, she would get really angry with you and tell you that you were lying, that you needed to stop lying or she was going to send you away to a school where'd they'd *make* you stop lying. But I never thought you were lying. I don't know what it was exactly, but it just didn't seem to me that you were lying; you really believed this friend was real. He ... he taught you things, for Christ's sake."

For a moment Piper had an image in her mind of the rosary beads her mother always had. And not just one. There was one in her bedroom, one in the kitchen, the living room, the entryway and one on Piper's nightstand. Together they would pray before bedtime. Piper closed her eyes as her father talked. She remembered feeling Elizabeth push the rosary beads under her pillow as her mother kissed her goodnight.

Piper furrowed her brow.

"Like what?"

"Well, for starters, horses. God, I never saw a kid handle a horse like you did. Even from the time you were, oh, about four, you would explain to us all about how a horse should be taken care of, what to feed it, how to treat its wounds, trim its hooves. At first, I thought it was funny, that you were just making it up or something. But then I started asking people who owned horses, and they told me all that stuff was true, but that some of the things I asked about were strange."

She raised one brow.

"Strange, how?"

He continued, "Well, you were describing the way they took care of horses back in the old days, hundreds of years ago. That's when I started to think that maybe you were talking with someone on the, well, on the other side, so to speak. I don't know, Sweet Pea, it just threw us for a loop."

Piper was trying to take it all in, but she couldn't believe her ears.

"What else, besides horses?"

"Flowers! God, you knew the names of plants and flowers that don't even grow in this part of the world. That's what convinced me. Christ, you talked about herbs that heal stomach problems and kill infections, plants that make a woman go into labor, which flowers smelled the best together—like perfume. It was unbelievable. You wanted a garden and you knew just how to prepare it, too. You planted vegetables, strawberries, flowers of all kinds. It really scared your mother, disturbed her, ya know? Neither of us knew the first thing about flowers or horses and here we have this little four-year-old ... it was really something."

Piper took a deep breath and turned her head toward the wall. She was feeling tired and a little sick to her stomach. *What does all of this mean, what's wrong with me?*

"Dad? Why did, or when did I become Piper? I'm still confused."

He looked at her and stroked her hair as she lay facing away from him.

"Well, that's a little more complicated, Honey. Maybe we

should leave that for another time."

She turned back to him abruptly, straining her neck.

"No! Dad, I need to know it all, please, don't stop now."

He sighed deeply and rubbed his tired eyes.

"What the hell am I doing here? I don't want to hurt you in any way. Maybe I don't know what's best for you, ya know? I mean, I love you more than anyone, Piper but maybe I ...." A tear rolled slowly down her cheek and onto the pillow. He felt such sadness for her, and so he continued.

"By the time you were almost seven, the doctors and the psychologists and teachers all agreed that you needed to be treated somehow, so that you could be, ya know, like a normal kid and not see ghosts anymore, if that's what was happening. I mean, it's not like you were miserable or anything. You were a lot of fun, and you were a great kid, too, the best! But it just seemed that you weren't going to have a normal life if things continued like they were. So there was this doctor, in Connecticut. He said he could help without medications or exorcisms or any of that bull. So we made an appointment and we went. At that time, Sweet Pea, the only thing I knew about hypnosis was what I'd seen on the TV, the stage kind, with the swinging wristwatch, ya know what I mean?"

She nodded and tried to smile but it took too much energy just trying to grasp what she was being told.

"So anyway, we get there and he says he's going to help you forget all that stuff about your friend and these memories you had about living in a village and losing your mother and the horrible things your brother did. It was all just supposed to go away. And most of it did. But the doctor, well, he said that when you were under, you regressed through two lifetimes before he got to the one where your friend lived. I wish I could remember the name. Well, he said that you struggled a lot in the two lifetimes since the one with your friend, your first life, your happiest one. He said that ... that ... you were trying to get back to that lifetime, to fix something. And until you could fix it, you were always going to be Piper. I didn't know what to believe, but ya know, I was out of ideas, so I had to believe it.

Your mother needed a valium that day. I really didn't know if I was going to go home with a wife and daughter that night or ... or what, I didn't know."

Piper looked at her father with love and whispered to him.

"It's okay Daddy; you're the best dad a girl could ever want."

He broke down then. The tears and the apologies strangled his words and he put his cheek against hers and tried his best to hold her as she lay strapped to the bed. Her tears mixed with his. *He was just trying his best. He was younger than I am now when I was born. Just figuring things out as he went along.*

When he composed himself enough to speak again he sat up and wiped her face, then his own.

"Agghhhh. You were Piper from that day on. And you know something, you were happy. Really happy. The doctor said that when you were under, he told you that you needed to stop talking about this friend and these other lifetimes, that you weren't supposed to remember them. But you put up a fight. You refused, something that doesn't usually happen in hypnosis, I guess—that's what he said anyway. He told us the only deal he could get you to agree to was letting you have your name back if you would leave your memories where they belonged—in the past. And when you woke up, you were Piper. And the friend, or the ghost or whatever it was ... just disappeared. Your mother and I didn't like the name change one bit. You probably don't remember, but your grandmother used to make comments. She would say, 'Piper? Que noma Pipe? Like-a under the sink?' She used to say that about our neighbor, too, 'Que noma Jackie? Like-a winter jacket, eh?'"

Piper smiled wanly at the sweet memory of her Italian grandmother and how the nuances of the English language confused her.

Her father looked up at the clock on the wall as he wiped his nose with the back of his sleeve.

"Your mother and I wanted what was best for you. We called you by that name ever since. Even went to the courthouse and had it legally changed, so that you could just be a normal kid. You don't remember the hypnotist or any of that other stuff?"

She shook her head no.

"I guess, because we explained it all in a way that a kid could understand, you just simply accepted it. Then, that year we bought you your horse. His name was Cocoa, remember? But you said his name was really supposed to be Victory, and well, you know the rest."

The door opened again and this time Dr. Randolph came in and told Piper's father that his wife wanted to see him. He looked at her to see if she would be okay and knew that he had done his best, what his heart said was right. He kissed her cheek and stood, looking directly into the doctor's eyes. No words were spoken but the message was clear that the woman in the bed was to be treated with the utmost respect.

The doctor dropped his eyes in deference.

"So, how are we feeling now?"

Piper looked at him and swallowed her contempt. With the friendliest voice she could muster, she spoke while looking him directly in the eye.

"I feel so much better. Thank you. I'd like some water and then I want to get some sleep."

That seemed to be the answer the doctor was looking for. *They don't know what to do with me, so they keep putting me back to sleep. The trouble is, I keep waking up.*

23

THE FIRST TIME SHE DROVE her car since Paul's death was a strange experience for her, as were all the firsts. The first holiday, the first-month anniversary, the first trip to the store to shop for herself, all stood out in her mind like a blinking neon sign. And the sign read: YOU ARE ALONE. She missed him deeply and played in her mind over and over their last conversation. *Now you get to remember your selfishness, and the guilt will be here every day for the rest of your life. And you know what? You deserve it.* The anger overshadowed the sadness for a little while, but never for long enough.

Since being released from the hospital, Piper had decided she needed to make some big changes in her life despite everyone's admonitions not to make rash decisions. *Yeah, like rash decisions are new to me. I'm an expert in the field.* Her mother had refused to discuss the matters concerning her childhood and her hypnosis therapy. *If ever there was a "Queen of Denial," it's my very own mother. Just my luck.* She thought this often when trying to get her mother to recount the conversations she heard through the closed bedroom door all those years ago. *"Oh, honey, it was just an imaginary friend. I've told you that before, don't you remember?"* This was the only answer that held any truth.

Piper quickly tired of the game and decided to take matters into her own hands. Did people forget that this is her life to live? Being home felt good, peaceful. *I'm grateful to be here in pain rather than in that place having no feeling at all. Funny how you can change your perception on something you never thought you could.*

Sharon came to visit the day after she got home, and like a true friend, brought lunch, flowers, and tissues.

"Hi, Chickadee!" she chirped.

Piper couldn't help but smile at this, her favorite nickname. She looked at Sharon, searching for any signs of pity or judgement but knew she'd find none.

"Hi. It's really good to see you. Thank you for coming out and thank you for ... ."

Her eyes welled up then but she didn't try to hide the tears. Now they were just a normal part of her every day, her every night, her every memory. Sharon placed the packages she had brought with her onto the countertop in Piper's clean unused kitchen, and grabbed a tissue from her supply. She handed it to her dearest friend and continued to locate dishes and silverware while Piper blew her nose.

"Thank you, again." Piper turned to Sharon.

"What for, darlin'?"

"For not telling me to stop crying. Everyone keeps telling me to stop, to look at my future, to remember the happy times. And guess what? I don't even know I'm crying sometimes. The tears just come. Plus, they don't get it. They can't. They just can't."

Sharon placed two heaping plates of Caesar salad on the kitchen table without another word. She just listened. And for the first time in a long time, Piper felt hungry.

The silence between them was not awkward, but instead rather pleasant. *Finally. Someone who gets it. I don't want to talk. I just want to feel better.* Piper looked at Sharon and saw comfort.

Later when they had moved to the great room and started a fire in the fireplace, each with a glass of wine, Sharon said, "I'm going to go get our cheesecake and when I come back we are going to make a list."

"A list?" Piper raised one brow.

"Yep. A list of things you are going to do to start feeling better. I'll be right back."

She grabbed Piper's notepad and pen off the coffee table and handed it to her.

Piper stared at the pad. At the top it read #Hustle and below that was a whole lot of empty space. Hustle. Ha. *I used to be all about that. Getting things done. Accomplishments. Climbing the ladder. Goals. Checkmarks. Next! And now, just getting through one hour, minute by minute. That's my thing. #Gamechanger.*

Sharon came back with plates of dessert. Without a word, she placed them on the coffee table, reached into her pocket, brought out a few tissues and handed them to Piper, who took them but just let them sit on her lap. The tears were earned and she was okay.

"So, what's it going to be? Your first item on that list. I want to hear it. And it's okay if it's small like maybe going to the mall and buying yourself a pair of shoes or a new lipstick."

Piper looked at her like she had two heads. But she softened, remembering who she was sitting with.

"Lipstick? I guess I could do that."

Sharon looked at her and nodded as she took a big bite of the lime-swirled decadence.

"Okay. So after that, can you think of something else that might make you feel a little better? Anything?"

Piper sat for a moment, Viceroy at her feet. Her constant companion.

"I guess I could get a trim at the salon. I haven't had one since before ...."

She looked down at the pad on her lap, the paper now with drops of despair soaking through. She had to shift her list over a bit. *1. Lipstick 2. Trim.*

"My lists used to be so ... bold. So confident. You know?" She looked at Sharon.

"Mm-hmm," Sharon knew she could just nod and keep her friend moving forward just like Piper could so quietly move her enormous horses around with only her presence or a simple word.

"So, let's see. I could go to Crop 'n Carrot. *3. Crop 'n Carrot.*"

She pinched off a bit of crust from her plate and tasted it. Comfort.

Piper looked at Sharon then and saw that one eyebrow

was raised and she was squinting to understand. They shared a genuine stress-relieving laugh. Piper remembered then that Sharon worked in the human insurance world, not equine. The only thing she knew about horses was that she was terrified of them.

Piper said, "Crop and Carrot is a tack shop. They have these...." She waved the rest of the sentence away knowing Sharon wouldn't know a boot jack from a martingale.

When dessert was finished and the wine glasses were refilled, Piper put the pad back on the coffee table. Sharon picked it up and read:

1. Lipstick: Ripe Raisin
2. Trim
3. C n C for Hooflex and Ivermectin
4. Find Dr. Corcoran

Knowing what Sharon was staring at, Piper offered an explanation.

"I was thinking maybe I could try to find that doctor. The one my parents brought me to. I don't know. Maybe he has some answers for me."

She looked up at Sharon, hoping against hope to not see pity or judgement; but this time she wasn't very confident that it wouldn't be there.

Sharon put her glass down and cleared her throat.

"Okay. Let's do this. Let's do this now."

"Really?"

Piper straightened a bit.

"You don't think it's crazy?"

Sharon shook her head emphatically.

"Don't use that word, Hon."

Piper laughed, "Oh yeah, not such a good choice."

She took the pad and pen back. She scribbled and drew a question mark. And then under #Hustle she added #Whothehellami?

24

D R. CORCORAN WAS IN Connecticut in the mid-seventies. According to Google, he still practiced there. So, three days after Sharon's visit, Piper decided she needed to pay this doctor a visit and try to get some answers as to why her parents felt the need to wipe out her memories and alter the course of her life. As she typed the address into her GPS she said to no one, "How dare they? It was my life. It *is* my life. And I want it back."

Shaking her head and taking a deep breath, she texted Sharon. *I'm heading to CT. Wish me luck?* She sat back, drew another deep breath, and closed her eyes. *Please, God.* Shifting into first gear, Piper set her eyes on the end of her driveway. "Here I go."

She wasn't on the road twenty minutes when her phone rang. It was her mother, and though Piper could understand that her parents did what they thought was best for her, she was still very angry with them for keeping it from her for all these years. She decided not to pick up the phone, and after a minute, a beep let her know there was a message for her. In fact, there were several messages that she hadn't listened to, not the least of which were the first three that Paul had left for her the day he died. Skipping over them that afternoon seemed like a good idea at the time because she knew that any important information would be in the last couple. She had never deleted them and now was afraid to listen to them, to hear his voice. Losing her mind was something Piper thought might happen very easily and at any given moment. She knew she was fragile and wanted help before it was too late. She said out loud as her car reached 80 mph, "I wonder if crazy people know they're crazy."

When she pulled her car into the parking lot of the old brick building she thought to herself, *Oh God, what's going to happen today? Am I going to be able to handle this? Do I have a choice?* She tossed her keys into her purse and cleared her throat; then she checked her makeup in the rearview mirror, noticing the deepening wrinkles, before stepping out into the sobering January wind.

Stepping into the warm building, she let out the breath she realized she'd been holding since she parked her car.

"Cold out there, huh?"

She turned to see an elderly man waiting to leave through the door she had just walked through.

"Uh, yes. Freezing is more like it." She tried to smile but her face felt frozen. She looked into his ocean blue eyes and for a fraction of a second she sensed that she knew him. In her mind's eye was a gentleman with a wooden case and glass vials with clear liquid in them. His eyes were the same as this man in front of her. The scent of jasmine, lemongrass and tea reached from behind her nose and begged her to stay in the moment. To focus. She paused and wanted to ask if she knew him from somewhere. He was looking at the floor.

"Your gloves, Madam. I'll get those for you." He bent down and picked up the gloves Piper hadn't realized her frozen hands had dropped.

"Oh. Thank you. I ... I feel like I know you from ....?"

The man's eyes slowly blinked as if in slow motion and he straightened his small frame.

"You'll need those gloves, Madam. Keep an eye on them!"

And with that, he was gone. Piper stood for a moment as the door closed behind him and she tried to recall the scent-ache but it, too, was gone. She looked around to see if anyone else was there. She shook her head and walked to the directory on the wall. First Floor – Dr. Corcoran – Clinical Hypnosis. Suite

111. Piper let out a deep breath.

"Found you."

She stood with her hand on the doorknob and hesitated. *What am I doing? This is crazy.* She turned the knob and pushed the door inward slowly, daring herself to turn back. Standing inside the warm suite with its sage green paint and latte colored furniture, she knew she was where she needed to be. *This is good. This is big. #Hustle.*

"Hi, I need to see Dr. Corcoran please," she said to the mousy receptionist who looked tired and bored, clearly not happy to be at work on this particular day. She didn't look up at Piper but simply asked, "Can I help you?"

"Uhh, I don't have an appointment, but it's very—"

Barbara, as the name plate on her desk announced, looked over her glasses at her as if she were used to this kind of doctor's office travesty and pointed to the orange vinyl chairs in the waiting room.

"Have a seat." She took her time finishing whatever it was she had started before Piper arrived and then disappeared into another room.

Piper took a breath and let it fill her cheeks like she did as a kid, only then she used Kool-Aid and loved the way it stained her tongue red or purple or orange. There were diplomas on the wall from several different universities, all very impressive, and she wondered what this doctor could offer her in terms of moving forward with her life now.

After a few minutes, a man appeared in the doorway from which Barbara had not yet returned.

"Good morning, can I help you Ma'am?"

Piper stood up and thought for a moment she must have the wrong office. *This guy is my age, maybe younger.*

She stood up and took a tentative step forward. "Hi. I was hoping to speak with ... with someone named Dr. Corcoran, but perhaps I have the wrong address."

The doctor stepped into the waiting area, closer to Piper.

"Well, I'm Dr. John Corcoran, Jr. What's your name?"

Piper resisted sticking her hand out to shake his because

his hands were on his hips.

"My name is Piper and...."

Her mind was trying to figure out if the scent of Play-doh was more important than figuring out if she was in the right place.

"Piper? Wait. Not Piper *Turchino*?" His expression went from anticipation to confusion to realization and back to anticipation.

She stood motionless for another moment, hoping it wasn't noticeable, as she tried to grasp what she saw in her mind's eye: Jacks, a rubber ball, Play-doh and a garlic press.

"Yes. That's my maiden name. Am I...."

Her mind whirled then. Since her hospital stay she had been working on positive affirmations that began with "I am"; now it seemed she had no idea who or what she was, so instead starting a question with "Am I" seemed like a good start.

She looked into the doctor's eyes as they closely scanned her face and realized there was a lot going on in his mind. This confused her even more

"You are in the right place. I can assure you of that. Please come in."

He backed up so she could walk in front of him and told her to step into the office on the left.

As she stepped inside, she was greeted by some pretty impressive diplomas and certificates. They all read Dr. John Corcoran, Jr. She looked at him as she sat in one of the chairs in front of his mahogany desk. In a sheepish tone she said, "Actually, I think I might be looking for your father."

The doctor flinched but caught himself and smiled.

"My father died three years ago, and I took over his practice. But I'm sure I can help."

"Oh, I'm sorry," she interrupted him.

He sat in the chair next to her, which surprised her a bit. She assumed he would sit behind his desk. He turned the chair toward her, shifting his weight until he was sitting at the very edge, his knees practically touching hers. He seemed excited to see her.

"So tell me, Piper, what brings you here?"

She looked nervously down at her hands, which were holding one another like scared children.

"Well, I'm ... I'm having a ...." She cleared her throat and looked up at him.

"I had a nervous breakdown after my husband's death a couple of months ago, and since then I've learned a lot of things about my past that I was never aware of. My father told me that my parents brought me here in the seventies to see you, or rather, your father."

Dr. Corcoran almost jumped out of his chair, clearly having a hard time waiting for her to finish her sentence.

"I'm so happy you're here. I wondered if this day would ever come. But ... do you know how much my father talked about your case? You, I mean, and what he learned from you?"

She shook her head and smiled, a little embarrassed.

"Well, let me tell you, my father regarded you as a gift, a pearl in the sand, he used to say. 'If you could see how she shines!'

"When he got sick, he took your records and put them in a safe deposit box for me and instructed me to seek you out. I tried, but I kept running into dead ends. Finally I found your parents in Massachusetts, but they said ... they said that ... well, that you had passed away."

Now it was Piper's turn to jump out of her chair.

"What!? They told you I died?!" Her thoughts spun and the scent of lavender rushed in behind her nose, but she ignored it, trying hard to comprehend the possible meaning of such a profound lie.

"Well, I guess maybe they didn't want me to dig into your past, so to speak, which, of course, is what I wanted to do. I'm sure they were just trying to protect you."

She nodded her head and said, "Yeah, that seems to be the recurring theme here."

He realized that this was a bit overwhelming for her and asked, "Can I get you some tea or water? Coffee?"

She shook her head. "No. Thank you, though."

He sat back down and motioned for her to do the same. She sat down hard, looking pale; but when he began to speak again, the color flooded back into her beautiful face.

"Can you tell me something, Piper?" He asked, and she responded with a nod. "Tell me what your father told you, what you know."

She looked at him and shrugged her shoulders like a kid who doesn't want to confess to something she'd been caught doing. His reassuring smile, though, was encouraging.

"Well, my father told me that when I was little, around four years old, I had an imaginary friend or a ghost who visited me at night. And my mother was really scared by it, so they tried everything they could think of to get it—whatever it was—to go away. And when they couldn't, they brought me here, to your father."

He nodded at her as if he knew there was more that she needed to tell him. But she looked down at her hands, hoping he would break the awkward silence. He let out a raspy breath, almost whistling.

"That's all he told you? I mean, was there anything more you can remember?"

She shook her head as if to say, *Isn't that enough!?*

Dr. Corcoran sat back in his chair and visibly relaxed.

"Do you remember anything? From the past I mean, from your past life?"

She looked at him to see if he was serious and then remembered where she was and what he did for a living. She shook her head no. "Well, I guess ... I guess that's the whole point, right?"

He laughed gently and nodded humbly.

"Yes, I guess it is. How do you feel about this information you recently learned? Oh, and I'm sorry to hear about your husband, by the way."

Piper nodded, hating when people said that, especially if they didn't even know Paul. She shrugged her shoulders and felt like she was in the principal's office back in high school, not knowing what to say.

"I don't really know. I mean, it's all so confusing right now. That's why I'm here. I'm just looking for answers and I don't think my parents are prepared to give me what I need."

John nodded at her then and waited to see if she wanted to say anything more. After a moment he leaned forward and said, "Well, I can assure you that whatever you need to know and I can help you with, it's yours for the asking. I'll be more than happy to waive my fees. It really is an honor to sit here with you. I still can't believe you're here."

The intercom on the desk suddenly crackled, interrupting like a waitress who waits until you have a mouthful of food before asking how everything is. John reached over his desk and hit a button on the phone and instructed Barbara to hold all his calls and let his next client know he'd be a few minutes.

Piper felt, for the first time in a month, that she might have a decent chance at getting some answers; perhaps even some peace. He looked at her and realized that a few minutes weren't going to do much for either one of them.

"Piper, do you think you can stick around for an hour or so until I'm finished with my next client? I want to continue our conversation, and I can clear my schedule for the afternoon if you have the time."

She nodded and said, "It seems all that I have these days is time. I'll just go get some coffee and I'll be back later." He showed her to the waiting room and looked into her eyes.

"You'll be back?"

She nodded her confirmation and left.

When she got back into her car, she exhaled loudly and closed her eyes.

"Thank you, God." She started her car and glanced down at her phone. It was mocking her from the console with its message alert chirp, begging her to check her voicemail. *No,* she thought. *There's only one person I want to talk to right now and that's Dr. John Corcoran, Jr., thank you very much.* The engine turned over and she set the heat to high as she drove from the parking lot.

She found a coffee shop. The sign read: One Lump or Two.

She turned off the engine and closed her eyes momentarily. *That's something I would have thought was clever just a year ago. It's amazing what a year can do to you.*

Paul had always gotten a medium coffee, cream only, and two jelly donuts, an order he never deviated from all the time she had known him. She took a deep breath, thinking how this was another first. As she swung open the door and stepped into the building she was greeted by the comforting smell of freshly brewed coffee. It was a smell that made her think of her grandparent's house at the holidays, studying for college exams, and of course the early mornings of horse shows.

There were a few elderly people sitting at tables, which were painted soft pastel colors, and Piper thought, *Why did they get to live to be old?*

"I'll have a small regular and a medium. She stopped midsentence and look down.

"Sorry. Just the small coffee."

The girl behind the counter whose crooked name tag read Amanda looked at her with bright eyes.

"Don't be sorry. Be happy because life's too short. That's what my professor always says." Piper looked at the girl and thought how cute she was with her black ponytail and her One Lump Or Two visor with its little sugar cubes and coffee cup printed in brown and pink. *She looks like she could be my daughter.*

"That's a great sentiment. What class does your professor teach?" she asked the girl.

"History Through Poetry. It's a cool class," she answered as she poured the coffee. Piper nodded and said, "Sounds cool." She took the coffee and handed the girl a five-dollar bill.

"Keep the change—for laundry."

The girl flashed her a beautiful, toothy smile, truly surprised.

"Have a great day!"

"You too, Honey." Piper made it to her car before she broke down and cried. She put her coffee in the cup holder before pounding her fists against the steering wheel. Her head hanging between her shoulders she cried, "Paul, I miss you so much! Why did you leave me? Was I that awful? Oh Paul, I know I was. I'm so sorry, please, I'm so sorry. I need you. All I want is you. You're the only one who understood me and now there's no one."

She picked up her phone and flipped it open. She quickly dialed her voice mailbox, then snapped it shut again. She needed to hear his voice in the way that an addict needs her drug, but she knew it would render her useless. She had to hold herself together until she had time to talk to Dr. Corcoran. She wiped her eyes with the napkin she had grabbed before she left the coffee shop and started the car again.

Driving around town, she figured, would keep her mind busy for the next forty-five minutes until she was to go back and try to find out who she had been, who she was supposed to be, who she might be once again.

The salt-stained gray streets lined with dirty snow banks greeted her at every turn and she wished she hadn't agreed to stay. She only wanted to be at home on her farm with a fire in the fireplace, but knew she'd be just as sad there, too.

As she watched people go about their daily lives she was struck with contempt and resentment. *How come they get to be happy and normal, just going on with their lives? Doesn't anyone understand what I'm feeling, doesn't anyone care?*

She wondered what it would be like to just become the woman she saw hurrying from her green minivan to the grocery store with a toddler in one arm and a baby in the other. *Where does she live? What's her house like? What does her husband do for a living? Does she love him?* She shook her head, knowing it was just self-pity and that it was part of the grief process, but she hated the feeling just the same. She sipped her hot coffee and felt it warm her insides, making her relax a little bit. It was almost time to go back to the hypnotist's office. She drew a deep breath. *I can do this.* She decided she was glad she had agreed to stay. *I wonder if I'll ever forgive them for this.*

Barbara didn't look up when Piper arrived back at the office, and she didn't much care. She was tired of miserable people and hoped that she would never give off the vibe that this woman was sending out. Glancing at the clock, she realized that she had returned ten minutes early. She began to turn toward the magazine rack but quickly looked back at the clock. It was the decorative sort she often saw at Home Goods and thought would look great in her office. It was purely decorative with Roman numerals and hands that were tipped with fleur de lis on a tea-stained parchment-looking face. The pendulum seduced her with its tick-tock rhythm and she stood staring. She squinted to see the words at the center of it: Paris, France.

Dr. Corcoran saw his patient at the door. *My father's pearl in the sand.* He was a little surprised that she had kept her promise to come back. He silently waved from behind the middle-aged man who was leaving so as not to seem too eager to see him out the door. Piper was absorbed first by the clock but then by the faint sound of horse hooves striking stone. It made her heart skip. For the first time in a long while she felt unforgotten. She turned toward John.

"Hi." It was all she could think to say. He raised his eyebrows.

"Hi. Glad you came back."

He led her back to the vanilla-colored office.

After settling back into their respective chairs, John picked up a thick folder from his desk. Piper glanced at it and knew it must be old. It was tattered on the edges and had pen marks and a faded red ink stamp that read: Confidential.

John watched her as she looked at the folder.

"So this is your file. It's almost as old as you are. I think you might be interested in it. Maybe not today, but at some point." He looked expectantly at her.

With her eyes still on the word "Confidential," she shook her head as if he had asked if she'd like to see autopsy results. To her way of thinking, that's exactly what the notes were.

"Maybe someday?" She knew it was non-committal but she didn't think she could handle what might be in there.

"Okay. That's fine, just thought I'd ask." He looked at her with anticipation, wondering if she'd change her mind.

She looked at a Princeton University degree on the wall:

Doctorate of Psychology.

"What do I do now?"

He shifted in his seat, crossed his legs.

"Well that depends. What do you want to do? Why did you come here?"

She looked at him directly now.

"Originally I thought I wanted to know what happened before my parents brought me here but I don't know. It's a little confusing and I ...." She looked at him for help.

"All right, I can tell you this. You're safe here and there's nothing to be scared of. If you think it will help you I can regress you, and record our session, which is what I do for all my clients and we can go from there." He paused for a moment.

"What do you think?"

She was stunned to think that in a matter of an hour or so she might have the answers to questions that had kept her awake for the last month and kept her from herself for almost forty years. She gripped the tops of her thighs out of nervousness, shrugged her shoulders again.

"I can't imagine ever going on without knowing. It's just that ... it's just that I feel like I'll never be able to un-know it. You know?"

He let out a laugh that spoke of relief and gratitude, as this was something he thought he had lost a chance of ever doing when her parents told him she had died.

"Yes. I do know. But I really think that's the whole point. Life has a way of surprising us. And sometimes in really good ways. Let's get started?"

Before long he had Piper sitting in the reclining chair in his office and assured her that it would help her relax more than lying flat on the couch by the bookcase.

"I don't know why most psychologists insist clients lie on a couch. You're not taking a nap here. You'll be fully awake and aware."

"I suppose you don't use a wristwatch either." She looked up at him.

"Only for paying customers," he said through a laugh.

She rolled her eyes as she tried not to smile. *What am I doing? Everything I thought was real might not be and everything I find out could be worse than—no, nothing could be worse than being without Paul.* The sob caught in her chest. Embarrassed, she put her hands over her face and tried to compose herself before the tears came.

John gave her a moment and then as if there had been no interruption, he continued. "Okay. Here's what we're going to do. I'm going to ask you to relax and close your eyes. Take a nice deep breath in through your nose. Hold it for a count of one and then slowly let it out through your mouth. Let all the tension drain from your body. Just picture it like water flowing off your fingertips. And then another breath. In through your nose, hold for a second, and then out through your mouth. Good. Then I will give you suggestions to help you relax even more and you will follow my voice as you get more and more relaxed. Then we begin the regression. It's as simple as that. You will be in complete control at all times. There's absolutely nothing to worry about. When I ask you to come back, you'll do it slowly, and you may or may not remember what you told me during the session but that's what the recorder is for. Okay?"

Piper nodded, not looking at him. She had already closed her eyes and again she could hear hooves on stone. The scent of lavender began to wash over her and a sense of peace enveloped her like a snug cocoon.

John's voice was quiet and comforting as he suggested her eyelids were so heavy that even if she wanted to she wouldn't be able to open them. After several minutes of suggestions that she was very relaxed and going deeper and deeper into the forest he began to take her back. Back before she could consciously remember.

"Now I want you to go back in your mind to yesterday morning. You see how you can be any place and in any time in your mind. It doesn't matter where or when you are now, your mind can bring you there—where and whenever you want to be." She nodded her head and took another deep breath.

He continued. "Now, Piper, bring me back to 1979 in your

house with your mother and father. I want to know what your bedroom looked like; can you describe it for me?"

She said in a clear and calm voice, "It's pink and it has two windows. My bed is under the windows, and I have stuffed animals on it. My cat is there, Valentine! And my Holly Hobby oven, and my saddle. It's new. I just got it for Christmas."

"Good girl." Dr. Corcoran's eyes, for the first time in his career, brimmed with tears, knowing his father was right there with him, guiding him as he guided her. "Now, can you tell me about your friend? The one who comes to visit with you."

"Yes! He's my best friend. His name is Vander and he is older than me. He's nine. He says that God promised we would always be together. But he's telling me that he has to stop coming to visit with me because people will think there's something wrong with me. But I don't want him to go. I love him." Tears seeped out from under her lids and. John moved her forward. Or rather, backward.

"Okay. Now let's go back before that time, Piper. Tell me about when you were four."

"My name is Catherine and I'm in pink pajamas in my bed. My mother is rubbing my back and telling me to go back to sleep, but I don't want to sleep because Vander is making funny faces at me and scaring the kitten."

"Okay. Let's go back further now. Can you go back further?" John's voice, ever steady, moved her back again. "It's okay. You are safe and you can go back even farther. She took a deep breath and visibly relaxed, her arms resting by her sides now, and said, flatly, "Now I am Francine. I'm with my sister on the rocks at the shore. I'm teasing her about being afraid to go out on the rocks and I'm afraid, too, but she doesn't know I'm afraid, too. She's begging me to stop fooling around but I want to prove that I'm not a scaredy-cat like her. I keep telling her to go farther and farther. And then ... and then she falls on the rocks and her head is bleeding. No! No! She's bleeding and she's falling into the waves. And I have to help but now we are both in the water and it's dark."

John's eyes blinked slowly, and though he was covered in

goosebumps and wanted to tell her that it was okay, that she is more than paying in this life for anything wrong she did in all the others that came before, he just moves her on.

"It's okay. That was a long time ago and now you are safe. Let's go back even further. Can you go back before you were Francine?"

Whimpering and clutching her jeans with her hands, Piper nods.

"I'm in my shop in the piazza. I have a lot of customers and they all demand the same thing. I wish I had more but I have to wait for the ships to bring it. They are all shouting for the fever tree, the holy bark. They shout at me. 'The malaria is killing me! It is killing our children!' I don't have enough for every one of them and they are pulling at me and hitting me with their fists. I don't have time for this. I have another job. Don't they know I would help if I could? I have to get home to my farm and my wife. She is expecting our first child any day now. But they are hitting me with their fists. I don't have time. I want to help, but they are cursing me and they pull me from behind my desk. Why can't they understand that I just don't have enough of the medicine bark for them all? One man drags me into the street and they are stealing everything I have, They are kicking me. I don't have time to be kicked and dragged! I have work to do. I am biting someone's leg now and he smashes my head with his boot!"

Piper moved uncomfortably in the chair and put her arms up to protect her head.

"Okay, Piper. That's good. Let's move on again. Send love and healing to yourself in this time. You did what you could do. Some people will never appreciate the sacrifice of others. It's just how it is. You are safe. Let's go back further."

For more than a few moments Piper sat in silence, eyes closed comfortably, and breathing calmly. John sat back and waited. He knew it was this next lifetime that was the most significant. The one that he sometimes wished he could join her in.

"Tell me, Piper. Where are you?"

"At home on our farm. Peyrinne! My beautiful girl!"

John leaned forward. "Is Vander there with you?"

"Yes! Vander! I'm so sorry! I didn't know! I should have listened to you! I'm sorry!"

"What didn't you know?" John's voice was just loud enough for Piper to hear him.

"Marek! My brother. Oh, my sad brother. He needed me. He wanted a place to sleep. He was so tired and hungry. Père died a few days ago, and we are all so tired and sad, so sad. I'm begging Vander to let him stay with us but he is stubborn. I'm telling him that I would open my home to his brothers and their wives and children. I have no patience! He raises his voice to me and says that Marek has the devil in him. I am so angry with him. How can he say these things about my poor brother who just lost his father? I am running outside to Marek, and I'm holding him in my arms and telling him he can stay with us. He is drunk again with the ale from that filthy tavern and he needs a bath. But I love him and he needs me. I am all he has left. Vander is leaving, taking Pieferet out in the dark. He shouts to me to make sure Marek sleeps in the barn. Marek curses him. I am helping him into the house, and I'm yelling at my children. Don't look at your uncle like that! He's not a dog! He needs his family!"

John pushed gently, "What now, Piper? Why are you so upset?"

"I'm in my bed alone. Vander did not come home. I am worried. He is never gone for this long. I must have fallen asleep but then there's a loud noise! And I can hear someone moving in the loft and yelling! I don't know what. I'm climbing the loft with the lantern, calling to my brother and my children. Are you fine, what is the matter? And Vander's there! He's dragging Marek away and when he does, I can see Peyrinne! Oh God, my Peyrinne! Her bedclothes are torn and she has blood on her legs! No! No! Vander doesn't see me and he throws Marek out the loft and knocks me down the ladder! The lantern! The fire, it's burning the table and the floor. The children! Luuk, Philip, Peyrinne! Vander! The children! Oh thank God, he's coming down the ladder with Peyrinne in his arms and puts her in mine. I smell his fear and his hatred. He goes back to the loft for the twins. The flames are so hot, and I can't breathe. Marek! He's not moving. I can't help him! Marek, how could you hurt my child!? Vander's coming, he has the boys."

Piper clutches the arms of the recliner, turning her knuckles white. "I am running out into the night air. No! Vander only has one of the boys. It's Luuk, and he is screaming for Philip but the flames ... the flames! It's too hot. We are choking on the smoke and run outside with Luuk and Peyrinne. The whole house is burning, and I cannot get close to it. Vander's running toward it! No, Vander don't go in there! Philip! My son! Philip! Vander! He is trying to get through the flames. I can hear my son—my beautiful, sweet boy! Philip!" Piper writhed in the chair, hands clawing at her face, kicking out at invisible flames.

John swallowed hard. He knew what would come next. He had read the notes a hundred times over the years. When his father first told him about Piper, when John Jr. decided to study hypnotherapy, he remembered her. She was the little girl whose parents brought her to the house to play with him. Or at least, that's what he thought she was there for. His mother put out cookies and tea like she did whenever they had company. She would tell John, "Go get your game of jacks and the two of you can play for a little while so the grown-ups can talk, Johnny." He remembered how the little girl was reluctant at first but when she decided to play, she played for keeps. He liked that about her. There were only five visits but each one was special, especially the second one when she told him, "My friend Vander likes you. He says you will have to wait but someday you will remember this day and smile."

He looked at her as she scooped up six jacks in one bounce of the small red ball and said, "I'm smiling now, though."

Catherine bounced the ball on the linoleum floor of the kitchen. Bounce, bounce, bounce. Suddenly, she grabbed it mid-bounce and held it tightly. Shaking her head, she said, "No. He says it will be a long, long time from now. And the smile will be way bigger."

Many years later, sitting with his father in the office, looking at the notes, he asked, "What do you think her friend meant by that?"

John Sr. looked over his glasses at his son proudly and said, "I'm not sure, Johnny. I think maybe she meant that Vander knew you would be here continuing my work."

Over the years, John Jr. read the notes time and time again, trying to glean some meaning from her words. He not only thought there was more significance to it, he felt it. And the day he got up the nerve to contact her parents to see how Piper was doing, he realized he would never find out.

"Leukemia." Elizabeth Turchino's voice was cold and she made it quite clear she did not appreciate the phone call from the doctor's son. In her mind, the doctor did his job, was paid, and that was the end of the story.

John was still remembering his disappointment when he asked, "Piper, what's happening?"

"Philip is screaming for me. 'Maman!' He is calling, 'Maman help me; I'm so scared! Maman help me, it's burning!' Vander is trying to get through the hell fires and he can't. He's screaming for our son. 'Philip, my son, Père loves you! Philip!' And then the screaming stops."

Piper covered her face in the chair, eyes still shut. She sobbed and clutched at her hair. "Vander is holding Luuk and crying. He's looking at me with Peyrinne. There's blood still dripping down her thin legs. I ... I can't stop screaming for my son."

John said gently, "Okay. Move forward now, Piper; tell me what happens next."

"We are burying him, my little brave boy. Vander is carrying his body and moaning. Peyrinne is holding my hand. She won't talk to anyone. Luuk is there, my only son! My beautiful son. We wrapped Philip in the blanket I knit before Peyrinne was born. It doesn't cover all of him, but it's all we have left from the fire. It was out on the fence drying when the fire happened. Luuk is holding his brother's burned hand, and my heart is broken. I cannot go on. I can't watch my love bury our son. But Peyrinne is pulling at me, and I don't want to go. I want to die. I want to be with my Philip. Vander is putting him in the ground. No, Vander! I can't watch you do this. He is taking his wedding medallion off. It's in the dirt now with our boy. He doesn't want to hurt him; he puts the dirt on him so gently, but he is dead and it's my fault. It's all my fault! I can smell the dirt now: it's in my nose and I brought flowers, but I don't like the way they smell today. Nothing can be happy or beautiful anymore. I want to crawl into the dirt with my little one! Vander is on his knees praying, but God doesn't hear him. He never hears us! Why does a woman have to bury her father, brother, and son in the same week? There is no god that would let that happen! I would give anything to listen to Vander and tell Marek to leave us, to find his own way. We all have to find our own way...."

John stepped in again. "Okay, Piper, you're right, we all have to find our own way. Now, I want you to listen to my voice. I am going to count now and when I get to five, you will slowly come back and you will be safe and refreshed here in my office. One, two ..."

Piper whimpered and nodded.

"... three, four, and five. Open your eyes, Piper."

She blinked at the light and looked at Dr. Corcoran, confused.

"What happened? Did we start yet?"

He smiled at her. "Yes we started *and* finished. See how easy that was? You went back to your lifetime over a century ago when you were, believe it or not, Piper."

She looked out the window then and realized that the sun was very low in the sky. Looking back at the doctor she said, "I do. I do believe it."

25

THE MORNING SUN GLINTED on the cobblestones after the night's warm rain. The city was just waking and sounds of daily life found her through the stone building: shod hooves on the streets, hawkers selling their wares, merchants chatting outside their shops. Piper managed to get out of the narrow bed and walk to the parlor without the aid of her cane. *Funny, how something I have done my whole life without thinking now takes great concentration.* But today was Friday—her favorite day as she would have visitors as usual at week's end. *My Gabriela will bring the little one to visit mid-morning. I hope she brings the tea and oranges. Oh, and the pastries and flowers!* How she loved the flowers and the sweet smell of freshly washed baby's skin. The very thought of tiny fingers and toes, giggles and hair like spun gold soothed her aching heart. She looked at the charcoal portrait on the wall, which spoke to her of a precious time long gone by. In the silver frame she stood next to Vander with Peyrinne and Luuk in front of them, all smiling. She was wearing her best dress and her only necklace, the one with the pearl. The portrait was drawn in front of their first storefront, Perfumerie Bleu. *How proud he was that day,* she thought, shaking her head and smiling at forlorn memories.

"How time marches on. But why do we follow?" Piper spoke aloud.

Vander seemed to be looking at her through the paper in the frame, those eyes so loving and so pained, the grief of losing Philip never losing its grip on either of them. How she longed to hear his voice; it had been so long. Thirty-four years had passed since she buried him, almost as long as they were married. The years had been kind to her and her family had grown so. Never did she think she would live to see her grandchildren having children, never mind seeing those children become parents, too. But here she was, waiting for them to visit on this beautiful summer morning, the sun shining through her window, promising a beautiful day.

She folded her hands in her lap and noticed that they still bore a slight resemblance to the hands that had held her mother's when she was ill, the hands that scrubbed her brother's bed linens, cooked the family's meals, placed a wedding medallion around Vander's neck, and held the tiny hands of her children as they took their first steps. But now these hands were wrinkled and gnarled with arthritis, painful and slow. She caressed one with the other, the way he used to. Closing her eyes, she visited that sweet time when they had had their whole lives ahead of them, so young and so eager to begin their journey together. *One never knows what's around the bend in the lane, but if you have a true friend you can get through anything.* Thinking then of Philip and how his life had just begun when he was taken from her, she smiled to know that he and Vander were together, probably riding Pieferet and Henk through fields of lavender and gold in heaven. *My sweet boys*, she thought. How she ached for them, all of them.

The knock at the door startled her, bringing her back to her small flat on Rue de Verneuil.

"Coming," she said but the door was already opening. In rushed the second youngest of her great-great grandchildren, two-year-old Jacque.

"Grand-mère!" He ran to her despite his mother's admonitions to be careful and not knock her over. She bent forward in her chair and hugged him with a love so deep, she didn't want to let go. She inhaled deeply, loving the smell of his soft skin.

"Did I ever tell you that you have your Père's eyes, my love?"

He wriggled free of her and sneezed as he always did when she wore perfume. They all laughed at this, as if they had forgotten to expect it. He rubbed his nose and went in search of some trouble to get into. His mother, Gabriela, lumbered in, heavy with child and laden with packages.

"Oh Grand-mère, I am out of breath!" she said. Piper looked at her with empathy.

"I remember that feeling. Can I help you, Love?"

"No, you stay right there. I'm fine, just wishing this baby would hurry." She looked at Piper and stopped.

"Are you feeling well?"

Piper, realizing she must be disheveled, having risen only an hour before, ran her fingers through her hair, to the gray bun that sat on the top of her head.

"Oh, don't worry about me, I'm just old." She meant to be lighthearted but knew it didn't come across that way.

Gabriela came closer and sat with her at the table.

"I brought your favorites: croissants with fresh raspberries and blackberries. Are you hungry?"

She nodded and took the packages from her.

"Jacque, come to the table and have breakfast with your grand-mère," she said. He was busy playing with the toys she kept for him and all her grandchildren.

"Gabriela, tell me. Have you been to the factory to see René, to try the new scents? I'm trying to be patient waiting for him to bring them to me. I think he feels I am too old to have a hand in the business, but I'm still sharp and my nose still works just as well as it always has."

Her great-granddaughter laughed aloud and touched her arm.

"Of course, you are not too old! That's your factory and where would René or any of us be without you and that nose of yours?"

Piper laughed at the sense of humor she appreciated so. Together they sat in the midmorning sun and shared breakfast.

When she and Vander had settled in the city so long ago,

Piper had thought, *I will just curl up and die in this place made of stone. No fields, no space for a garden, no fresh eggs from my own hens, and far too many people!* But life moved her along as it always had, and while it took some time, she reluctantly adapted to life in the city. They boarded Pieferet in a stable used by the city's coachmen, to which Piper walked every day to groom him and bring him apples from the market, shining them with her apron on the way. To be sure his hooves were not being eaten by the cobblestone streets she soaked them in a bath of sea salt, lavender, and geranium oils.

Vander continued to farm his fields of lavender, making the long trek to the countryside often. In the city, he entered into the business deal he had hoped Piper would have been agreeable to years prior, and this partnership changed their lives in so many ways. His flowers were considered to be of the highest quality because of the soil in which they grew, rich in limestone and not far from the sea. Endless cartloads were bought by soap makers, "noses," glove factories, and the tanneries of Grasse and Marseilles to hide the putrid odors that came with the processing of leather goods. Word of his fine flowers reached far. He was visited by alchemists from across the sea, bringing more business than he knew what to do with.

Piper became involved only to help him with his workload, hoping it would be necessary only temporarily. But as months melted into years, and the children grew more independent, she began to really enjoy her work; so far from anything she had ever imagined doing. Mixing essential oils, experimenting with fragrance, it seemed she had developed a unique gift that was quite sought after.

On more than one occasion, she was asked to leave her "husband's paltry little business" to work in the grand perfumeries of Marseilles and Grasse by businessmen who, no matter their status and wealth, did not possess her natural ability. She felt, however, that they were just trying to squelch their competition. To these requests, she literally and figuratively turned up her nose.

The money came and with it distinction. Neither of them

being the sort to take blessings for granted, they banked most of the money, and graciously ignored the attention, living comfortably in the small apartment in which she still lived.

"Grand-mère, I brought you some of that glöggi you love so much. You know what I call it, don't you?" Piper tilted her head to the side, anticipating a comical punch line from her firecracker of a great-granddaughter. "Turpentine with a cinnamon stick," the young lady said. They both had a good laugh at that as Gabriela brought out the cobalt bottle and placed it on the table.

"Oh my love, you know it brings back such memories. Will you open it for me? I just want to smell it."

Gabriela smirked at her and said, "Uh-huh, that's what you always say." She popped the cork off and held the bottle out to her beautiful great-grandmother who closed her eyes and drew a deep breath. "Did I ever tell you of the night your Tantine Peyrinne was born, and how your Papa Vander made us some glöggi to celebrate? He was all thumbs that evening, so nervous. He and his father, Philip, were at my hearth—oh the mess I had to clean up the next day! He spilled a handful of raisins onto the stove and in all my life I never smelled such a sickening smell!"

Gabriela laughed, "I wish I could have heard you scolding him. You should create a cologne of burnt raisins for clumsy men—to warn all women, Grand-mère. If my Jean had been wearing it when I met him ...."

Piper had that familiar feeling of connecting with another woman simply because she was a woman. *How we are so much alike, wanting the same things, having to endure the same pain, the same heartache. God, please have mercy on this young one; spare her from tragedy.*

When their visit was cut short by a knock at the door, Gabriela scooped up her fussing toddler, kissed Piper on the cheeks and bade her farewell. René entered and greeted everyone in his customarily cheerful way, bringing with him a sense of jovial comfort and familiarity. When the apartment was quiet again, he greeted Piper, his old friend, the wife of his grandfather's partner. "I am here on business, Madam, so it is my wish that you do not try to seduce me with that beautiful smile. My wife would have my head!"

She laughed out loud, exposing the few teeth that she had left and said, "You are a devil, René. I have always known it! Now, have a seat young man. Would you like something to eat?"

He shook his head no and sat next to the old woman who had made his family very wealthy. He took from his leather shoulder bag the wooden box that was so dearly familiar to Piper that the sight of it made her heart skip a beat. He carefully slid the lid from it and extracted five glass vials, setting each one down carefully on the thick wooden tabletop, where Piper's family had, for decades, shared meals, planned their lives, and dreamed aloud.

She gently placed her gnarled hand on top of the cool glass and smiled at him. On each vial was a blank label which ultimately would bear, in René's hand, Piper's notes and possible names for the fragrance within. She delighted in the naming process, feeling that a scent's name should convey a feeling or a wish for the customers who wore her perfumes. Some of her favorites had been shipped to the farthest reaches of the world: Guérit le Cœur, Toujours L'amour, Les Ailes d'ange, and her favorite, which Vander had named, Piper Bleu Toujours.

René raised his eyebrows and nodded, asking if she was ready to begin. Winking in return, she lifted the first vial and handed it to him, so that he would remove the stopper for her. He held the vial for a moment then held it under her nose. She inhaled and asked him to dab a little on her wrist which he did with a sly smile, making her giggle and roll her eyes.

"Renard," she accused. He sat back and waited for her remarks, pen in hand. Closing her eyes she inhaled the mixture of violet, rose, and lemongrass, and pictured the gardens of her youth. She opened her eyes wide. As she conveyed her approval with the slightest nod and the very shine in her eyes, René noted on the label that this vial held a possibility. The next three were met with definite disdain as the elderly woman, who in her youth had never quite mastered the art of hiding her displeasure, wore on her face a clear lack of interest. The last vial was unopened when she reached for it.

"Hand it to me René," she said in her most authoritative voice.

René furrowed his brow and asked, "Are you sure it wouldn't be better if I ...."

She leaned forward for the vial and he let her take it from his hands, hoping she wouldn't drop it. He always saved his highest hopes for last, and she knew this time was no different. She struggled with the stopper but was determined to pry it loose. She dabbed a small bit of the liquid on her clean wrist and took a long, deep breath. Immediately her mind filled with images of a time very familiar to her but nothing she could actually place as memories: a handsome dark-haired gentleman, a tall, beautiful woman who wore her hair down about her shoulders in the daytime—how scandalous. She saw horses that looked similar to Pieferet and Henk, a vineyard, and there was love mixed with much sadness.

Upon opening her eyes, René asked, "And where did you go just now?"

She smiled at him and wondered the same thing. The second time she inhaled the fragrance, she stared at René, not being able to place all of the scents.

"Almond, violet, myrtle and ...."

He smiled at her and winked before he said, "Well, my dear, I have stumped the nose of all noses, eh?"

Not to be trumped, she took another deep breath and let it fill her nose. "It ... it *is* familiar, but ...."

René sat back and laughed at her furrowed brow.

"Any guesses, Madam?"

Shaking her head and looking defeated, she handed the vial back to him. Just as he opened his mouth to speak, she blurted out, "Grapes!"

He nodded to her and said, "Yes, madam! Grapes." After a moment's silence, he asked, but didn't need to. "Well, what do you think, young miss?"

She couldn't help but take another bit of the fragrance

and dab it on her neck and her other wrist. "Oh René, this one is going to turn heads. And allegiances!"

They both giggled at the thought of Paris's elite leaving the shops of Guerlain and Mollinard and running to Perfumerie Bleu for their new favorite fragrance. "This one needs a special name. I'll have to think about it. Leave me this vial so I can have it with me for a couple of days."

René packed four of the vials into the wooden case and before sliding the lid back into place, looked into Piper's eyes and said, "You know we shouldn't do this, leave this vial around. You know better than anyone it could be stolen. I bet they have someone watching this very house right now."

She looked back up at René and nodded, knowing he was right; the perfume industry was a ruthless one, and she would have no way of fending off an intruder. She knew, too, that poisons were commonly mixed with perfumes to rid a particularly pesky, or, in this case, extremely successful competitor. Be it in love, business, or otherwise, poisoning had become commonplace.

She gently handed René the vial and asked that he just dab some on her gloves so that she could keep it with her.

"Oh, of course, my dear lady. Now I won't have to drink heavily worrying about someone coming here to kill you for this formula. And to think I started my day imagining the worst I had to worry about was hiding a tryst from my darling wife."

Piper laughed again, heartily, knowing René's wife was anything but darling. And she had no doubt that if she ever did catch René being unfaithful, he would walk *himself* to the guillotine.

He left the sweet-smelling gloves under her pillow for her and bid her a good week.

"I will see you next Friday and I hope that by then you will have found the perfect name, Love."

She kissed his cheeks and wished him a relaxing weekend with his wife. Laughter rang in her ears as she lay down for an early afternoon nap, a sense of finality settling about her shoulders.

26

T HREE MONTHS AFTER LEAVING Dr. Corcoran's office, Piper
signed a purchase and sale agreement on the farm. When
she handed the paperwork back to her real estate agent as they
sat at the kitchen table, she thought, *I can't believe I'm selling
what's left of Paul's dream. And mine, too.* She shook the thought
out of her mind and smiled, glad at least to be moving on.
Trying to live on the farm without him was just too painful,
and Dr. Corcoran suggested that she might try starting over
someplace new.

Kim looked at her and said, "Now, about the other property. Have you called an inspector yet?"

Piper rolled her eyes comically and replied, "That's at the
top of my to-do list; well, right under dealing with the life
insurance company and settling some debts, catching up on
my work, and calling the auctioneer about the winery equipment."

Kim nodded. "I understand, but you don't want to drag
your feet either."

Piper nodded back. *Does this woman have any clue what I've
been through? No, I guess no one really does.*

She saw Kim to the door, promising to get an inspector
out to the tiny Cape house she planned to purchase. Not
wanting to be alone, she hopped into her car and thought that
she wanted nothing more than a hot cup of coffee and a friend
to talk to. She dialed Dr. Corcoran's number and when he
answered, she smiled.

"John! Hi, it's Piper. How are you?"

He was surprised to hear her voice. She had gone to see him for a follow-up appointment a month after her first session; but since then, they hadn't spoken.

"Piper, hi. I'm well; how are *you* doing?"

She started the car and headed out the driveway, juggling her phone and the seat belt, exhibiting her lack of patience in fine style.

"I'm ... okay, I guess. I just signed a purchase and sale agreement on the farm and I feel, uhh, I feel good!"

"Well that's good news. Wow, I didn't think you'd act so fast, but really, I think it will prove to be good for you. Change, I mean. Change can be really good."

"Me too, John. I just wanted to thank you for everything and for listening and understanding and helping me piece things together."

He replied with a lilt in his voice that surprised him.

"It's been my pleasure. Really, it has. When do you think you'll be coming back in? Any idea?"

She didn't need to think about her response as she already knew.

"I'd like to come down this week sometime if you can fit me in."

Without looking at his schedule, John replied, "Of course I can! Barbara's out today so let me know what's good for you and I'll make it work."

Piper rolled her eyes, thinking of the extremely unpleasant secretary.

"Wednesday afternoon works for me, maybe around 2:00?"

Pulling onto the snow-lined street, she had a sense of really moving forward and it felt good. She acknowledged it and took a breath. *Moving again ... thank God.*

"Perfect, I'll see you then." John took a breath and penned in: Piper 2:00 p.m.-Close.

Tossing her phone onto the passenger seat and gripping the wheel with the gloves Paul had given to her one Christmas, she felt a weight being lifted from her. She really was piecing things together and moving on. It was painful, and she knew she had to grieve. And she would grieve, but right now she wanted to keep her wits about her so that she could figure out her past.

"It's the only way I can think to live the rest of my days as a whole person," she had said just before the voice on the speaker asked if she'd like to try a turbo shot with her coffee.

"No thanks. Just a small regular, please."

She paid at the window and headed back to her farm.

When she pulled into the driveway, she tried to imagine how the farm must look to the soon-to-be owners. It really was a beautiful home, set so nicely on the lot, shielding the stable from the street, and surrounded by old-growth trees, something she and Paul had both insisted on keeping. Sitting in the car for a few moments before getting out, she caught a glimpse of the crocus and tulip foliage, their beautiful green life peeking from the otherwise colorless landscape. She closed her eyes and prayed, *I really hope they won't sell off the vineyard for the land, Paul. I hope someone will continue what you've started. I'm sorry I can't be the one to do it, Honey. I just can't be here without you. I hope you understand.*

Back in the house, she was greeted by Viceroy.

"Hi, Vice! You staying out of trouble, old man?" He barked and wriggled, not insulted in the least. She went to the kitchen and got him a cookie, then went up to her office to catch up on some work.

Opening her email before working was something she long ago vowed she would never let herself do, but since Paul's death, she was turning over new leaves in every area of her life. She clicked on her inbox and scanned the thirty-seven junk emails, deleting them with a sigh. She kept, but didn't open, the ones from Sharon, her mother, or Kim. Deciding she didn't want to answer emails at the moment, she went to iTunes and downloaded some new songs for her iPod. *Sorry Paul, can't help it. I like foreign rock music—got tired of the American stuff.* There was just something about some of these bands that she really connected with.

She went to the site Sharon kept telling her about. At first Piper thought she was saying U2, but then Sharon sent her a link for YouTube and had been addicted ever since. She typed in Ville Valo and saw that there was a new posting of him performing an old Finnish folksong. She shrugged her shoulders, thinking, *I won't understand a word of it, but if he's singing it, I'm sure it's beautiful.* She clicked on it and sat back. The opening notes of the song played and she closed her eyes, waiting for the deep voice she loved. Her nose filled with the scent of roses and a sense of deep longing filled her heart. She was unaware that she was clutching at her collarbone by the end of the song. After clicking back on iTunes to try to download it and not being successful, she went back to Google and searched for a downloadable version of it. No luck. Hands trembling, she wrote down the name of the song, following Dr. Corcoran's orders to keep a log of her scent memories and what may have triggered them for their next session. Odottaa sinua valo. *What does that mean, I wonder?*

She shrugged her shoulders and tucked the piece of paper into her purse. After listening to the song again, she decided that catching up on work could wait one more day at least. *I need to take care of some things. I've been putting off too much for too long. I have to do this.*

She took her cell phone and brought it into her bedroom. Lying down on the bed, she noticed the afternoon sun slanting through the window in a way that announced spring as unmistakably as the tulips and crocuses. She caressed Paul's pillow, thinking how long it had been since he had slept next to her. With trembling fingers, she dialed her voicemail, something she did almost daily. But this time she decided she wanted to hear what Paul had said in those first few voicemail messages back in November, on the last day of his life.

At the prompt, she input her password and hit the pound key. Her heart began racing, and she was afraid the familiar feeling might lead to another anxiety attack and flipped her phone shut. Quickly, she opened the bottle on her nightstand and put half a Xanax under her tongue. After redialing, she took a deep breath and said, "Please God, help me get through this."

Once again, she typed in her password and hit pound. She skipped over her mother's three recent messages, not really wanting to hear her cheerful voice calling her Catherine. She was not Catherine. She knew that one day she would need to confront her mother and get to the root of this pain. This betrayal. But right now, she knew, was not the time.

When she heard Paul's voice, she sucked in her breath and pulled his pillow closer to her.

"Hey, Beautiful! I didn't get to see you this morning, well, not awake anyway. You must have been tired—you didn't move at all when I came downstairs this morning. Was I snoring again last night or something? Sorry, Hon. All I know for sure is that I'm so excited about tonight and I can't wait to see you in your new dress. I hung it on the bedroom door for you. Call me when you get this so I know you're okay. Love ya."

The mechanical voice told her the message had been recorded at 11:11 on November 20th. She hit the number nine to save it as she had done each of the last few months, not listening to the messages, but not wanting to lose them either.

"Hi, again. It's just me. Where are you? I wish you'd get back and give me a hand. Time is flying and I'm starting to get nervous. Give me a ring so I know how long you'll be. Oh, and I wanted to tell you later tonight, but I can't wait. I have a surprise for you, Babe."

The scent of Paul's cologne and even his skin was there in her nose, her memory. In her heart. She wiped tears from her eyes and sniffled. *Paul. I need you. Why did you leave me?* After hitting nine again, she sat up and drew in a deep breath, the next message being the last. Knowing that she was going to hear a voice that really no longer existed except on some database somewhere, she felt panic rising in her throat despite the sedative.

"Next message," said the mechanical voice.

"Hey, where the hell are you, Piper? It's 2:15. I thought you'd be back by now. You've got me worried. Please, Piper. As soon as you get this, call me right back. Love you."

And that was it. She saved that message, too, and rolled onto her side. She closed her eyes. *There. I was flying out of state to get what turned out to be the wrong friggin' labels and he had a surprise planned for me. I didn't deserve him. I don't deserve anything except what I've got: an empty house and an empty heart ... a name that's not even mine. Past lives to deal with. God, please help me through this.* And when her now daily afternoon medication mercifully kicked in, she drifted into a dreamless sleep, not feeling the gentle hand resting on her forehead.

27

RAND-MÈRE, we're here. Can you hear me? I wish you'd open your eyes so I can know you've seen him. I brought the baby, he's here. Grand-mère, please, just open your eyes for me."

Piper wanted to open her eyes, but her lids felt so heavy, so dry. And then came the sound of a newborn's cry; how she loved it.

I am here my love, my heart. Don't be afraid, I've come for you. We will all be together soon. Vander! She wanted to open her eyes, but she knew she would not see him. He wouldn't be there. But he *was* there, somewhere behind her eyelids, and she heard his voice so clearly. *Piper...* the cry of the baby again. She thought, *I want to see him. The baby, Vander, I want to see him first.* She struggled against the weight of her lids and the lure of his voice, and let in the light, just a little at first. When she was helpless to keep it at bay, the sunlight infiltrated this sweet interlude, bringing her back to her bedroom on Rue de Verneuil. Her eyes opened wide, flooding her thoughts and washing away that beautiful voice she would know anywhere.

"Grand-mère! Oh, Grand-mère, you're awake. I thought ... I thought you were ...."

Piper blinked at her great-granddaughter but couldn't summon the energy to speak. The sound of the baby again reached her heart, and she looked into Gabriela's arms. *So tiny,* she thought, *so beautiful. I will watch over you little one.*

"Grand-mère, this is Claude, Claude Vander, for Papa.

Can you believe this is your ninth great-great-grandchild?"

Piper looked at the beautiful woman who had glistening tears on her pink cheeks. *Don't cry for me. I am fine, just old.* The baby hiccupped and brought a soft smile to her face which made Gabriela cry harder.

"Oh please don't leave us, Grand-mère. What will we all do without you?"

Piper prayed silently for the strength to speak. It took several moments but finally she said, "Don't cry love. It is how God wants it. It's my end, but only the beginning for you," she nodded at the baby and continued, "And for him, too. A very long time ago, my mother told me that little girls grow, have children and raise them but then go to heaven to watch over their grandchildren and great-grandchildren. I guess I must be late!"

Gabriela laughed out loud and leaned forward to stroke Piper's wrinkled cheeks, dry as flint. But before she could say anything the baby was squawking again.

"Grand-mère, I must feed him. He is always hungry it seems. Luuk is here. I'll get him and then I'll be right back." She nodded to Piper as if to ask if she understood.

Piper nodded to Gabriela, then dropping her gaze, looked for the first and last time into the eyes of the boy, who when grown, would turn her tiny perfumery into a legendary business known the world over.

Luuk, her beautiful boy, now an old man himself, came through the bedroom door and stopped. He turned back toward the safety of the parlor but knew he must go in: she had seen him. With reddened eyes and nose, he sat in the chair by her bed, not wanting to look at her. His chest heaved with each breath as he stared at his feet. She thought he looked like the little boy she had scolded once so very long ago when he cut most of his sister's hair off with the wool shears while she slept. *Oh, how he cried then,* she thought. *Why are they all so sad for me? I am old! Do they think I should live forever? Don't they know my heart aches for Vander and for my little Philip, too?* She lifted her hand and touched his wrinkled face, wiping his tears away the way she had when she explained to him that God gave girls long hair as a special gift for all the hard work and pain they had to endure in life. It's what made them feel pretty and that he shouldn't be jealous because his hair was not long and dark like Peyrinne's and Maman's. That his hair was like Père's and Philip's and that's why she loved it so much.

"You are my straw boy, just like Père and Philip," she had told him and held him close. She knew how to make him feel better when he was a child, no taller than the sheep in the stable yard. But now, there was no solace.

"Luuk, don't cry. It's just my time, the way God wants it. Don't be sad, you know I have lived long. I lived a good life."

He squeezed her hand gently and nodded.

"Yes, Maman, That's why it's so hard. We'll be lost without you."

She shook her head no.

"Sshhh ... don't say such things. You are a *fine* man and have raised a beautiful family. Your sons are big and strong and so very smart. And your grandchildren, Luuk! They remind me of your father when he was young."

Fresh tears fell, and, this time, Luuk wiped hers away and kissed her cheek like he had done a thousand times before. She closed her eyes and pictured him by the sea with the large sweater she had knit for him before he was born, before she knew he had company in her womb. She laughed as she recalled for her son how she and Vander thought she was going to give birth to a giant, her belly had stretched so.

"The sweater didn't fit you two until you were in your fourth summer," she laughed.

"That was the year Philip ...." Her voice broke off, remembering his shining eyes and soft skin.

"The year Philip found the pearl in the sand. How proud he was to show it to me, cupping his little hands and holding them up for me. He said, 'Maman,' for you! Do you remember, Luuk?"

He nodded his head slightly, eyes glazed and reddened.

"I remember everything about him Mère, everything."

Piper nodded. "I have kept that pearl all this time. I want your granddaughter to have it, Luuk. Give it to Anna and tell her I will be watching over her."

The noon day bell rang in the belfry of the church she had last attended the Christmas before. As if it were intended as a reminder to her that time was not a patient friend.

"Peyrinne. Is my Peyrinne here?"

Luuk nodded and stood.

"I'll get her now. I love you, Maman."

I'm so tired, she thought, *and I want to sleep.* She closed her eyes, and, as her lungs drew shallow, raspy breaths, she heard a little boy's sweet, sweet voice. *'Mère! Mère! I have been waiting for you!* (Philip! My heart, my son!) *Mère, it is so beautiful here, you will see. The flowers are much sweeter, and the colors—oh! So many! You will love it. I've missed you, Mère, so much and I heard you calling to me through the fire. I was so scared in the night when Papa couldn't pull me from the flames. But God wanted it that way. I heard Him tell me I must stay. And when you cried in the night and wanted to stop living, God let me show you how to live again. It was my chore to show you the way and I have! I've helped with things you don't even know about yet. But you will, I'll show you, Mère! Pieferet and Henk miss you so but I take good care of them. Their coats are shinier than ever, you'll see how I make them shine!*

"Mère, I'm here." It was Peyrinne, her voice so gentle. "Mère, can you open your eyes for me?"

Piper knew she could open them but also knew that once she saw her beautiful daughter, she would not want to close them again. *Philip, wait for Maman!* She was torn between the two worlds, each so close and tugging at her heart. "Peyrinne," she whispered and took a deep breath, slowly opening her eyes. "You are wearing the new scent. It smells right on you. *Parfait.*" She looked up at the dark, watery eyes over her bed. *How funny to have your child taking care of you,* she thought. "Did René tell you the name of it?" Her daughter nodded and raised her kerchief to her eyes, blotting away tears to make room for new ones to fall.

She said, "I love it, Mère. And it is. *Notré Vie Belle,* it *is* a beautiful life."

The two women sat this way for a long time, in the bedroom of the apartment they had lived in together until Peyrinne left for university, something young women rarely did. In the dim light of the room, love whittled away time and age, accomplishment and fear, courage and scars. And as with all matters of the heart, only what truly mattered was all that was left. Together they were simply mother and daughter, entwined forever, their bond never to be severed. They shared memories and laughter, joy and tears, hopes and sorrow. And when it was finished, when her time was near, Piper nodded her exaggerated approval and slipped painlessly away into the warmth of the light and the ocean of ceaseless love that sometimes gives and sometimes takes away.

Don't cry for me, Peyrinne, my heart. It is only this life and there is so much more.

28

O N HER WAY DOWN Route 84 to her appointment with Dr. Corcoran, Piper kept looking over her shoulder at the back seat where she had left her notebook.

"It's not going anywhere, Ding-a-ling. Just drive."

She was aware that she now spoke to herself aloud quite often. And she really liked it. Positive affirmations were something she used to laugh at. But that was before. Before her life changed in ways she could not have imagined even just a year ago.

She took a deep breath. Gripping the wheel and pressing the accelerator, she picked up speed and turned on the radio. *Vander, I want to know more about you, and Philip, Luuk, and Peyrinne, too.* She felt it a bit odd that this thinking didn't seem crazy to her; nor did observing herself now as more than just a person—more than just flesh and bone and ego-driven human. She was curious to find out what else there was to learn about herself, whatever it might be. Sharon had said to her on more than one occasion, "Chickadee, this is your new normal. I'm here while you figure it all out."

Piper realized that resisting the changes only made the changes seem like punishment and therefore more painful. She decided that she was in control now. And not in the way she had tried controlling everything in her life until Paul's accident. No, this was more in the way of controlling how she reacted to that which she could not control. In short, she was willing to try anything to feel better again.

John had asked her to keep a log of all her scent-aches and her poetry to see if there was a connection. More pieces of the puzzle as it were. She was going to arrive early, a habit she had gotten into when she was young and needed to feed Victory and braid his mane and tail before a show. She always hated the feeling of being late. She quoted aloud something her beloved riding instructor always said, "Early is on time and on time is late."

After getting her coffee from One Lump or Two around the corner from John's office, she sat in the parking lot as she had done on her previous visits. This time, though, she wasn't forlorn or feeling shattered. In fact, she felt good, alive again. She took the notebook from the backseat and flipped it open, thumbing through some of the older poetry she didn't want to read at the moment.

January 9th. Her heart quickened and she immediately took a deep breath and held it until her heart slowed its pace, not unlike the way *she* would get her horse to slow when he tried to rush a fence. January 9th. *The hospital.* She thought how wonderful it would be to tear those ugly pages out of their spiral-bound place in her life and she resisted the urge to slam the notebook closed. Knowing it was part of her experience, her lesson, an essential step toward wherever it was she was going, she smoothed the pages and decided she would not judge herself and what she wrote from her hospital bed.

"Compassion."

She looked at herself in her rearview mirror and nodded. John coached her on being gentle with herself and using only loving thoughts and words. And as much as she stumbled through the minefield of criticism in her head, she slowly began to become her own friend. And she really did like herself. This surprised her in a way she hadn't expected.

Running her fingers over the words, smoothing the pages flat, she could feel the indentations her pen had made that night, her anger burning through her and onto the page.

Paul
Tides wash you from my skin
And flesh from your bone
Waiting for you is my penance
God's love turned to stone
The breath in my body stale
My lifeblood ends here
Darling, turn not the tides
My only solace this fear
Come to me in the storm
Hold me in the fray
Reap not what you've sown
I have given it all away
Lonely hearts
On wings of pain
Cry into the dark
I need you again
The moon pulled her tide
Before time grew old
The candles flicker
My blood runs cold
Where are you my Love
I hear you in the night
My heart feels your weight
As this dream takes flight.

She whistled through her teeth and thought, *I was in a very dark place that night.* Looking back at some of her older poetry dating back to her time with Darrick, she saw how much she really had grown since meeting Paul. Her world had changed when they met and it was a good change, one that she felt she deserved at the time. But now she wasn't so sure. Looking up at the clock on the dash she realized that because of her earliness, she was now going to be late.

Shoving the notebook aside and finishing her coffee, she scolded herself.

"Only you Piper, only you." And then, "It's okay. You're on time, not late."

She parked in a handicap parking space, again feeling like maybe the world did in fact owe her something for what she'd been through. Out of breath by the time she climbed the stairs, she rushed into the office only to realize that the clock in her car was a few minutes fast and she was, in fact, early as usual. Rolling her eyes, she hung her coat in the waiting room but didn't feel like sitting still so she decided to take a closer look at the diplomas on the walls.

Reverend Fr. John A. Corcoran.

Piper raised one eyebrow. *Father? Hmm.*

"A priest?" she said, not loudly but still surprising herself just the same.

Another diploma hung near the reception desk, but she had never bothered to look at any of them before.

The Sorbonne, Paris.

Just then she heard footsteps. A young woman was talking with John and making an appointment for next month. *Babs must still be out.*

John wished his client a great day and turned toward Piper, smiling.

"Hi Piper, how are you?"

She turned toward him and smiled back.

"I'm here so I guess that means I'm good. Or at least getting there."

John nodded, "I've been looking forward to today. Come on in."

When they reached the room in which he had hypnotized her twice before, Piper let her impatience get the better of her.

"I have to ask you something."

John extended his arm so that she could enter the room before him. She nodded thank you and walked in, took a seat, and said, "Was your father a *priest?*"

He looked at her and laughed genuinely, nodding. "Yeah, he was a priest for about nine years before meeting two people who he said changed his entire world." Piper nodded, hoping he would continue, which he did.

"One of those people was Pierre Doucette, one of his psychology professors in Paris who introduced him to hypnosis and ultimately past-life regression therapy."

He stopped there to see if she would ask who the other person was. He stepped behind his desk and straightened some paperwork that didn't need straightening. Her eyes widened and she shook her head ever so slightly, waiting.

"And who was the other person?" she blurted out.

He smiled before looking up at him, waiting to see if she would venture a guess. When she didn't, he looked directly at her and said, "My mother."

Piper covered her nose and mouth as she laughed, not wanting him to take offense, but not being able to hold it in either.

"I know. It's a strange thought, but love finds a way I guess," he said.

She sat back and looked down at her nervous hands.

"Yeah, I guess it does."

He came back around the desk then and sat in the chair opposite her, not seeming much like a doctor to her at the moment and continued, "Do you believe that, too?"

Piper looked down at her hand where her wedding ring used to sit. "I'm not sure what I believe anymore. That's why I'm here, John."

Taking a deep breath, he leaned forward, hands out in front of him, fiddling with a pencil. He said, "There's more to this, Piper. You see, my father was a *devout* Catholic, my grandparents made sure of it. But from an early age he had, well, he had experiences that he just couldn't explain. I mean literally, he *couldn't* explain them without catching a beating with the belt, or worse. My dad saw spirits and heard voices and I guess today you'd say he had some psychic abilities. But back then, when he was growing up in an Irish Catholic household—boy, you just called it trouble. One of his grandmothers was a very well-known healer from the Mac Veigh family. She was punished publicly for healing people, which under British rule had become illegal. According to Dad, though, she helped a lot of people with figuring out what was happening in their life, interpreting signs in nature and making medicines from memory. They were from books her father had owned that were confiscated by the king's soldiers. He had been a doctor, too, as was his father. Dad learned quickly that these weren't things to be talked about unless you wanted to be punished. So he did what was expected of him and joined the priesthood. But he said that the day he arrived in Doucette's classroom, he was liberated. He said that to know other people take this stuff seriously and that he wasn't the devil incarnate, really freed him. And of course meeting Ciara, and falling in love with her didn't go over well with the church either, so ... well, the rest is history."

Piper looked at him with kindness and said, "Wow. That's a beautiful story. Thanks for sharing it with me."

He snapped back into professional mode and said, "Sure, but there's one more thing."

She looked at him, one eyebrow raised and feeling apprehensive but hoping that whatever that one last thing was, it had a happy ending.

"You know how your mother brought you to see a priest when you were very young?"

She nodded, not quite catching on.

"That was my father."

She sat up straight in her chair and felt her heart begin to race.

"He was pastor at St. Vincent's for just a couple of years before leaving for Paris, and he was the priest your mother brought you to see. That's why, when your parents brought you here, to Connecticut years later, he felt it must be fate, that it was part of God's plan that he help you. What he didn't realize at the time was that you were helping him in so many ways, too. 'A pearl in the sand,' he called you. He said that you were the first patient who made him truly believe, without a doubt, that past lives exist. His notes were filled with exclamation marks and pure excitement. He told me once that he prayed for you each and every day of his life, that he regarded you as an old soul, if you will, and someone who was destined to do good in this life."

Piper's eyes began to water, and she wished she had remembered to bring some tissues with her.

"Wow. I ... I had no idea," was all that she could say. John walked to his closet and took out a box of Kleenex and tore off the cardboard top. He handed her a tissue.

"Yeah, it's a cool story, isn't it? Imagine my surprise when you just showed up out of the blue a couple of months ago!"

She laughed, and said, "Yeah, now, I can see why you were so surprised."

After a moment, she said, "Oh, I remembered to bring the notebook with the poems and the journal of my scent-aches."

His eyes widened in anticipation as he took the tattered notebook from her. "Great, let's get started."

29

"OKAY, PIPER, you know the routine. I'll count backwards from ten, and you are just going to take some big, deep breaths and just let all the tension run out of you. Let it just run like water down your arms and off your fingertips."

She nodded, eyes closed, and took a deep breath. When Dr. Corcoran reached one, she was under and her breathing was calm and quiet. He started recording, grabbed his notes and a pen, and began their final hypnosis session.

"Piper, bring me back to Rue de Verneuil when Vander was with you. Bring me to his final days, and tell me about it. What are you feeling?"

Her breathing quickened and she shifted in the recliner.

"I see him by the kitchen table. He's holding his chest, and he can't breathe very well. I know he doesn't want me to see that he isn't well, but he hasn't been well all week. He's telling me to go ahead to the factory and check on the new bottles to see if they are acceptable. But I won't leave him; his breathing is worse now, and I can see him bending forward— he is uncomfortable and I'm getting scared."

John interrupted and encouraged her to move forward a day so that she would not dwell on her fear.

"Vander is on the bed, and the doctor is here. I know it isn't good when the doctor won't leave. I want him to leave and I know if he does, Vander will be better. The doctor is telling me his humors are unbalanced, and he needs to be bled, he has too much blood. But I don't want the doctor to do it. I want to sit with Vander and nurse him back to health like I have our whole lives. I'm telling him to go out to the parlor and wait there."

John sat back as he watched Piper's face turn pale and solemn.

"Go ahead, Piper. Tell me what's happening."

"I'm sitting with Vander and I'm telling him it's going to be all right. I tell him he has to be all right because I need him here with me and the children and the grandchildren need him, too. He can't breathe now and I'm so scared and worried. He's holding my hands and wants me to sing him a song. It's his favorite, but it makes me so sad."

"Why does it make you sad? What song is it, Piper?"

"It's the one my father taught all the men in our new village. He learned it far away where he and my mother met before they came to France. After Maman went to heaven, Papa went to the tavern every night, singing this song down the lane."

"Okay. It's okay. Can you sing it for me?" he asked her. She nodded, her lower lip quivering. Her breath hitched as she drew it in.

> Tämä ikivanha lupaus
> Suurin koskaan tiedä - henki puhelut
> Ja kuuntelen sinua
> Sinun siniset silmät paloi
> minun muisti elämien sitten
> Odotan sinua
> Etsi sinua valossa
> Salvia, rovio, jäätyneiden järvien
> Odotan sinua
> Minä odotan sinua
> Vuosisatojen avautua ja minä
> odotan sinua
> Odottaa sinua valo

Her voice faded and then stopped. She sat, covering her face with her shaking hands.

John spoke gently and noticed he was holding back tears. He cleared his throat. "It's okay. Move forward, Piper, and tell me what's happening."

To him, she looked like a little child after being told something upsetting, perhaps after a scolding.

"He's slipping away from me, and I can't stop him. He's very pale now, and he's clutching his chest. I'm telling him I will get the doctor now but he holds my hand, and he's shaking his head. He wants me to stay with him. He's telling me I am his love now and I will be forever. 'God's promise' he's saying, 'God's promise.' And I want to go with him. I can't be here without him. But he tells me no, I have to take care of everyone and everything like I always have. I'm asking his forgiveness for letting Marek stay with us and ruin our perfect life in the country. He is telling me 'No. It's not your fault, Piper.' And I … I am so sad because he is slipping away from me."

Tears poked their way out from under her closed lids.

"His eyes are open, but he's not there. Oh God, he's not there, my love, my heart. Vander!"

Piper was shaking all over and Dr. Corcoran asked her to move forward but she couldn't. She wouldn't leave that moment in time. He had read his father's notes over and over through the years. He shook his head and waited a bit, but he knew she would not leave him. Piper would not leave him then and it was apparent to him that she never left him. In that lifetime or any other. No one would do. Not even Paul.

He decided to end the session.

"… 8, 9, 10. Okay Piper, when you're ready you may wiggle your fingers and toes and feel yourself here in this room, in this chair. When you are ready you may open your eyes and feel refreshed and awake."

After a few moments, her eyes opened and she blinked in the dimly lit room and focused on John.

"Hi," she said, feeling a bit embarrassed as she had during the previous sessions because she didn't clearly remember what had transpired.

"Hi!" he responded and flipped through her notebook.

After a moment she asked, "What're you looking for?"

But he was concentrating intently on the pages in front of him so she sat back silently. He shook his head when he got to the end of the pages and sat back with a quizzical expression. She raised her eyebrows, waiting for any sort of information.

"That's interesting," he said and flipped through the pages again, this time a little quicker. He shook his head and said, "Hmmph."

She laughed and asked, "What's 'hmmph' mean—good or bad?"

He snapped out of his own trance and smiled, "Oh nothing bad, I just ... well. You were singing a song in another language but it definitely wasn't French."

Piper laughed out loud and color came flooding back into her cheeks.

"I may have lived in France a hundred years ago but I definitely don't speak French beyond what I learned in high school. And I *certainly* don't know any other foreign language. Are you sure I was singing a song? That's not something I do well, either!"

He laughed and nodded.

"Yes, you were singing all right, and it was beautiful. I just don't know what language it was." He leaned forward and hit the rewind button on his recorder to find the spot at which Piper was singing.

She leaned forward, astonished. "Wait! Go back!"

He rewound it again, and asked, "Do you know that song? What is it? Tell me!"

She furrowed her brow and listened closely. "I ... I don't know ... it does sound familiar though, but I don't know why." She wrinkled her nose and asked, "Is that Russian?"

He looked to see if she had anything else to offer. She shook her head and shrugged her shoulders. He stood up and walked to the window, then turned back to her.

"I guess we have a little research to do. But I'll tell you, that's going to bother me until we figure out that song."

She rolled her eyes and said, "You? I'm the one who was

singing it!"

He responded with a friendly, "Touché."

He sat back down with the notebook and looked over the notes she had kept regarding the scent-aches, and read some of her poetry out loud. She winced at several of the lines, realizing how dark it all sounded, her soul spilled onto paper.

Salvation beckons as the
Endless tide refuses to turn
Oceans of chance and regret
The years, how they burn
I have waked joy at the funeral of time
Show me the flame
Hold still the line
Hours tick and drone
Here inside this skin
Alone at the birth of night
This, my forever sin.

After going through the recording and the journal together, Piper was feeling mentally exhausted, but relieved that the session hadn't ended on a sad note. *At least I was with Vander when he passed. And he knew how much I loved him. I think I must have been a good wife. Oh Paul ... .*

On her way back to the highway, she decided to stop for a sandwich and pulled into a plaza in the middle of town. The warm spring sun flooded her windshield, and she was momentarily blinded. She sat for a moment, behind the wheel, in a parking space and let the sun warm her face and make her feel unforgotten. Pulling her wallet from her purse, she stopped suddenly.

"Oh my God, I completely forgot!" She quickly opened the change purse on her wallet and there among her nickels and pennies was the tiny slip of folded paper she put there so she wouldn't forget to bring it to her session and show it to John. With shaking hands, she dialed his number, hoping he hadn't left yet.

"Hello, John Corcoran speaking."

She let out a sigh of relief when she heard his voice. His was the only voice among billions on earth that she trusted right now. The thought frightened and consoled her at the same time.

"John! It's me, Piper. I totally forgot to show you something."

She unfolded the paper. "It's ... it's ... oh my God, it's the song I sang when I was under. I wrote down the name of it a couple months ago. It brought on a scent-ache, but I didn't have my notebook with me, so I just put it in my wallet so I wouldn't forget, which is, of course, exactly what I just did."

He laughed gently and reminded her that her mind had been on lots of other things lately. "Well, Piper, it's a step in the right direction and that's a good thing. Where did you hear this song anyway?"

"I was looking for songs by this singer from a Finnish band that I like, and this was one of the songs that came up. I had intended to find out more about it, but ... well, that was the day I finally listened to Paul's messages on my phone, and well, let's just say it was a rough week after that."

He reassured her that everything was going to be okay, that she was piecing it all together and that it always takes more time than we would like. "When you get home, e-mail me a link to that song. I'll try to do some research, too. Sound good?"

She said it did and hung up, not feeling in the least bit hungry.

Back at the farm, once all the animals were fed, stalls were cleaned, and she had forced herself to have a bowl of soup, she decided to Google the song that she simply could not stop thinking about. In her office she said a quick prayer to God to let her find what she was looking for. She played the song twice, holding her breath almost the entire time, and wondering how some people, like Ville, could have such beautiful voices and others were just simply not meant to sing: namely, herself. *Not my super power, I guess.* Then she searched for the lyrics, and upon finding them, thought, *Great, but I don't know what these words mean.* Clicking back to the search engine, she typed ikivanha lupaus *English translation*. She scanned the screen in front of her, hungry for the answers she, until recently, hadn't known she needed.

> This ancient promise
> Most never know - the spirit calls
> And I listen for you
> Your blue eyes burned
> In my memory from lifetimes ago
> I look for you
> Look for you in the Light
> The sage, the pyre, the frozen lakes
> Wait for you
> I wait for you
> The centuries unfold and I
> wait for you
> Wait for you in the Light.

Her eyes stung and in her heart she felt a longing so deep it was profoundly beautiful in its very stillness, having been caged like a tiny fledgling for centuries, waiting. Set free by such a hauntingly familiar voice, it beat its delicate wings, fanning a procession of scents and memories that played out like a beautiful story Piper's grandfather might have told her at bedtime. Or one that John's great grandmother might have told.

A blue-eyed woman on her sickbed, a broken husband, a lost boy, the scent of burnt raisins, a young girl in a lonely garden, a baby's tiny fist clenching its father's thumb, the scents of lavender and honey, a young boy kneeling by a hurt girl in a meadow, wiping her tears away, twin boys with hair of spun gold glinting in the summer sun, one of them holding a tiny pearl up for his mother to see, vast fields of purple meeting a cloudless blue sky, a houseful of love, the stench of ashes and death, moonlight illuminating white ribbon around a dark horse's neck, a hatful of berries, a golden medallion taken from around a neck and lowered into a grave by a sobbing man, his remaining son begging him to stop, a woman, fallen to her knees, whose eternal grief keeps her from ever having another child.

For the first of many times in her life, Piper felt certain that she was alive for a reason, that her life meant something. She knew without a doubt that even the anxiety she was feeling creep into her throat was all a part of being alive. The anxiety, fear, sadness, despair, and loneliness were all just part of life, as were joy, excitement, anticipation, and love. For once, she embraced it all and all at once. Racing down the stairs, heart beating like Valo's hooves, she looked at the clock in her kitchen which read 9:37 p.m. She dialed the phone and ran her fingers through her dark hair.

"Kim! Hi! It's Piper. Sorry to call you so late, but I need to talk to you about the farm. I've decided to stay."

30

TIME IS A RELATIVE THING, moving us along at a snail's pace, but, upon looking back, how it seems to have flown by. A whisper on the breeze, such are the decades. Ten years passed, and time moved Piper gently along on the tides of change. Singlehandedly, she transformed the vineyard into a Friesian breeding facility and riding school for children. Horses and children require, and also teach, great patience. She folded her friends inward, close to her heart, blending them into her life like the siblings she never had. Loneliness was not the constant companion she thought it would be in the absence of Paul. She dated men of substance and morals through the years and on a few occasions thought she might marry again, but knew that it wasn't as important to her as it once was. Replacing Paul could never happen, and finding Vander wasn't meant for this lifetime. So she righted herself and forged ahead with both of them deep in her heart, letting them guide her along her path.

It was in her 51st autumn that she received a phone call from her dear friend, John Corcoran, whom she had kept in touch with through the years, attending his wedding and children's christenings, birthday parties, and Christmas dinners.

"Piper. Hi! We're getting off the turnpike now, and I always take the wrong road to get to your place. Remind me which one it is?"

She giggled like a little girl and could picture John's wife sitting in the seat next to him growing impatient and giving him a hard time, something she had excelled at early in their marriage.

"You are one of the brightest men I know, and yet you couldn't find your way out of a wet paper bag, my friend. It's your third left, and I'm about two miles down on the right. You've been here at least fifty times. Do you want me to stand at the end of the drive and flag you down?"

He rested his head on the headrest and laughed aloud, "No, I don't think that'll be necessary. Oh, don't let me forget, I have a surprise for you."

The scent of roses and a feeling of dread filled her as her throat tightened. She was flooded with the memory of Paul's voicemail so long ago.

"Okay, I'll see you soon. Drive safe."

She hung up the phone in the stable's office. She returned to the indoor arena where Philip stood quietly with an eight-year-old child perched on his back. His ears came forward as she approached and she gently ran her hands down his long, sleek black neck. "Okay, Tori. Ask him to walk on, using your legs. Don't tug on his mouth; he's doesn't like that. That's it! Well done! Can you believe a horse that size will do anything you ask as long as you have the patience to ask it the right way?"

The little redheaded girl looked at her, shook her head no and tried to hide a smile, but several bright white teeth poked their way into the daylight.

Piper smiled back at her and said, "Patience is a virtue and you must practice, practice, practice, just like you did with your posting and look how wonderfully you do that now."

Freckles disappeared into dimples on the girl's face as she unabashedly smiled now at the compliment.

When the lesson was over and she heard John's car in the drive, Piper bade the girl and her mother a good week.

"I'll see you next Saturday and I think that's when we will try our first canter. You'll like it, and I think you're more than ready. Good job today, young lady."

John and his family rounded the house just then and headed for the stable yard. His wife, not the outdoorsy type, followed slowly behind, picking her way slowly through the yard as if there might be snakes lying in wait. Piper laughed to herself how some people can seem completely mismatched and yet make it work. John was a good man: Salt of the earth; and he fell in love with a demanding woman whom he loved taking care of.

"To each his own," she said under her breath, out of earshot. He held a child's hand in each of his. Kayla didn't want children and after the many years of trying to negotiate with her, to no avail, he became a "big brother" to two little boys from the city. He loved to bring them to the farm when he had time, and his wife granted permission.

"Hi!" he said when they were still a hundred feet away.

"Look who I brought!"

Piper smiled and waved.

"Hi, boys. It's so good to see you again. I hope you brought your boots so you can ride."

They looked up at the tall woman in boots and breeches and nodded their shy little heads, moving closer to John's legs. He stroked their blonde heads.

Piper said hello to Kayla without waiting for her to look up and acknowledge her, and gave John a hug. She held him close and felt that he had lost weight since their last visit.

"You look great, John," she said as she stood back and held him at arm's length.

He looked bashful then and said, "Oh? Thanks!"

Kayla forced a smile on her flawlessly made-up face. Piper had hoped that Kayla would soften, and learn to see life as something to enjoy rather than something to conquer. She also remembered what it took for her to soften, and knew that not everyone sees second chances as miracles. John informed Piper via email a month before to say that Kayla's cancer was back, this time in the liver.

"Hi. Beautiful day," Kayla said without looking directly at Piper.

Piper responded, "Yes, it sure is."

Their conversations were never more than small talk and

false pleasantries and so she led them toward the stable, noticing that Kayla had worn high heels to the farm. She invited her to take a seat in the heated observation room, which had a coffee maker, a television, and a sofa, luxuries most stables didn't have.

The boys relaxed a little bit and stood on tiptoes to peer into the stalls of the giant horses they were excited to see. John watched Piper as she admired the curiosity and eagerness of the twins. He knew how she had longed for children of her own, but knew that her riding school provided for lots of relationships with little ones whose lives would be forever bettered for having known her.

"Can we ride now?" one of the boys asked.

Piper nodded and took two lead lines down from the hook on the wall near the rear door of the twenty-five-stall stable that had for a short time been the winery building.

"Let's go get you a couple of ponies your size, like we did last time. What do you say?" she asked them. Their little faces brightened as they nodded their approval. She handed them each a cotton lead line and instructed them to go into the feed room and get a scoop of grain to put into the coffee can that hung by baling twine on the wall. They hurried inside and quarreled over which one would scoop the grain and which one would hold the can.

She looked at John who said, "Kids!" They shared a laugh and a bond that was obvious to everyone who saw them together.

After the kids caught the ponies in the paddock, she talked them through a thorough grooming and helped them tack up; tasks that should only take ten or fifteen minutes, instead taking a half hour.

"Living in the moment. You should try it sometime, John," she teased.

"Interesting concept. Did you come up with that on your own?" he teased back.

It was a defining moment in his career—a concept he pioneered back in the early 2000s which created a movement in the holistic healing world to help people take control of their lives, their anxiety, their pain. It was the very concept that had transformed Piper's life and helped her fulfill her dreams.

The boys mounted Cheerios and Triscuit, two Chincoteague ponies Piper had bid on while attending a pony-penning day auction in Virginia on a trip with Sharon and her daughters two years earlier. She told the children they could ride out in the meadow if they promised to keep it to a trot. They nodded their helmet-clad heads and she led the way. John followed with his camera, the fall foliage the perfect backdrop for pictures he would share with the boys' mother.

As they watched the ponies trotting in zig-zag lines for the inexperienced riders, John said suddenly, "I almost forgot, geez. They say the memory is the first thing to go." He reached into his coat pocket and took out a folded piece of paper.

She took it from him and asked, "What is it?"

"It's something you inspired me to write."

Her furrowed brow begged for more information.

"It's a poem, for you." John handed her an envelope with a single folded page inside.

"A poem? For me?" she asked, genuinely surprised.

He couldn't help himself then. He said, "Maybe it's the hearing that's the first thing to go."

She lovingly pinched his arm and unfolded the paper. He watched as her eyes moved from side to side while she read. When she finished she looked up at him and said with a nod of heartfelt approval, "Thank you, John. It means more than you know. When did you start writing poetry?"

He looked up at the sky as if he was searching far back in his memory.

"When I learned that Kayla was sick again. I remembered how writing helped you get through everything and look what it did for you. I wrote a lot for Kayla and my mother. I wrote for myself and this one I wrote for you."

She thanked him again, refolding the paper and putting it into her coat pocket. "It's really quite good, my old friend."

31

Piper, Once & Again
By J.A. Corcoran, Jr.

Love settles on wisdom's shoulders like a cloak
She wears with pride, so familiar, a dear friend
Each line on her face a story untold
Every tear cultivating a tale
Youth sneers at their elders so sure are they
"Time will never catch them," she whispers
The widow at the gate watching
As children catch ponies in the meadow
Her own never born
Memories of a lost love fill her
She hears him call her on the wind
Time, she knows, stops for no one
This journey a beautiful gift
He has waited lifetimes
But she will not make haste
"Have patience," she laughs
It's Almost time, my love,
Almost

Piper placed the sheet of paper she had read a hundred times over the years in her nightstand and gently closed the drawer. She touched Paul's face in the photo that sat by her bed as she had every night over the last 30 years. She crawled under her covers and settled on her side. As she lay there in her bed, the moon a nightlight outside her window, she thanked God for all the blessings in her life and drifted steadily to that state between waking and sleeping, feeling the hand on her shoulder. *I am here, love, and I am so proud of you. My beautiful Piper, my heart of hearts. I am waiting.*

⌒

No! No! Wait! Piper sat up straight in bed and felt her heart beating in her chest, her hair hanging down in her face. She grounded herself. She drew a deep and gratitude-filled breath. She wasn't an old woman. She hadn't allowed the solitude to seep into her veins so deeply that she closed herself off from living.

No. She decided that life didn't happen to her. Indeed, she happened to life. She had become open to all the surprises the universe wanted to show her.

Thank you, thank you. Thank you.

She eased herself back down onto her pillow and rolled onto her side. John's warm hand slipped into hers and she felt a tear slip down her cheek as she drifted off again into that ceaseless ocean that sometimes gives and sometimes takes away.

CPSIA information can be obtained at www.ICGtesting.com
Printed in the USA
BVOW08s1323110716

455133BV00003B/22/P